YOU ARE DESTINED
TO BE TOGETHER
FOREVER.

Saint Odd

By Dean Koontz

The City · *Innocence* · *77 Shadow Street*

What the Night Knows · *Breathless* · *Relentless*

Your Heart Belongs to Me · *The Darkest Evening of the Year*

The Good Guy · *The Husband* · *Velocity* · *Life Expectancy*

The Taking · *The Face* · *By the Light of the Moon*

One Door Away From Heaven · *From the Corner of His Eye*

False Memory · *Seize the Night* · *Fear Nothing* · *Mr. Murder*

Dragon Tears · *Hideaway* · *Cold Fire* · *The Bad Place*

Midnight · *Lightning* · *Watchers* · *Strangers* · *Twilight Eyes*

Darkfall · *Phantoms* · *Whispers* · *The Mask* · *The Vision*

The Face of Fear · *Night Chills* · *Shattered*

The Voice of the Night · *The Servants of Twilight*

The House of Thunder · *The Key to Midnight*

The Eyes of Darkness · *Shadowfires* · *Winter Moon*

The Door to December · *Dark Rivers of the Heart* · *Icebound*

Strange Highways · *Intensity* · *Sole Survivor*

Ticktock · *The Funhouse* · *Demon Seed*

ODD THOMAS

Odd Thomas · *Forever Odd* · *Brother Odd* · *Odd Hours*

Odd Interlude · *Odd Apocalypse* · *Deeply Odd* · *Saint Odd*

FRANKENSTEIN

Prodigal Son · *City of Night* · *Dead and Alive*

Lost Souls · *The Dead Town*

A Big Little Life: A Memoir of a Joyful Dog Named Trixie

DEAN KOONTZ

Bantam Books | New York

Saint Odd

An Odd Thomas Novel

Copyright © 2015 by Dean Koontz

Published in the United States by Bantam Books,
an imprint of Random House, a division of Random House LLC,
a Penguin Random House Company, New York.

Title page art from an original photograph by Luis Brito

A signed, limited edition has been privately printed by Charnel House.
Charnelhouse.com

BANTAM BOOKS and the HOUSE colophon are registered trademarks
of Random House LLC.

LIBRARY OF CONGRESS CATALOGING-IN-PUBLICATION DATA

Koontz, Dean R. (Dean Ray)
Saint Odd : an Odd Thomas novel / Dean Koontz.
pages ; cm.—(Odd Thomas)
ISBN 978-0-345-54587-9 (hardcover : acid-free paper)
ISBN 978-0-345-54588-6 (eBook)
1. Thomas, Odd (Fictitious character)—Fiction.   2. Cooks—
Fiction.   3. Mediums—Fiction.   I. Title.
PS3561.O55S25 2015
813'.54—dc23
2014038145

Printed in the United States of America on acid-free paper

www.bantamdell.com

2 4 6 8 9 7 5 3 1

First Edition

Book design by Virginia Norey

This book is dedicated to Frank Redman,
who has more than once reminded me
of Odd Thomas.

The only wisdom we can hope to acquire
Is the wisdom of humility. . . .

—T. S. Eliot, *East Coker*

Saint Odd

YOU ARE DESTINED
TO BE TOGETHER
FOREVER.

One

Alone in the vastness of the Mojave, at two o'clock in the morning, racing along at seventy miles per hour, I felt safe and believed that whatever terror might await me was yet many miles ahead. This would not be the first time in my strange life that safety proved to be an illusion.

I have a tendency to hope always for the best, even when I'm being strangled with a little girl's jump rope knotted around my neck by an angry, three-hundred-pound Samoan wrestler. In fact, I got out of that difficult situation alive, primarily by getting hold of his beloved porkpie hat, which he considered the source of his good luck. When I spun the hat like a Frisbee and he let go of the jump rope to try to snatch his chapeau from the air, I was able to pick up a croquet mallet and surprise him with a blow to the genitals, which was especially effective because he was wearing only a thong. Always hoping for the best has generally served me well.

Anyway, under a full moon, the desert was as eerie as a landscape on an alien planet. The great black serpent of highway undulated over a series of low rises and gentle downslopes, through sand flats that glowed faintly, as if radioactive, past sudden thrusting formations of rock threaded through in places with quartzite or something else that caught the Big Dog motorcycle's headlights and flared like veins of fire.

In spite of the big moon and the bike's three blazing eyes, the Mojave gathered darkness across its breadth. Half-revealed, gnarled shapes of mesquite and scatterings of other spiky plants bristled and seemed to leap forward as I flew past them, as if they were quick and hostile animals.

With its wide-swept fairing and saddlebags, the Big Dog Bulldog Bagger looked like it was made for suburban marrieds, but its fuel-injected, 111-cubic-inch V-twin motor offered all the speed anyone could want. When I had been on the interstate, before I had switched to this less-traveled state highway, a quick twist of the throttle shot me past whatever car or big rig was dawdling in front of me. Now I cruised at seventy, comfortable in the low deep-pocket seat, the rubber-mounted motor keeping the vibration to a minimum.

Although I wore goggles and a Head Trip carbon-fiber helmet that left my ears exposed, the shrieking wind and the Big Dog's throaty exhaust roar masked the sound of the Cadillac Escalade that, running dark, came up behind me and announced itself with a blast of the horn. The driver switched on the headlights, which flashed in my mirrors, so that I had to glance over my shoulder to see that he was no more than fifty feet behind me. The SUV was a frightening behemoth at that distance, at that speed.

Repeated blasts of the horn suggested the driver might be drunk or high on drugs, and either gripped by road rage or in the mood for a sick little game of chicken. When he tooted shave-and-a-haircut-two-bits, he held the last note too long, and I assured myself that anyone who indulged in such a cliché and then even lacked the timing to pull it off could not be a dangerous adversary.

Earlier, I had learned that the Big Dog's sweet spot was north of eighty miles an hour and that it was fully rideable at a hundred. I twisted the throttle, and the bike gobbled asphalt, leaving the Caddy behind. For the moment.

This wasn't the height of bug season in the Mojave, so I didn't have to eat any moths or hard-shelled beetles when I muttered unpleasantries. At that speed, however, because I sat tall and tense with my head above the low windshield, the warm night air chapped my lips and stung my cheeks as I bulleted into it.

Any responsible dermatologist would have chastised me for speeding barefaced through this arid wasteland. For many reasons, however, there was little chance that I would live to celebrate my twenty-third birthday, so looking prematurely aged two decades hence didn't worry me.

This time I heard the Escalade coming, shrieking like some malevolent machine out of a *Transformers* movie, running dark once more. Sooner than I hoped, the driver switched on the headlights, which flared in my mirrors and washed the pavement around me.

Closer than fifty feet.

The SUV was obviously souped. This wasn't an ordinary mama-takes-baby-to-the-playground Caddy. The engine sounded as if it had come out of General Motors by way of Boeing. If he intended to run me down and paste me to the Caddy's grille—and evidently he did—I wouldn't be able to outrace whatever customized engine made him king of the road.

Having tricked up his vehicle with alternate, multi-tonal horns programmed with pieces of familiar tunes, he now taunted me with the high-volume song-title notes of Sonny and Cher's "The Beat Goes On."

The Big Dog boasted a six-speed transmission. The extra gear and the right-side drive pulley allowed better balance and greater control than would the average touring bike. The fat 250-millimeter rear tire gave me a sense of stability and the thirty-four-degree neck rake inspired the confidence to stunt a little even though I was approaching triple-digit speeds.

Now he serenaded me with the first seven notes of the Kingsmen's "Louie Louie." And then again.

My one advantage might be maneuverability. I slid lower in the seat, so that the arc of the windshield sent the wind over my helmet, and I made more aggressive use of the three-lane highway, executing wide serpentine movements from shoulder to shoulder. I was low to the ground, and the Escalade had a much higher center of gravity than the Big Dog; if the driver tried to stay on my tail, he might roll the SUV.

Supposing he was smart, he should realize that by not mimicking me, by continuing arrow-straight, he could rapidly gain ground as I serpentined. And with easy calculation, he could intersect me as I swooped from side to side of the road.

The third blast of "Louie Louie" assured me that either he wasn't smart or he was so wasted that he might follow me into a pit of fire before he realized what he had done. Yet another programmed horn blared several notes, but I didn't recognize the tune, though into my mind came the image of that all-but-forgotten rocker Boy George.

When brakes caterwauled, I glanced back to see the Escalade listing, its tires smoking, as the driver pulled the wheel hard to the right to avoid going off the north side of the pavement. Carving one S after another down the straightaway, I cornered out of the current curve, grateful for the Big Dog's justly praised Balance Drive, and swooped into the next. With another squeal, the Caddy's tires laid a skin of hot rubber on the blacktop as the driver pulled hard to the left. The vehicle nearly skidded off the south shoulder of the roadway, listing again but, as previously, righting itself well before it tipped over.

Resorting to his basic horn, the driver made no attempt at a tune this time, but let out blast after blast as if he thought he could sweep me off the bike with sound waves.

Recounting this, I might convey the impression that I remained calm and collected throughout the pursuit, but in fact I feared that, at any moment, I would regret not having worn an adult diaper.

In spite of whatever drugs or beverages had pushed the SUV driver's CRAZY button and filled him with murderous rage, he retained just enough reason to realize that if he continued to follow my lead, he would roll the SUV. Arrowing down the center of the three lanes, he regained the ground that he'd lost, intending to intersect my bike between connecting curves of my flatland slalom.

The Big Dog Bulldog Bagger wasn't meant to be a dirt bike. The diet that made it happy consisted of concrete and blacktop, and it wanted to be admired for its sleek aerodynamic lines and custom paint job and abundant chrome, not for its ruggedness and ability to slam through wild landscapes with aplomb.

Nevertheless, I went off-road. They say that necessity is the mother of invention, but it is also the grandmother of desperation. The highway was raised about two feet above the land through which it passed, and I left the shoulder at such speed that the bike was airborne for a moment before returning to the earth with a jolt that briefly lifted my butt off the seat and made my feet dance on the floorboards.

Hereabouts, the desert wasn't a softscape of sand dunes and dead lakes of powdery silt, which was a good thing, because crossing ground like that, the Big Dog would have wallowed to a halt within a hundred yards. The land was mostly hard-packed by thousands of years of fierce sun and scouring winds, the igneous rocks rich with feldspar, treeless but in some places hospitable to purple sage and mesquite and scraggly plants less easily identified.

Jacked up on oversize tires, more suited to going overland than was my bike, the four-wheel-drive Escalade came off the highway in my wake. I intended to find a break in the land or an overhanging escarpment deep enough to conceal me, or a sudden spine of rock, anything I could use to get out of sight of my lunatic pursuer. After that, I would switch off my headlights, slow down significantly, travel by moonlight, and try as quickly as possible to put one turn in the land after another between me and him. Eventually I might find a place in which to shelter, shut off the bike, listen, and wait.

Suddenly a greater light flooded across the land, and when I looked back, I saw that the Escalade sported a roof rack of powerful spotlights that the driver had just now employed. The desert before me resembled a scene out of an early Steven Spielberg movie: a remote landing strip where excited and glamorous scientists from a secret government agency prepared to welcome a contingent of benign extraterrestrials and their mother ship. Instead of scientists and aliens, however, there was some inbred banjo player from *Deliverance* chasing me with bad intentions.

In those harsh and far-reaching streams of light, each humble twist of vegetation cast a long, inky shadow. The pale land was revealed as less irregular than I'd hoped, an apparent plain where I was no more likely to find a hiding place than I would a McDonald's franchise complete with a playground for the tots.

Although my nature was to be optimistic, even cheerful, in the face of threat and gloom, there were times, like this, when I felt as though the entire world was death row and that my most recent meal had been my last one.

I continued north into the wilderness rather than angle back toward the highway, assuring myself that it wasn't my destiny to die in this place, that I would find refuge ahead. My destiny was to die thirty miles or so from here, in the town of Pico Mundo, not tonight but tomorrow or the day after, or the day after that. Furthermore, I wouldn't die by Cadillac Escalade; my end would be nothing as easy as that, nothing so quick and clean. Having argued myself into a fragile optimism, I sat up straight in my seat and smiled into the teeth of the warm night air.

As the SUV gained on me, the psycho driver resorted to one of his custom horns again. This time I recognized the title notes of "Karma Chameleon" by Culture Club, which had been fronted by Boy George. The song seemed so apt that I laughed; and my laughter would have buoyed me if it hadn't sounded just a little insane.

The nitrogen-gas-charged shocks, the rubber-isolated floorboards, and the rubber handgrips all contributed to a smoother off-road ride than I had anticipated, but I expected that I was headed for one kind of mechanical failure or another, or for a collision with an unseen thrust of rock that would dismount me, or a community of rattlesnakes that, flung into the air in the midst of copulation, would rain down upon me, hissing.

I was suffering a brief remission in my characteristic optimism.

Ahead, a long but slight slope led to a narrow band of blackness before the Escalade's lights revealed a swath of somewhat higher land that shimmered like a mirage. I couldn't be sure what I was seeing; the sight was no less baffling than an abstract painting composed of geometric forms in pale beige and black, but in case it might be what I needed, I accelerated.

I had to weave among bushy clumps—a colony of pampas grass—that were half dead from too little water, their narrow five-foot recurved blades perhaps sharp enough to cut me, the numerous tall feathery panicles waving like white flags of surrender.

Evidently the nutcase pursuing me did not belong to the Sierra Club, because the Escalade barreled through the pampas grass without hesitation, leaving a path of crushed and shredded vegetation, gaining fast on me.

The ceaselessly repeated signature notes of "Karma Chameleon" and the roar of the SUV's pumped-up engine were so loud, I knew that it must be close, maybe ten feet behind me. I didn't dare glance back.

With but three or four seconds to make the right move, I saw that my suspicion about the terrain ahead was correct. I hung a hard right just before the brink.

The Big Dog fishtailed, the rear tire chewing away the lip of the abyss for a moment before it got traction.

Whether the driver's attention suddenly shifted to the land ahead, whether he remained intently focused on me, in either case the Escalade had too much mass and momentum to come to a stop in time, and it was far less maneuverable than my bike. The wind of its passage swirled dust and dry bits of desert vegetation over me, and the big SUV launched off the rim of the ravine, still blaring "Karma Chameleon" as it briefly took flight.

With its four-piston billet calipers, the Big Dog could stop on a dollar if not a dime. I propped it with the kickstand and swung off and stood at the brink as the spotlight-equipped Caddy, now dropping nose-down like a bomb, illuminated its terminal destination.

Carved by millennia of flash floods and Mojave winds and seismic activity, the crevasse appeared to be about thirty feet wide at the top, less than ten at the bottom, about fifty feet deep. The plunging SUV tested the bedrock at the bottom, and the bedrock won. The last title note of the Culture Club tune came an instant before the crash of impact, the vehicle lights went out, and in the sudden darkness, the SUV shed pieces of itself, which rattled and clattered across the rocks.

I said, "Wow," which isn't witty enough for movie dialogue, but it's what I said. I'm no Tom Cruise.

After a few seconds of darkness, the fire bloomed. It wasn't an explosion, only low capering flames that quickly danced higher, brighter. The ravine proved to be a trap for tumbleweed that mounded along its bottom, and the spherical masses burst into flame faster to the west of the wreckage, apparently the direction in which gasoline spilled from the ruptured tank.

The walls of the ravine were steep but navigable on foot. The stone shaled away treacherously as I quickly sidled down with all the grace of—I don't know why this unlikely image occurred to me at the time—a penguin on stilts. Too many years of watching old Warner Bros. cartoons by Chuck Jones can instill in you a silliness gene by proxy.

Perhaps equally silly—I was in my Good Samaritan mode. The driver had tried to kill me, sure, but his homicidal rage might have been the consequence of inebriation, and he might have been a peach of a guy when he was sober. I couldn't let him bleed or burn to death just because of his idiocy behind the wheel of the SUV. Sometimes I am hampered by having a moral code, but I have it nonetheless, like a burr under the brain, with no way to pluck it out.

Fire flared to both sides of the Escalade, and lesser flames crawled under it, but the interior wasn't yet ablaze. There were so many tinder-dry tumbleweeds that the ravine would be aglow for quite a while.

As I neared the vehicle, I saw painted on its tailgate neatly formed characters in a pictographic language reminiscent of ancient Egyptian hieroglyphics, white against the black paint. I halted and reconsidered the meaning of the encounter with the unknown driver.

A couple of months earlier, on a mountain in Nevada, I had found it necessary to explore a well-guarded estate where, as it turned out, kidnapped children were being held for the purpose of ritual murder by a satanic cult. Before I found the kids, I discovered a stable filled with antique breakfronts instead of horses, and in those breakfronts had stood thick glass jars the size of crocks, filled with a clear preservative, the lids fused in place with an annealing torch. In those jars were souvenirs of previous human sacrifices: severed heads, wide-eyed and open-mouthed, as if in the grip of eternal shock and terror, and on every forehead a different line of a pictographic language exactly like that on the tailgate of the Escalade.

Small-town boy meets big-time evil.

The driver of the Escalade hadn't encountered me by chance. He had learned what route I was taking, when I would take it, and he'd set out in pursuit of me, no doubt intending to avenge the damage I had done to the cult. I'd killed a number of them. But their resources were impressive—in fact otherworldly—and we were far from finished with each other.

My code of conduct didn't require me to save the lives of vicious murderers any more than it required me to feed myself to a shark just because the shark happened to be hungry. In fact, I felt obligated to kill murderous sociopaths if that was the only way to prevent them from slaughtering more innocents. Usually, that turned out to be the only way, because few of their kind responded well to reason or to stern warnings, or to the wisdom of the Beatles, which tells us that all we need is love.

The doors of the Escalade had buckled but hadn't popped open, and if anyone had clambered out of a shattered window, I had not seen him. The driver—and passenger, if there was one—were all but certainly still inside. Maybe dead. At least badly injured. Perhaps unconscious.

As I retreated, the crackling fire under the vehicle abruptly found its way inside, and with a *whoosh,* the interior filled with flames. I saw no thrashing shadows in the Escalade and heard no screams.

I couldn't imagine how they had known I was going home to Pico Mundo or when I would make the trip, or what I would be driving. But as I had unusual talents, abilities, and connections, so did they. I might never learn *how* they had located me. What mattered now was that they were looking for me; and if they had found me once, they could find me again.

They wouldn't have tried to find me and kill me en route, however, if they had known where I would be staying when I got to Pico Mundo. Instead, they would have waited for me there and cut me down when I arrived. The safe house waiting for me was still safe.

Climbing the shale slope proved more difficult than the descent had been. I kept glancing behind me, half expecting to discover a pursuer, some grotesque nemesis with hair afire and smoke seething from his twisted mouth.

At the top, I looked back and saw that the flames, a bright contagion, had spread maybe sixty yards to the west, from one crisp tumbleweed to another. The shale must have been veined with pyrite, for in the walls of the ravine, in the throbbing firelight, ribbons of yellow glimmered brighter than the surrounding stone. The burning Escalade screaked and twanged. As its metallic protests echoed and re-echoed along the crevasse, they were distorted, changed, until I could almost believe that I was hearing human voices, a suffering multitude crying out below.

I had not seen their faces. I had not killed them, only given them the chance to kill themselves. But still it seemed wrong that I should not know the faces of those I allowed to die.

The noise and the blaze must have disturbed a colony of bats. Just then, no doubt having recently returned to their cave in a ravine wall after a night of feeding, they burst into agitated flight, shrieking as they soared on rising thermals, many hundreds of them, perhaps thousands, their membranous wings snapping in accompaniment to the crackle of the flames. They rose to the top of the ravine, then descended, only to rise again, surged east and then west and then east again, as if confused and seeking something and failing to find it, their shrill cries both angry and despairing.

Life had taught me to believe in omens.

I knew one when I saw it.

The bats were an omen, and whatever they might portend, it would not be an event marked by benevolence, harmony, and joy.

Two

I came home to die and to live in death. My life had begun in the desert town of Pico Mundo, California, and I had remained there until I was twenty, when I lost what mattered most to me. During the twenty-one months since then, I had traveled in search of my purpose, and I had learned by going where I had to go. That I had come full circle shouldn't have surprised me, for we are born into time only to be born out of it, after living through the cycles of the seasons, under stars that turn because the world turns, born into ignorance and acquiring knowledge that ultimately reveals to us our enduring ignorance: The circle is the essential pattern of our existence.

The Green Moon Mall stood along Green Moon Road, smack between old-town Pico Mundo and its more modern neighborhoods. The structure was immense because it was intended to serve not just our town but others in the area that were too small to support a mall of their own. With sand-colored walls and curved planes and rounded corners, the architect meant to suggest adobe construction. In recognition of the Mojave heat, there were few windows, and the most glass to be seen was at the several entrances, where pneumatic doors once whisked aside to welcome shoppers.

The mall had been closed for a long time, contaminated by its history of mass murder. Many feared that to reopen it would invite some unhinged person to attempt to rack up a larger kill than the nineteen who were murdered on that day. Of the forty-one wounded, several were disabled for life. Starbucks, Crate & Barrel, Donna Karan, and other retailers had bailed on their leases, having no desire to be associated with a place of such horror. The mall owners, with common sense that was rare in modern America, had taken no tenants to court, instead announcing that the building eventually would be torn down and the land repurposed for upscale apartments.

After parking the Big Dog bike on a nearby residential street, I visited the mall more than an hour before dawn, carrying a pillowcase in which were a bolt cutter, a crowbar, and a sixteen-ounce hammer with a rubberized grip that I'd brought with me from the coast. I found my way by flashlight down a long, wide ramp that led to an immense segmented garage door through which countless eighteen-wheelers had once driven with loads of merchandise for the department stores and the many smaller shops.

The moon was down, the glimmering constellations so distant, and even in May the Mojave night was as mild as baby-bottle milk. On flanking concrete walls that loomed higher as the ramp descended, pale reflections of the flashlight drifted alongside me as if they were spirit companions.

I knew a great deal about the ghosts that haunted this world. I saw those who had died but who, for whatever reasons, would not or could not cross over to whatever came next. My life had been shaped by those lingering dead, by their regrets, their hopes, their needs, their melancholy. In my twenty-two years of life, I had come to regard even angry spirits with equanimity, reserving my dread for certain still-living human beings and the horrors of which they were capable.

To the left of the enormous roll-up door was one of ordinary dimensions, secured with both a mortise lock and a large padlock. I propped my flashlight against the door frame, with its beam angled upward.

Using the long-handled bolt cutter, I severed the shackle from the case of the padlock. I unhooked the padlock from the slotted strap and threw it aside.

The rimless lock cylinder could not be gripped with lever-wrench pliers and pulled out of the escutcheon. From my shirt pocket, I took a wedge-shaped steel tap with a broad head, and I pounded the tap into the keyway of the mortise lock. The poll of the hammer rang off its target, the pin tumblers in the keyway shrieked as the guts of the lock were distorted, and the stricken door clattered in its frame.

I had no concern that the racket I raised would draw unwanted attention. The deserted mall was surrounded by a vastness of empty parking lot, which was these days encircled by chain-link fencing crowned with concertina wire to discourage romantically inclined teenagers in cars, homeless people with their worldly possessions packed in shopping carts, and whatever creeps might be drawn to the place by its history of violence. The police chose not to patrol the property anymore because, after all, everything on it was scheduled for demolition in a few months.

My version of the "Anvil Chorus" was brief. When I'd driven the tap fully into the keyway, the deadbolt rattled loosely in the latch assembly, and a narrow gap opened between door and jamb, although the bolt remained seated in the faceplate. I applied the crowbar and worked up a sweat before I broke into what had been the subterranean loading docks and the employee parking lot beneath Green Moon Mall, leaving my tools behind.

I am a fry cook, at my best when working the griddle, master of the spatula, maker of pancakes so light they seem about to float off your plate. I am a fry cook and wish to be nothing more, but the many threats I face have required me to develop skills not needed in the kitchen of a diner—like breaking and entering.

Stained concrete underfoot, overhead, on all sides, the ceiling supported by columns so thick that I couldn't have gotten my arms around one: As a deep-sea diver in his pressurized suit and armored helmet might nevertheless sense the tremendous tonnage of the ocean pressing upon him, so I felt the great mass of the two-story mall and the anchoring pair of three-story department stores above me. For a moment, I felt buried, as if I had died on that day of violence and now must be a spirit haunting this elaborate catacomb.

Here and there lay small piles of trash: the splintered boards of a broken packing crate, empty and moldering cardboard boxes, and items not easily identified in the flare of the beam and the dance of shadows.

The rubber soles of my sneakers failed to disturb the absolute silence, as though I had no substance. Then a short-lived rustling sound rose from my left. It must have been a rat disturbed in a nest of trash, but nevertheless I said, "Hello?" The only response was the echo of that word, which in the colonnaded darkness returned to me from all sides.

When last I'd been here, the place had hummed with activity

as numerous trucks off-loaded merchandise and harried stock-room clerks prepared it for delivery to the holding rooms and the sales floor, using forklifts and electric carts and hand trucks.

The elevated loading dock ran the full length of the enormous structure. I climbed a set of steel rungs embedded in the face of it, crossed the dock, and pushed through a pair of extra-wide double doors into a spacious corridor with concrete walls painted white. Two freight elevators waited on the left; but even if they were still operative—which I doubted—I didn't want to be boxed in one of them. I opened a door labeled STAIRS, and I climbed.

From a ground-floor stockroom, I proceeded into what had been a department store. Silence pooled in the cavernous build-ing, and I felt as if something akin to sharks swam through the waterless dark, circling me beyond the reach of the flashlight.

Sometimes entities appear to me that no one else can see, inky and undulant, as quick and sleek as wolves, though without fea-tures, terrible and predatory shadows that can enter a room by the narrowest crack between a door and jamb or through a key-hole. I call them bodachs, although only because an English boy, visiting Pico Mundo, once saw them in my company and gave them that name. Seconds later, a runaway truck crushed him to death between its front bumper and a concrete-block wall.

He was the first person I'd ever known with my ability to see the lingering dead and bodachs. Later I discovered that bodachs were mythical beasts of the British Isles; they were said to squirm down chimneys at night to carry off naughty children. The crea-tures that I saw were too real, and they were interested not solely in naughty children.

They appeared only for horrific events: at an industrial explo-sion, at a nursing-home collapse during an earthquake, at a mass

murder in a shopping mall. They seemed to feed on human suffering and death, as if they were psychic vampires to whom our
terror, pain, and grief were far sweeter than blood.

I didn't know where they came from. I didn't know where
they went when they weren't around. I had theories, of course,
but all of my theories bundled together proved nothing except
that I was no Einstein.

Now, in the abandoned department store, if bodachs had been
swarming in the farther reaches of that gloomy chamber, I would
not have seen them, black forms in blackness. No doubt I was
alone, because in that desolate and unpopulated structure, there
were no crowds for a gunman to cut down in the quantities that
appealed to bodachs. They never deigned to manifest for a single
death or even two, or three; their taste was for operatic violence.

Back in the awful day, when I'd come out of the busy department store into the even busier promenade that served the other
shops, I had seen hundreds—perhaps thousands—of bodachs
gathered along the second-floor balustrade, peering down, excited, twitching and swaying in anticipation of bloodshed.

And I had come to think that they were mocking me, that perhaps they had always known I could see them. Instead of putting
an end to me with a runaway truck and a concrete-block wall,
maybe they had schemed to manipulate me toward my loss, toward the fathomless grief that would be born from that loss. Such
grief might be to them quite delicious, a delicacy.

At the north end of the mall, the ground-floor promenade had
once featured a forty-foot-high waterfall that cascaded down
man-made rocks and flowed to the south, terminating in a koi
pond. From sea to shining sea, the country had built glittering
malls that were as much entertainments as they were places to

shop, and Pico Mundo prided itself on satisfying Americans' taste for spectacle even when buying socks. No water flowed anymore.

By flashlight, I walked south along the public concourse. All the signage had long ago been taken down. I could no longer remember what stores had occupied which spaces. Some of the show windows were shattered, drifted glass glittering against the bases on which the large panes had stood. Other sheets of intact glass were filmed with dust.

I had come there with determination, but as I approached the southern end of the building, I moved slower, and then slower still, overcome by cold that had nothing to do with the temperature of the abandoned shopping mall. In memory, I heard the gunfire, the screams, the piercing cries of terror, the *slap-slap-slap* of running feet on travertine.

At the south end of the concourse lay another vacated department store, but before it, on the left, was the space where once Burke & Bailey's had done business, the ice-cream shop where Stormy Llewellyn had been the manager.

A tattered hot-pink awning with a scalloped edge overhung the entrance. In memory, I heard the hail of bullets that had shattered the windows and doors, and I saw Simon Varner in a black jumpsuit and black ski mask, sweeping a fully automatic rifle left to right, right to left.

He had been a cop. Secondarily a cop. Primarily an insane cultist. There had been four of them. They murdered one of their own, and I killed one of them. The other two were now in prison for life, where they still worshipped their satanic master.

In that moment of my return, I felt as though I were a spirit, having perished in a forgotten conflict, my body shed and left to decompose in some far field. I was unaware of moving my legs, and I no longer either heard or felt my feet stepping across the dirty travertine. I seemed to float toward the ice-cream shop, as if the white beam before me came not from the flashlight that I held but from some mysterious distant source, levitating and transporting me toward Burke & Bailey's.

The broken glass had been broomed into small jagged piles. Even under a thin film of dust, the sharp edges of the shards sparkled. I thought, *Here lie your hopes and dreams, shattered and swept aside,* and could not raise a ghost of the optimism that previously I had been able to conjure even in the bleakest moments.

As I crossed the threshold, I saw in memory Stormy Llewellyn as she had been that day, dressed in her work clothes: pink shoes, white socks, a hot-pink skirt, a matching pink-and-white blouse, and a perky pink cap. She'd sworn that when she had her own ice-cream shop, which she expected to secure by the time she was twenty-four, if not sooner, she would not provide her employees with dorky uniforms. No matter how frivolous the outfit she wore, she was an incomparable beauty with jet-black hair, dark eyes of mysterious depth, a lovely face, and perfect form.

Was. Had been. No more.

I think you look adorable.

Get real, odd one. I look like a goth Gidget.

She'd been standing behind the service counter when Simon Varner opened fire. Perhaps she had looked up as the windows shattered, had seen the ominous masked figure, and thought not of death but of me. She had always considered her own needs less than those of others; and I believe that her last thought in this world wouldn't have been regret at dying so young but instead concern for me, that I should be left alone in my grief.

Maybe one day when I have my own shop, we can work together. . . .

The ice-cream business doesn't move me. I love to fry.

I guess it's true.

What?

Opposites attract.

Until now, I had not returned to Burke & Bailey's after that dreadful day. I knew that suffering can purify, that it's a kind of fire that can be worth enduring, but there were degrees of it to which I chose not to subject myself.

The tables and chairs were gone, as well as freezers and milk-shake mixers and other equipment. Attached to the back wall was the menu of flavors, topped by Burke & Bailey's newest offering at that time: COCONUT CHERRY CHOCOLATE CHUNK.

I remembered having referred to it as cherry chocolate coconut chunk, whereupon she had corrected me.

Coconut cherry chocolate chunk. You've got to get the proper adjective in front of chunk *or you're screwed.*

I didn't realize the grammar of the ice-cream industry was so rigid.

Describe it your way, and some weasel customers will eat the whole thing and then ask for their money back because there weren't chunks of coconut in it. And don't ever call me adorable again. Puppies are adorable.

At the end of the long counter, I opened a low gate and entered the work area from which Stormy had been serving customers when the shooting started. The flashlight revealed vinyl tiles littered with plastic spoons, pink-and-white plastic straws, and dust balls that quivered away from me as I moved.

I relied on intuition to stop at the very place that Stormy had been standing when she'd been cut down. The stains underfoot were more than a year and a half old, and I considered them only briefly before moving past them and sitting on the floor.

This was the still point around which my life turned, the axis of my world. Here she had died.

I switched off the flashlight and sat in darkness so complete that it seemed as if all the light had gone out of the world and would never return.

After her death, her spirit had lingered for some days this side of the veil. My grief was so heavy, so bitter, that I couldn't endure it, and for a while I lived in denial. Lingering spirits look as real to me as do living people. They are not translucent. Neither do they glow with supernatural energy. If I touch them, they have substance. They do not talk, however, and Stormy's silence should have at once told me that her spirit had left her body and that before me stood the essence of the girl I loved, her splendid soul, but not the girl complete and physical. My denial was close to madness; I imagined conversations between us, made meals that she could not eat, poured wine she could not drink, planned a wedding that could never be consummated. By my desperate longing, I held her to this world days after she should have passed on to the next.

Now, sitting on the floor, behind the counter in the ice-cream shop, I spoke to her, unconcerned that with my paranormal talent I might draw her back into this troubled world. Those who pass to the next life do not return. Not even the power of love, as intense a love as any a man had ever felt for a woman, could open a door in the barrier between Stormy and me.

"It won't be long now," I said softly.

I felt that she could hear my words even a world away. That may sound weird to you, but stranger things have happened to me. When you have come face-to-face with a senoculus, a six-eyed demon with human form and the head of a bull, you grow more open-minded about what might and might not be possible.

Besides, I have no choice but to believe that all our lives are woven through with grace, because only then could the promise made to me and Stormy come true.

Six years earlier, when we were sixteen, we went to Pico Mundo's annual county fair. At the back of a carnival-arcade tent stood a fortune-telling machine. We dropped a quarter in the slot and asked if we would have a long and happy marriage. The card given to us couldn't have been more reassuring: YOU ARE DESTINED TO BE TOGETHER FOREVER.

Framed behind glass, that card had hung above Stormy's bed when she still lived. I carried it now in my wallet.

I whispered again, "It won't be long now."

I don't believe it's possible to imagine a favorite scent, to recall a fragrance as vividly as one can hear a tune in the mind's ear or see in the mind's eye a place visited long ago. Nevertheless, as I sat there in the lightless shop, I smelled the peach-scented shampoo that Stormy had used. After a shift cooking in the Pico Mundo Grille, when my hair had sometimes smelled like hamburger grease and fried onions, she gave me that same shampoo; but I hadn't been able to find the brand anymore and hadn't used it in months.

"They're coming to Pico Mundo. More cultists. Inspired by those who . . . murdered you. They aren't content anymore with quiet rituals and human sacrifices on secret altars. What happened here has shown them a more thrilling way to . . . practice their faith. In fact, I think they're already in town."

No sooner had those words escaped me than I heard laughter in the distance and then voices echoing through the mall.

I started to get to my feet, but a blush of light rose across the face of the darkness, and I stayed below the counter.

Three

The voices abruptly grew louder when the new arrivals entered the former ice-cream shop. Unless others were present who did not speak, there were three of them, a woman and two men.

Fearing that they might lean over the counter or come to the end of it to shine their flashlights along the service area, I eased into a space once occupied by an under-the-counter refrigerator or other piece of equipment, into cobwebs that clung like a veil to my face and tickled my nostrils toward a sneeze.

As I wiped the veil away and imagined poisonous spiders, the woman asked, "What was the body count, Wolfgang? I mean in this store alone?"

Wolfgang had a voice perhaps roughened by countless packs of cigarettes and more than a little whiskey taken neat and therefore scalding. "Four, including a pregnant woman."

I had thought they must have found the door through which I'd forced entry, the tools that I'd left behind. But they didn't seem to be searching for anyone; evidently they had entered the mall by a route different from mine.

The second man had a soft voice, naturally mellifluous but too honeyed, as though he must be so practiced in deceit that even when he was in the company of his closest comrades and speaking from the heart, he could not change his tone to match the circumstances. "Mother and child taken together. Such admirable efficiency. Two for the price of just one bullet."

"When I said four," Wolfgang replied with a note of impatient correction, "I wasn't, of course, counting the unborn."

"Incunabula," the woman said, which meant nothing to me. "It wasn't in the newspaper count of nineteen. Why would you think it had been, Jonathan?"

Rather than reply, the corrected efficiency expert, Jonathan, changed the subject. "Who were the other three?"

Wolfgang said, "There was a young father and his daughter. . . ."

I had known them. Rob Norwich was a high-school English teacher who sometimes had Saturday breakfast with his daughter, Emily, at the Pico Mundo Grille. He loved my hash browns. His wife had died of cancer when Emily was only four.

"How old was the child?" the woman asked.

"Six," Wolfgang replied, adding a sort of sigh to the end of the word, making two syllables of it.

I wondered who these people were, for what purpose they had found their way into the mall. Perhaps they were merely three more of those legions whose patronage made hits of torture-porn horror movies, on vacation and eager to satisfy their morbid curiosity by touring mass-murder sites. Or maybe they were not as innocent as that.

"Just six," the woman said, as if relishing the number. "Varner would've been well rewarded for that one."

Simon Varner, the bad cop, the gunman on that day.

Wolfgang had all the facts. "Her father's face was blown away."

Jonathan said, "Any chance the coroner determined which of those two was shot first, Daddy's girl or Daddy himself?"

"The father. They say the daughter held on for about half an hour."

"So she *saw* him shot in the face," the woman said, and seemed to take smug satisfaction in that depressing fact.

One of the flashlight beams traveled up the long list of ice-cream flavors on the back wall, which I could still see from the nook in which I hid, and at the top it came to rest for a moment on COCONUT CHERRY CHOCOLATE CHUNK.

"Victim four," said Wolfgang, "was Bronwen Llewellyn. Twenty years old. The store manager."

My lost girl. She disliked the name Bronwen. Everyone called her Stormy.

Wolfgang said, "She was a good-looking bitch. They showed her photo on TV more than any of the others because she was hot."

The beam traveled across the flavor list, to the wall and down, lingering for a moment on a pattern of blood spray that once had been scarlet but was now the color of rust.

"Is this Bronwen Llewellyn important?" asked Jonathan. "Is she why we've come here?"

"She's one reason." The light moved away from the blood-stains. "Ideally, she'd be buried somewhere, we could dig her up, use the corpse to mess with his mind. But she was cremated and never buried."

In addition to seeing the spirits of the dead, I have a gift that Stormy called psychic magnetism. If I drive around or bicycle, or walk, all the while thinking about someone—a name, a face—I will sooner than later be drawn to them. Or they to me. I didn't know these three people, wasn't thinking about them before they arrived; nevertheless, here they were. This might have been unconscious psychic magnetism—or mere chance.

"Who has her ashes?" the woman asked.

"I don't know. Several possibilities."

Their footsteps retreated from the ice-cream shop, and distance dimmed the lights they carried.

I came out of hiding, rose to my feet, and hurried to the gate at the end of the counter. Regardless of the risks, I needed to know more about those people.

Four

Revealed only as shadowy forms wielding swords of light, the trio moved leisurely toward the north end of the mall, pausing to fence with the darkness and illuminate one point of interest or another.

I dared not switch on my flashlight. Their conversation gave me some cover, but if I followed blindly in their wake, I was likely to step on something that would make enough noise to attract their attention.

My dilemma was resolved when a hand laid on my shoulder made me turn my head, whereupon I came face-to-face with a softly glowing man *who had no face.* Eyeless sockets regarded me from a mask of bullet-torn flesh and shattered bone.

After so many years of supernatural experience, I was by then immune to the sudden fear that others would have experienced at the unexpected touch of a hand in the dark. Likewise, the hideous face—or the absence of one—inspired no fright, but instead sadness and pity.

I could assume only that here stood the spirit of Rob Norwich, who had died in the ice-cream shop almost two years earlier, the father of six-year-old Emily, who had also died. If the child had moved on from this world, her father had not.

Never before had a spirit appeared radiant to me, and I thought he manifested in this manner so that, by accompanying me, he might serve as a lamp to reveal the way. Aglow or not, he could be seen only by me, and the light that he emitted, although it revealed the floor around us, most likely also remained invisible to Wolfgang and Jonathan, and to the nameless woman.

His face in death resolved into the countenance he possessed when alive, the wounds closing up. Rob had been thirty-two, with receding blond hair, pleasant features, and eyes the soft green of cactus skin.

He cocked his head as if to inquire whether I understood his purpose, and I nodded to confirm that I did and that I trusted him. The dead don't talk. I don't know why.

Quickly he led me to the nearby escalator, which was powerless now, only a staircase of grooved steel treads that angled over the dry formation that had once been the koi pond. I followed him up to the second floor, for the moment heading away from the creepy trio that interested me.

I feared that the escalator, so long out of service, would creak or clatter underfoot. The treads were firm, however, and they weren't littered with debris.

At the top, I followed Rob Norwich to the right and then north, keeping away from the storefronts, staying near the railing beyond which, had there been more light, I could have looked down into the ground-level promenade. Here and there lay scatterings of trash, but guided by the spirit's radiance, I was able to step over or around the debris without making a sound.

On the lower promenade, the suspicious trio halted, flashlights concentrated on something beneath the upper concourse on which I stood. Bullet-pocked walls, perhaps. Or an interesting pattern in a spray of blood.

Hoping that their faces might be at least half revealed in the backwash of light, I leaned against the railing and peered down at the group. But the angle was too severe for me to see much about them.

I don't know what gave me away. I'm sure that I didn't make a sound. Perhaps I disturbed some small piece of litter that rolled between the balusters and fell past one of the men below, because abruptly he turned his flashlight toward me. The bright beam found my face and dazzled me so that I couldn't clearly see him or any of them.

Rob Norwich, my most recent friend among the dead, put a hand on my shoulder again, and I turned to him as, in the concourse below, Wolfgang shouted, "That's *him*. Get him. *Kill him!*"

Any remaining illusion I had that these people might be mere horror junkies, touring the mall because of its bloody history, evaporated. Although they hadn't known that I was there, they had come because they were associated with the demonic cult that I had infiltrated in Nevada, and this place inspired them. They were in Pico Mundo to honor the mass murderers who had shot up Green Moon Mall back in the day, to honor them by committing some greater atrocity elsewhere in town.

Because of the events in Nevada, they knew that I might be the only one who could foil them. This chance encounter—if anything in life occurred by chance—gave them an opportunity to waste me, thereby improving the odds that their specific intentions wouldn't be known until it was too late for anyone to stop them.

My ghostly companion, who served also as my guiding light, hurried toward the nearer of the two abandoned department stores that anchored the shopping mall, the one at the south end. He must have had an exit strategy in mind for me, but I didn't follow him.

Rob had been a good man in life, and I didn't worry that his spirit might be malevolent. He was not intent on leading me into the arms of my enemies.

The lingering dead, however, aren't entirely reliable. After all, for whatever reasons, in spite of the certainty that they can't undo their deaths and that there is no satisfying future in the haunting business, they're either reluctant to leave the beauty and wonder of this world or afraid of stepping into the next one. They are not acting rationally regarding the most important issue before them; therefore, trusting in them without reservation was even less likely to work out well for me than trusting an IRS auditor to help me find beaucoup tax deductions that I might have overlooked.

Now that Wolfgang and his two comrades knew where I was, they would most likely head to the south escalator, by far the nearest route to the second-floor promenade. I was unlikely to make it into that empty department store before they could cut me off.

Instead, daring to hurry through the darkness, I went north and made considerable distance before stumbling over something and knocking it aside, whereupon I heard the woman shout, "He's going that way!"

I no longer had a reason to risk the darkness. I switched on my flashlight, cupping one hand around the lens to make it less visible from below.

As I reached the end of the promenade, I heard booming footsteps and rattling metal: someone running up the north escalator, which evidently wasn't in as good condition as the one at the south end that I had climbed so quietly. Suddenly a light speared upward, searching for me, as the person on those stairs reached the halfway point.

The doors to the northern department store, pneumatic sliders, no longer operative, were frozen in the open position. I raced through them, into what had once been a temple to luxury goods, where the god of excess consumption held court. Many of the display cases had been left in place, and I ducked behind them, hunched and hustling, until I heard my hunters shouting to one another, and then I halted and switched off the flashlight.

Now what?

Five

My psychic magnetism worked best when I was seeking someone whose face and name I knew, though one or the other would usually suffice. On a few occasions, I had conjured in my mind the image of an object for which I was searching, and eventually I was drawn to it, though not in as timely a fashion as when my quarry was a person.

As the three hunters spread out in the department store, I pictured the pillowcase that contained a bolt cutter, a crowbar, and a hammer. I had left it just inside the door through which I'd broken into the mall.

When I felt the urge to move, I set out once more, hunched and scuttling as silently as possible. I followed the display cases, all with glass fronts and tops but with solid backs that would shield me from the cultists—unless one of them stepped into the aisle along which I traveled. At an intersection with other rows of cabinets, I turned right, moving steadily away from what little illumination the distant flashlight beams provided when they ricocheted off the walls and columns and glass displays.

Forward into darkness.

I had never before counted on psychic magnetism to make my way through pitch-black rooms, but only to lead me eventually to that which I sought. Now I decided that having paranormal abilities wouldn't mean much if, on the way to my goal, my wild talent could run me head-on into a wall, send me tumbling down a staircase, or drop me into an open shaft. Surely I could trust it now, had to trust it, just like Spider-Man trusted his web-spinning ability to swing from skyscraper to skyscraper even though the briefest interruption in his production of spider silk could drop him eighty stories to the street below.

Of course, Spider-Man was a comic-book character. He couldn't die unless the company that owned him was in the mood to flush away a multibillion-dollar property. I was a real person, and I wasn't worth multiple billions to anyone.

I ventured into lightless realms, although tentatively at first, sliding one hand along a display case. My other hand was extended in front of me, alternately anticipating a wall where empty air should be and feeling the floor to avoid a sudden drop-off or debris.

At the rate I was going, I wouldn't escape the three searchers, and even if I did elude them, I'd die of thirst or starvation before I got to the pillowcase of tools that I pictured in my mind's eye.

I had always assumed that my gift was just that, a *gift*, not the result of a rare gene or of some beneficial brain damage related to my mother's consumption of martinis during her pregnancy. A gift like mine seemed to come from some higher power, and whatever the source—whether God or space aliens or wizards living in a parallel Earth where magic worked—it must be a *benign* higher power, because I was motivated to help the innocent and afflict the guilty. I had no desire to use my abilities to amass colossal wealth or to rule the planet with either a velvet glove or an iron fist.

Taking a deep breath, all but totally blind, trusting in my psychic magnetism as Spidey trusted in his web spinning, as Wile E. Coyote trusted in products sold by Acme to snare or kill the Road Runner, I rose somewhat and, in the hunched posture of an ape, hurried forward. If trash of any kind littered the floor, I didn't once set foot on it. If there were obstacles in my way, I didn't collide with them. Intuitively, I turned this way, that way, this way, marveling at my ability to navigate successfully and with hardly a sound.

I had always been in awe of Stevie Wonder and Ray Charles, blind men who sat at their pianos and never played a bad note, absolutely certain of where the keys were in relation to their fingers. I dared to feel a connection with them, though I had no more musical talent than a rock; standing taller, moving rapidly and successfully through total darkness, I thrilled to the experience as sometimes I had thrilled to Stevie's and Ray's piano work.

The searchers fell far behind me. I couldn't see even the most indirect glow of their lights. I couldn't hear them, either, though perhaps because my heart was pounding so hard that the blood-rush roar in my ears was like my own private Niagara.

With my right shoulder, I brushed against something, only the slightest contact, but it alarmed me, and I stopped. I turned, felt around me as if in a game of blind man's bluff. I discovered a doorless doorway, the cold metal jamb slightly oily to the touch.

I thought I knew where I was. This must be the stockroom that had once supplied the sporting-goods department, from which stairs led down to the employees-only level under the mall. On the day of the mass murder, when I'd passed through this place in the grip of psychic magnetism, desperately seeking the gunman, Simon Varner, before he could kill, I had encountered a pretty redhead busily pulling small boxes off packed storage shelves. She'd said *Hey,* in a friendly way, and I'd said *Hey,* and I had kept moving through the door and onto the sales floor, expecting the dreadful sound of gunfire at any moment—which had come only a few minutes later.

Now I heard a voice. A woman. But not the redhead. One of the searchers. She was shouting, excited. I was too far away to hear exactly what she said, but I caught the word *footprints.*

The mall had been abandoned for many months. Time might have laid a thin carpet of dust, probably not everywhere but here and there, revealing part of the route I had taken.

Suddenly, out there beyond the stockroom, a flashlight flared, another, a third. They were closer than I expected.

Picturing the pillowcase full of tools once more, I hurried across the stockroom, stopped, felt a door jamb where I expected it, and stepped blindly onto the first step of the two flights of stairs that led down to the mall's underworld. Using the railing to steady myself, I descended as far as the mid-floor landing before I heard voices above, perhaps not in the stockroom yet but approaching it.

I hustled down the last flight, eased open the fire door just far enough to slip through, closed it as quietly as possible, and switched on my flashlight. Here in the wide service corridor, dust hadn't settled as it had in the high-ceilinged, cavernous sales floor above. I'd left no footprints on my way in; and I would leave none on my way out.

From the stairwell behind me came an eager voice, footsteps descending.

If I followed the route by which I had originally entered the mall, there was nowhere close to hide. The two freight elevators featured open-work steel gates instead of solid sliders. Farther away were the double doors to the loading dock, which I couldn't possibly reach before the cultists arrived and saw me.

I turned in the opposite direction, where there were rooms on the left side of the corridor. I hurried to the nearest door, opened it, switched off my flashlight, and crossed the threshold as I heard my pursuers spilling out of the stairwell.

As I quietly shut the door, a stench rose around me, the stink of rot and feces and sulfur and—strangely—ammonia so intense that I gagged and my eyes watered. I dared not step farther into whatever living nightmare might await me, but I couldn't flee to the corridor, either. I eased to my left and pressed my back to the wall.

The hinges immediately to my right made a grinding bone-on-bone sound as the door opened. The nameless woman rattled off a series of colorful words to express her disgust at the malodor and at the sight that her flashlight revealed.

Approximately forty feet on a side, the room offered foot-deep mounds of whitish matter streaked with gray and mottled with yellow, nearly all of it heaped toward the back half of the space. The stuff glistened in many places, lay dry and cracked and pocked in others, and busy beetles scurried across it, like minia-ture mechanical moon rovers exploring the surface of an airless world. Here and there, bristling from the hideous mass were dark, twisted, spiky things that, after a moment, I realized must be dead bats that were especially interesting to the beetles.

The woman's flashlight beam traveled up to a wall-to-wall grid of metal rods suspended a foot below the true ceiling, from which perhaps merchandise had once been hung while it awaited delivery to stores overhead. The filth-encrusted rods were less interesting than the bats depending from them. The flourishing colony hung for the most part in sleep, but the traveling light encouraged a few to open eyes that glowed like yellow-orange jewels.

Wolfgang, the guy with the whiskied voice, cursed and said, "Close the damn door, Selene."

Fortunately, Selene didn't slam it. She eased the door shut as though she had accidentally lifted the lid of Dracula's coffin and, being without garlic or a pointed stake, hoped to slip away before the thirsty count bestirred himself.

I heard the trio talking in the corridor, but I couldn't make out what they were saying.

Inhaling the disgusting odor of dung and rot and musk, I stood with my back to the wall and waited for one of the bats to squeak. One of them did. Then another.

Six

Amaranth.

Between the rescue of the kidnapped children in Nevada and my return to Pico Mundo, I lived for two months in a cozy three-bedroom seaside cottage with Annamaria. It was in this charming house, in late May, on the night before I would ride the Big Dog motorcycle across the Mojave, that I had the dream of the amaranth.

Having met in late January, on a pier in the town of Magic Beach, farther up the coast from where we lived now, Annamaria and I were friends, never paramours. But we were more than friends, because she was, like me, more than she appeared to be.

During the four months that I had known her, she'd been eight months pregnant. She claimed that she had been pregnant not merely eight months but a long time, and she said that she would be pregnant longer still. She never spoke of the father, and she seemed to live without worry about her future.

Many things she said made no sense to me, but I trusted her. She wrapped herself in mystery and had some purpose that I *could not comprehend. But she never lied, never betrayed, and compassion shone forth from her as light from the sun.*

Neither a great beauty nor plain, she had flawless skin, large dark eyes, and long dark hair. She never wore other than sneakers, elastic-waist khakis, and baggy sweaters. Because she was petite in spite of her swollen belly, she always looked like a waif, though she claimed to be eighteen.

She sometimes called me "young man." I was four years older than Annamaria, but this habit of hers also seemed right.

I knew her only hours when she told me that she had enemies who would kill her and her unborn child if they got the chance. She had asked if I would die for her, and I had surprised myself by saying at once, "Yes."

Although she pretended that I served as her valiant protector, she did more to pull me out of one dangerous place or another than I ever did for her.

On the night that I dreamed of the amaranth, Annamaria and I and the nine-year-old boy named Tim slept in our separate rooms in the cottage. A golden retriever, Raphael, shared the child's bed. Rescued three months earlier from horrific circumstances, Tim now had no family but us. I've written of him in the seventh volume of these memoirs and won't repeat myself in this eighth.

In Greek mythology, the amaranth was an undying flower that remained at the peak of its beauty for eternity. But the dream did not begin with the flower.

From a peaceful sleep, I plunged into a nightmare of chaos and cacophony. Screaming rose all around me. Some of the voices were fraught with terror, but an equal number seemed to shriek with a glee that was more disturbing than the fearful cries. Wound among all the human voices was another tapestry of grotesque sound, churr and howl and ululation, bray and squeal and clangor. Much light in many colors whirled and throbbed, yet did not illuminate. Racing streams of red and yellow and blue smeared across my eyes and blurred my vision. I could not understand what little I was able to see: a giant stone wheel, three or four stories high, rolling, rolling straight toward me at tremendous velocity; faces swelling like balloons about to burst, but then shrinking as they deflated; hundreds of hands simultaneously grasping at me and thrusting me away. . . .

Seven

The deserts of California and the Southwest provide a sustaining environment for a variety of bats. Earlier, I hadn't been surprised to see them swarming out of a cave mouth at the bottom of the ravine into which the Cadillac Escalade plunged, but I had not the slightest expectation of finding them in a shopping mall basement, not even if the mall was long abandoned and awaiting a wrecking crew. There must have been an exit from this room by which they left to hunt after nightfall and by which they returned each day before dawn, perhaps a ventilation shaft, maybe a chaseway for plumbing or electrical cables.

I had thought the first flight of bats must be an omen, and after this more intimate encounter such a short time later, I had no doubt that the bats augured something. The problem with omens is that they never come with an illustrated pamphlet explaining what they mean. I am no better at interpreting them than I would be at puzzling out the meaning of a conversation between a guy speaking Uzbek and a guy speaking Eskimo, which I tried to do once when a multilingual Eskimo and a multilingual Uzbekistani were arguing about which one had the best reason to kill me.

At that moment, just after Selene had shut the door, closing me in with the stench, I was less concerned about the meaning of signs and portents than about holding down my gorge, which seemed on the verge of leaving my stomach and erupting in a credible imitation of Mount Vesuvius.

I stood listening to voices in the corridor and to the squeaks and the ruffling of wings as the bats settled down after the brief annoyance of the opened door and the intrusion of the flashlight. I gagged, and the residents of the room didn't seem to appreciate the sound I made, perhaps taking it as criticism, and so I resolved not to gag again, as I was always loath to give offense.

Trapped between the cultists and the winged horde, I tried to remember everything that I knew about bats. My friend Ozzie Boone, the four-hundred-pound best-selling mystery novelist who mentored my own writing, had written a novel that involved murder-by-bats as a red herring. When Ozzie became fascinated with a new line of research, he insisted on sharing his enthusiasm, no matter how creepy the subject might be, though vampire bats weren't as disturbing as what he shared when he wrote a story in which the victim was murdered by a personal chef who fed him watercress salads infested with the tiny eggs of liver flukes.

Bats were the only mammals that could fly. Flying lemurs and flying squirrels, swooping from one treetop to another, were only gliding; they didn't possess wings to flap. Bats did not get tangled in people's hair. They were not blind. Even in absolute darkness, a bat could find its way by echolocation; therefore, I suppose that, considering my psychic magnetism, I should have felt some kinship with these creatures. I did not. I never had quite gotten a handle on that multicultural thing. Most of the species in the

Mojave were insect eaters, though a few fed on cactus flowers and sage blossoms and the like. There were vampire bats, too.

The vampires were small, maybe four inches. The size of a mouse. They weighed little more than an ounce. Each night, they could eat their own weight in blood. A vampire bat would never kill me, but a thousand might be seriously draining.

Maybe these were vampire bats. Maybe they weren't.

Of course they were. Other than griddle work, nothing ever came easy to me.

In the pitch-black room, the disturbed colony had grown quieter, most of the restless insomniacs at last joining their blood-crazed companions in slumber, lost in dreams that I would definitely not try to imagine. A soft brief rustle here. A thin squeak over there. The harmless little noises of the last few weary individuals getting cozy for their morning sleep.

Death by vampire bats would be less painful than you might suppose. Their teeth were so exquisitely sharp that you wouldn't even feel the cuts they made. People were rarely bitten by vampire bats, which mostly drank the blood of chickens, cattle, horses, and deer.

I didn't find the word *rarely* as comforting as the word *never.*

In the corridor beyond the closed door, the voices of the three cultists had faded completely away. Their silence didn't mean that they had given up their search for me and had gone back to their usual activities, like strangling babies and torturing kittens. No offense intended to the satanists who might be reading this, but I have found that those who worship the devil tend to be sneaky, more deceitful by far than your average Methodist—and proud of it. They might still be in the mall basement or garage, standing silently in the darkness, waiting for me to show myself, whereupon my life would be worth spit, and in fact less than spit.

Some people believe that a vampire bat is attracted by the smell of blood, that you have to be bleeding, even if from a tiny puncture or a scratch, before the little beasts will be drawn to you in a feeding frenzy. That is not true. Instinctively, bats know that any creature that sweats also bleeds. If a molecule or two of sweat, floating on the air, found its way into the folds of their nostrils, they would twitch their whiskers and bare their razor-edged teeth and lick their thin lips and, in the current situation, be pleased by the realization that someone had ordered takeout and it had been delivered.

I was perspiring.

Something crawled off my shirt and onto my throat and explored the contours of my Adam's apple. Over the years, after numerous shocks and horrific encounters, my nerves had become as steady as solid-state circuitry. I figured one of the beetles that had been eating the dead bats in the dung pile had found its way up my body, too light to have been felt through my clothes. Instead of shrieking like Little Miss Muffet, I reached up to my throat and captured the insect in my fist.

Because of the ick factor, I didn't want to crush the bug. But when I attempted to throw it back toward the dung pile from which it had come, the vicious little thing stuck to my hand with the tenacity of a tick.

Ozzie Boone had written a novel in which the villain threw one of his victims, an IRS agent, into a pit seething with carnivorous beetles. In spite of the tax man's flailing, stomping, and desperate attempts to climb out of that hellhole, the voracious swarm killed him in six minutes and stripped his bones of every last scrap of flesh in three hours and ten minutes, not as rapidly as piranhas might have done the job, but impressive nonetheless.

Sometimes I wished that my mentor had been Danielle Steel.

I opened my right hand, in which the beetle had gotten a death grip on my palm, made a catapult of the forefinger and thumb of my left hand, and flung the noxious little bugger back into the reeking darkness.

I hadn't heard a sound from the three cultists in a few minutes, and as I listened intently to the occasional bat rearrange its wings around itself as though adjusting its blanket, I wondered if the castaway beetle had been an outlier, more adventurous than others of its kind. Or even now were numerous others exploring my shoes and climbing the legs of my jeans?

If I have machinelike steady-state nerves, I unfortunately also have the imagination of an acutely sensitive, hyperactive four-year-old on a sugar high, a four-year-old with an understanding of death equal to that of a war veteran.

Although I felt certain I would die here in Pico Mundo within days, I told myself that the fatal moment had not yet arrived, and that it was not my fate to be beetled to death. I would have been reassured if I hadn't lied to myself often in the past.

I was about to bolt from beetles real and imagined, from bats sleeping or not, when I heard a door slam in some far region of the basement, and I concluded that the cultists must still be searching for me.

I had not seen their faces. Although I knew their first names, they were anonymous. A strange thought disturbed me: If they should kill me, and if we met eventually in some place beyond the grave, they would know me, but I would not know them.

Given more time to recall what I had learned about bats from Ozzie Boone, I remembered that a minimum thirty percent of any colony would reliably be infected with rabies.

Darkness so perfect it made my eyes ache, the fetid air so thick that the stink became also a foul taste, the whispery sounds of the carnivorous beetles feeding on the tiny carcasses of rabies-infected bats, the occasional ruffle of wings as members of the colony stirred in their sleep, the expectation that they would abruptly take flight and prove Ozzie wrong regarding their affinity for human hair: In that poisonous atmosphere, I became more disoriented minute by grim minute. Decomposing dung releases sulfurous gas, deadly in sufficient concentration, and if not ultimately lethal here, at least capable of making me lightheaded, even delirious. I grew convinced that a time would soon come when, like an astronaut in zero gravity, I would have no sense of up or down. If I dropped the flashlight, I just *knew* I wouldn't be able to locate it, and when I attempted to escape this room, the door wouldn't be where I expected to find it.

Alarmed by what I do not know, the entire colony erupted from the overhead grid of rods from which they hung, and they broke into what seemed to be chaotic flight, though according to Ozzie, there was always orderliness in bat formations, each individual aware of its assigned position.

At once I slid down against the concrete wall until I was squatting, trying to stay well below their flight path, the multitude of shrill voices giving rise to gooseflesh on my gooseflesh. Their squeaking is why people think of them as flying rodents, and although they really aren't rodents, I felt as if I were in some whacked-out low-budget movie about a rat storm.

Their wings beat fourteen times a second, another bit of trivia, courtesy of Ozzie. Although none of them brushed against me as they whirled around the room, I felt the wind of their passage, which stirred even more intense odors from the air as surely as a chef's ladle would stir more appealing aromas from a soup pot.

However they might have exited, they didn't leave by the door. The flutter of their wings inspired sympathetic vibrations deep in my ears, so that I shivered uncontrollably until their numbers had significantly diminished. Then the last were gone, silence fell upon the room in their wake, and I rose to my full height, shaken and nauseated.

When the bats erupted out of the mall by whatever route, they would quickly realize that dawn was coming. The day world was not theirs, and the moment that their alarm subsided and instinct guided them once more, they would return. Perhaps in the next minute or two. Agitated. Bats were capable of anger. Especially vampire bats. The males frequently fought. I didn't want to hang around to find out if they would ignore me or instead focus on me as the primary object of their rage.

The door featured a lever handle that worked with a minimum of noise. I opened it, wincing at the faint creak of the hinges, and faced a service corridor as pitch-black as the room behind me.

For a moment, I listened to the eerie quiet, cocking my head to the left, to the right. If Wolfgang, Jonathan, and Selene were still lurking in the immediate vicinity, they should have heard the exodus of the bats, even through the closed door, should have switched on their flashlights and found me when I was betrayed by the hinges.

I stepped across the threshold and eased the door shut behind me. By comparison to the wretched stink I'd just escaped, the air here smelled so sweet that I wanted to draw great noisy breaths, but in the interest of avoiding a bullet in the head, I refrained. After listening for another half minute, I clicked on my light.

Solid-state nerve circuitry didn't serve me well, because I jumped when, from behind, a hand gripped my shoulder. I turned and found Rob Norwich, my recent spirit guide, no longer glowing, but with his face again blown away.

Eight

Rob Norwich's eyeless sockets, fragmentary nose, lipless mouth, broken facial bones, and other elements of bloody ruin were, as far as I was concerned, not conducive to conversation, whether in that gloomy mall basement or in a sunny park.

"Sir," I whispered, "you have to stop coming up behind me. And I'd be grateful if you kept your face on."

The ravaged countenance faded, and the gentle features of the English teacher replaced it. His expression said, *Sorry.*

"Are those three still here somewhere—Wolfgang, Jonathan, and Selene?"

He shook his head.

"They've left the mall?"

He nodded.

"Sorry I didn't follow you to the other department store, sir, but going there wasn't the right thing."

He nodded again.

Having a conversation with a dead guy can be duller than you might think. Only someone in love with his own voice could be routinely enchanted by the experience.

Usually, lingering spirits come to me because, whether they realize it or not, they want me to talk them into moving on from this world. A couple of them have even been celebrities who were loath to leave this realm where they had been loved by so many. I have written about Mr. Presley and Mr. Sinatra in other volumes of this memoir, both of whom had been thornier problems for me than I imagined a former English teacher would be.

"Is there something I can do for you, Mr. Norwich?"

He shrugged.

"You're afraid to cross over to the Other Side. Is that it, sir?"

He held one hand out, palm down, and rocked it back and forth, a gesture of equivocation. Maybe he was afraid to cross over, maybe he wasn't. He didn't want to commit himself to an opinion. He was dead, but he wanted to keep his options open. Although he'd been an English teacher, he was acting like a lawyer.

"Sir, your wife and daughter are already over there. Do you believe that?"

He nodded.

"Don't you want to join them?"

He nodded. Then he held out both hands, palms up, and raised his eyebrows as if inquiring about something.

"You're wondering what it's like over there?"

He nodded vigorously.

"Well, not having been there, sir, I can't describe it. But my girlfriend, Stormy Llewellyn, she believed this life is the first of three. She called it boot camp. She said we're here just to prepare ourselves for a second life of service in some great adventure beyond our imagination. She thought it might be like *The Lord of the Rings* but with more magic, more danger, worse things than

Orcs, maybe with no elves, though she had nothing against elves, maybe like Tolkien with a noir edge, something that would have roles for Bogart and Mitchum if it were a movie. And John Wayne, for sure."

Mr. Norwich just stared at me.

It was my turn to shrug. "I'm not saying that's what it's like, sir. It's just Stormy's theory. Like Purgatory, see, but a lot more colorful than we usually think of it. Anyway, whatever the second life is like, once we get to our third and eternal life, then it's all very sweet, you know, lovely and wondrous and perfect and happy-making."

He cocked his head and regarded me as he might have a student who had failed to read an assignment and was trying to fake his way through a discussion of Milton's *Paradise Lost.*

"Just take the leap, sir. What have you got to lose—other than the misery of ghosting around in this life where you don't belong anymore?"

Mr. Norwich shook his head—no, I had not convinced him— and he dematerialized, there one moment but gone the next.

I hate it when they do that. I find it rude. You'd think he could have at least waved bye-bye or patted me on the head.

In the nearby suburban bat cave, the colony returned with a demonic symphony of squeaking and the beating of many wings, angry to have been spooked from their roosts.

"Okay, an omen . . . meaning what?" I asked.

But the closed door said nothing more to me than had the mute spirit of the English teacher.

With my flashlight, I found my way out of the service corridor, onto the subterranean loading dock, down to the employee garage, and to the violated door, where I had left the pillowcase containing my burglary tools.

Outside, the May sun had mostly risen. The cloudless sky was sapphire-blue in the west, lighter blue overhead, coral-pink in the east, reminiscent of an old Wurlitzer jukebox.

At the top of the ramp down which eighteen-wheelers had once driven daily, I stopped to examine my shirt and jeans, my shoes, expecting liberal splatters of bat dung. To my surprise, I appeared both to have escaped bombardment and to have avoided stepping in anything disgusting. Hesitantly, I combed one hand through my hair, but by some miracle, I had also escaped the indignity of a poo shampoo.

Nevertheless, I needed a shower, and I wanted one more than I needed it. But not yet.

Wary that one of the cultists might have been posted to watch for me, feeling dangerously exposed, I crossed what seemed like a hundred acres of blacktop to the exit. Earlier, I had used the bolt cutter to sever the chain that held shut the gate to the fenced parking lot.

I had left the motorcycle in a nearby residential neighborhood of modest homes shaded by massive old ficus trees. No one was abroad at that hour, except for one rangy coyote slinking down the center of the street, reluctant to give up the night's hunt, looking left and right, hoping to find a house cat for breakfast or perhaps even a small child who had disobeyed his mother and had come outside alone.

Somehow the driver of the Escalade, who had tried to run me down the night before, had known that I would be traveling on the state route, straddling a Big Dog Bulldog Bagger; therefore, it made sense that the other cultists also might be looking for the bike. I didn't have a master-of-disguise kit and didn't intend to prowl Pico Mundo incognito; however, calling attention to myself didn't make sense, either. Later that morning, I would need to ditch the Big Dog and find other transportation, but first I had an appointment to keep and no other wheels to get there.

After stowing the pillowcase and tools in one of the saddle-bags, I put on my helmet and goggles. I pulled away from the curb and headed toward the coyote. It backed off but wasn't in-timidated. As I drove past the beast, it followed me with a yellow-eyed stare of predatory calculation, sharp teeth revealed in a sneer of contempt.

Nine

Formed by the construction of a dam, Malo Suerte Lake was immediately east of Pico Mundo, a large deep body of water with a marina and sandy beaches along the north shore. Associated with one of those beaches, a grassy park offered picnic areas shaded by phoenix palms and by the spreading branches of massive live oaks.

The park had long been popular in warm weather, which was most of the year in Maravilla County, but as it offered no campground, I had never before seen anyone there laying out a picnic breakfast less than an hour after dawn. Ozzie Boone had draped a white cloth over one of the concrete-slab picnic tables designed and anchored to foil thieves. On the cloth he had arranged several chafing dishes warmed by Sterno.

I drove past him, past the Cadillac that had been customized to accommodate his bulk and weight, and parked the Big Dog out of sight behind an oak. I hadn't seen him in a few months, since he had picked me up at St. Bartholomew's Abbey in the Sierra Nevada, where I had for a while lived in the guesthouse, hoping to find peace and quiet among the monks, finding instead a kind of darkness new to me.

As a writer, Ozzie served as my mentor. As a man, he had long been a surrogate father, which I had often needed. My real father had no idea how to fill that role. He'd never shown any desire to do so.

"Dear Odd," he said, enfolding me in a bear hug, "the last time I saw you, I feared you'd lost weight, and now I'm certain of it. You're a shadow of your former self."

"No, sir. I still weigh the same. Maybe I appear smaller to you because you've gotten still larger."

"I am a svelte four hundred thirty-five pounds, and if I can stick to my diet, I hope to be four hundred fifty by September."

"I worry about you," I said.

"Yes, you are quite the worrier for one of such tender years. But if obesity were the worst that any of us had to worry about, the world would be an idyllic place. You've probably noticed that it isn't."

"Yes, sir. I've noticed."

In a bucket of ice were a carton of orange juice and two of chocolate milk. He had also brought two large thermoses of coffee. He offered those beverages to me, and at my request he poured coffee, black.

The mug was large and thick, emblazoned with the words PICO MUNDO GRILLE and the logo of that diner, where I had once worked. I figured that the mug might be intended not only as a welcome-back gesture but also as a subtle suggestion that I return to my old job and put down roots and cease roaming in search of what only home could offer.

When I looked up, I saw that he had been watching me as

I stared at the mug. He said, "This *is* where you belong, Oddie. With those who love you most."

"Sir, you've not only gained weight since I saw you last, you've also become psychic."

"One doesn't need to be psychic to read your mind, Oddie. In spite of all your complications, you are wonderfully transparent."

"I guess I'll take that as a compliment."

"As it was intended." He picked up a tall glass of chocolate milk, savoring two long swallows before putting it down and dabbing at his faux mustache with a paper napkin. "When you called, you were as mysterious as a character in one of my novels. You were so discreet, you might as well have been talking in code. Why couldn't we have breakfast in my kitchen?"

"I didn't want to endanger you, sir. Are you sure you weren't followed here?"

He sighed. "If I had been followed here, dear boy, I wouldn't *be* here. What trouble has found you this time?"

"The same trouble, sir. Cultists like those who shot up the mall back then."

Ozzie writes noir fiction, and in spite of his rotundity, he thinks of himself as someone who can be a tough guy when the need arises. He does indeed have impressive forearms and considerable courage. But unshed tears rose in his eyes when I mentioned the mall shooting, because he wasn't only my surrogate father; to some extent, he had also fulfilled that role for Stormy, who had been orphaned as a child.

"They've come in from out of town," I continued. "They want to make what happened here two summers ago seem like nothing."

"In a sense, it was nothing," Ozzie said, tears still standing in his eyes. "Everything barbarians do is nothing, no matter how loudly they insist it's something."

The coffee had cooled just enough that I could sip it. "Sir, I don't know how many of them are here to do this thing. I don't know their faces, and I only know three first names. I'm afraid it's happening sooner than later, too fast for me to get a handle on it."

He finished the glass of chocolate milk and put it down on the white tablecloth and placed the heels of his plump hands over his eyes, rubbing gently, as though he hadn't slept in a long time and was weary, but of course he was blotting the tears and pressing them back.

I said, "I had a set-to with others of their cult over in Nevada not long ago, and it didn't end well for them. They'd like to kill me, and I can't pretend there wouldn't be an up side to that, but I'd rather stop them first."

Lowering his hands from his face, Ozzie said, "Anything happens to you, there's no up side, son. Not for me. There's only so much eating a man can do to keep the world at bay before he loses all taste for food."

Rarely am I at a loss for words, but I didn't know what to say to that. I covered my speechlessness with a few sips of coffee.

Ozzie reached for the open carton of milk wedged in the bucket of ice, but then decided not to pour any more for himself just yet.

He said, "I imagine that through all your adventures, you still held fast to it."

I knew what he meant. "Yes, sir." I put down the mug, took out my wallet, and produced the card from the fortune-telling machine.

His hand trembled as he held the little pasteboard prediction.

He appeared to read it more than once, as though hoping the simple statement might be modified before his eyes. YOU ARE DESTINED TO BE TOGETHER FOREVER. But of course the words did not change. Considering the source of the promise and the importance of it, I was confident that it would not be broken and in fact that it would be kept sooner than later—as long as I did not fail to do what I had been called home to accomplish.

As I took the card from him and returned it to my wallet, I said, "Whatever happens next, what most concerns me is that none of my friends should die because of me. If I let that happen . . . I won't have earned what I've been promised."

We turned together toward the sound of a car on the lane that wound through the park. A police cruiser approached and pulled off the pavement to stop half on the graveled shoulder and half on the grass, in the oak shadows, behind Ozzie's Cadillac.

Wyatt Porter, chief of police in Pico Mundo, got out of the car, closed the door, and for a moment stood looking at us across the roof of the vehicle. I had been fortunate enough to have two surrogate fathers when I'd lived in Pico Mundo, and they were both joining me for breakfast in the park. I hadn't seen the chief since I'd left town about nine months earlier. The last thing he'd said to me was, "I don't know what we'll do without you, son." What we had both done was keep on keeping on, which is all any of us can do. He looked good for a man who had once been shot in the chest and left for dead, and I was happier than I can say to see how well he appeared to be.

He rounded the car and came to us. I found myself smiling, but the chief did not smile. He nodded at Ozzie, and then he stopped in front of me and said, "Do you believe in dreams, Oddie?"

The chief—and very few others—knew about my paranormal

talents. He and I had worked together on a number of cases over the years, though he had always concealed my contributions and spared me from being made a media sensation.

"Dreams?" I said. "Some are just the mind playing games with itself, and they're not to be taken seriously. But I don't think that's the kind you mean."

"I had this same one three times in the past week, before you called, and I'm not given to reruns of dreams."

As if to forestall what Chief Porter would say next, Ozzie asked him if he wanted juice or milk, or coffee.

Instead of answering that question, the chief said to me, "Three times before you called, I dreamed you were coming home."

"And here I am."

He shook his head. With basset eyes and bloodhound jowls, the chief's face was proof of gravity's effect. He looked as solemn as time itself when he said, "What I dreamed is that you came home in a coffin."

Ten

The five chafing dishes contained scrambled eggs with black olives and cilantro, ham layered with sautéed onion slices, home fries, seasoned and buttered rice that smelled like popcorn, and in the last one, tamales stuffed with shredded beef and cheese. A bowl of strawberries rested in a larger bowl of cracked ice, and beside the fruit stood a bowl of brown sugar with a serving spoon. Butter and jellies had been provided, too, and a basket of rolls, some sweet and cinnamony, some plain.

At the linen-mantled table, we sat together on concrete benches, on thick cushions upholstered in vinyl and supplied by our immense and immensely hospitable host. Ozzie sat at the very end of the slab, while Wyatt Porter and I sat across from each other. We ate and talked. At first, all the conversation was about amusing incidents in the history of Pico Mundo, moments we had shared; though humor marked those memories, they were also colored lightly by melancholy.

I felt there was something sacred about that breakfast; but at the time, I could not have explained what I meant. The air was dry and warm, with the faintest breeze to keep it fresh, and scattered through the oaken shade, across the ground and the table and the three of us, glimmered treasures minted by the sun, coins of golden light, and in the trees song sparrows and western meadowlarks trilled, but it wasn't the place and its atmosphere that hallowed the moment. Neither was it the sumptuous meal nor the memories that we shared, nor the fact that we were at last in one another's company again. All of those things contributed to the mood, but the heart of the moment, the truest reason that it felt so pure to me and seemed to have special meaning, remained elusive. Indeed, it would continue to elude me the entire time I spent in Pico Mundo.

When we got around to talking about why I had returned to town, the mood darkened.

The chief said, "We've been up against their kind before, this same madness, and we took losses, but we're still here."

Ozzie shook his head, and his extra chins trembled. "We can't endure more losses like those at Green Moon Mall. This is a town with spirit, but if it takes too many hits to the heart, it'll never be the same. Any town can die without actually drying up and blowing away. It can be as dead as a ghost town even with people still living in it."

Gazing into his mug as if he were a Gypsy and as if coffee could be read like the remnants of tea, the chief said, "They won't make a fool of me like the others did."

"Wyatt Porter, you were never a fool," Ozzie declared in a tone of voice that did not invite debate. "Every man is outfoxed sooner or later, about one thing or another. If criminals were never cunning enough to deceive the authorities, every cop's job would be nothing but make-work, and nobody would want to read my crime novels."

I said, "Whatever they're planning, they intend it to be the biggest news of the year. And they're not just wannabe satanists like those the summer before last. These fruitcakes who nearly put an end to me in Nevada are members of a cult first founded back in 1580 in Oxford, England."

"Fanatics with a long heritage of lunacy," Ozzie noted, "tend to be formidable. Their zeal is frenzied, but over generations they have learned to control and focus it."

"They're formidable," I assured him. "They're devoted to the demon Meridian, and though that sounds loopy, they're serious. It's not just fanboy stuff with them, not just freaky costumes, spooky altars with black candles, ritual sex and ritual murder. They don't just celebrate evil, they work hard to bring more of it into the world, to bring upon the world a tidal wave of horror that'll wash hope out of it forever."

Evidently Chief Porter had lost his appetite, because he stared at the unfinished cinnamon roll on his plate as if it were a rotting fish. "Why can't the bad guys be satisfied with just robbing a bank or sticking up a liquor store?"

"You have plenty of that kind of thing to deal with, sir. Think of this as just a little variety."

He shook his head. "No, year by year, there's less of the your-money-or-your-life kind of thing, less grab-the-purse-and-run, less normal crime. Guys who once broke the speed limit by ten or fifteen miles an hour—I'm talking ordinary Joes here, not drug runners or coyotes transporting illegal aliens—these days some of the idiots do ninety in a forty zone. When you try to pull them over, they make a run for it, though running makes no sense, 'cause we've got their license-plate number. They think they're stunt drivers, masters of evasion, and then they take out a school-girl in a crosswalk or an entire family in a van."

The direction of our conversation hadn't affected Ozzie's appetite. As he lavished butter on a cinnamon roll, he said, "Perhaps it's the YouTube effect. These police chases rack up a lot of views. Everyone wants a taste of fame."

"It's not just that," Chief Porter said. "A guy who once would have raped and killed a woman, now a lot of times he also has to cut off her lips and mail them to us or take her eyes for a souvenir and keep them in his freezer at home. There's more flamboyant craziness these days."

Giving the buttered cinnamon roll a reprieve, Ozzie said, "Maybe it's all these superhero movies with all their supervil-lains. Some psychopath who used to be satisfied raping and mur-dering, these days he thinks that he should be in a Batman movie, he wants to be the Joker or the Penguin."

"No real-life bad guy wants to be the Penguin," I assured him.

"Norman Bates was happy just dressing up like his mother and stabbing people," Chief Porter said, "but Hannibal Lecter has to cut off their faces and eat their livers with fava beans. The role models have become more intense."

"I'm not sure it's the role models," Ozzie said. "Maybe it's more related to the pace of change in recent years. Centuries-old ways of looking at the world, centuries-old rules, are jettisoned seem-ingly overnight. Traditions are mocked and banished. A man—or woman—with an unstable mind sees things falling apart. 'The center cannot hold; / mere anarchy is loosed upon the world.' To a psychopath, anarchy is exciting, the chaotic world reflects his chaotic interior life, confirms his conviction that anything should be allowed, that he can rightly do whatever he wants."

Chief Porter finished the cold coffee in his mug and grimaced either at the bitterness of it or at the subject under discussion. "For those of us with our boots on the ground, it doesn't matter what the causes. We're too busy dealing with the effects." He looked as weary as anyone I'd ever seen when he said, "Oddie, what should I be doing to stop whatever's coming? What do you need from me?"

"I don't know yet, sir. We just learned they're planning this for May, possibly this week."

"'We'?" The chief looked puzzled. "You have a new posse?"

"Something like that, yes."

"Other law enforcement?"

"Not exactly."

"When do I meet them?"

"At the right time. You've got to trust me on this, Chief. I don't like keeping anything from you, but that's how it has to be right now."

"This is my town to protect, son. I don't tolerate vigilantes."

"No, sir. That's not what this is."

We engaged in a staring contest, after which he sighed and said, "If I can't trust you, I can't trust myself. Forget your posse for now. What more do you know about the bad guys?"

"All I have is three names. Wolfgang, Jonathan, Selene. Those might not even be their real names. I never saw their faces. I'll let you know the moment I have any kind of useful lead."

Having presented his theories of societal collapse, Ozzie now addressed the buttered sweet roll rather than the chief or me—"Lovely"—and set about devouring it.

"Where are you staying?" Chief Porter asked.

"Not with any old friends in town. I won't put them at risk."

"Karla misses you, son. She'd love to see you."

Karla was the chief's wife, a kind and gracious lady who treated me far better than my real mother ever did.

"I'd love to see her, too, sir. We'll get together soon. When this is over."

My words drew Ozzie's attention from the cinnamon roll. "So you didn't come home to die."

I could have said to them that the prospect of my death wasn't what brought me home to Pico Mundo, but that were Death to find me in the course of this mission, I would have no regrets and, more to the point, would go through that dark door with more gratitude than fear. They might interpret those words as proof of a suicidal disposition. I was not suicidal, however, only full of longing for the girl whom I'd lost. No need to worry my closest friends.

And so I said, "No, sir. I came home because I'm needed here—and because she's here."

In spite of my assurances, Ozzie appeared no less worried. "Her ashes, you mean."

"Yes. And in a way, her, too. All my memories of her are here."

My surrogate fathers exchanged meaningful looks, but neither of them said anything. I figured they would be on their phones with each other by the time they left the park for the state highway.

We packed the chafing dishes and plates and utensils and leftover food in boxes and coolers, and we loaded them into the spacious trunk of Ozzie's customized Cadillac.

"Not the remaining strawberries," Ozzie said, taking possession of that bowl at the last minute. "A weary traveler needs a snack to see him through a tedious journey."

"You'll be home in fifteen minutes, sir."

"By the most direct series of streets, yes. But I may choose to take the scenic route."

"You didn't have to do all this," Chief Porter said to him. "A box of doughnuts would have been enough."

Ozzie pursed his lips and frowned in disapproval. "Doughnuts for a police officer would be such a cliché. I make an effort to avoid clichés in my life every bit as much as I eschew them in my books."

Although he was a warm-hearted man, Wyatt Porter had never been as much of a hugger as Ozzie Boone. He wanted a hug anyway.

I said, "Be sure to tell Karla I love her, and tell her not to worry about me."

"It's good to have you back, son. I hope your days of wandering are all behind you."

I watched them drive away.

My attention was drawn to the lake by a sudden thrumming of wings and a chorus of low hoarse croaks. Eight or ten migrating egrets touched down where beach met water and spread out along the shore, each respecting the other's hunting grounds. More than three feet tall, white but for their yellow bills and skinny black legs, moving slowly and with solemn deliberation, they stalked the shallows for their breakfast. They speared small wriggling fish from the water and tilted their heads to let the catch slide, still alive, down their long, sleek throats, and I wondered if even in the small brain of a little fish there might be a capacity for terror.

Eleven

The night before my return to Pico Mundo. The seaside cottage where I and Annamaria and young Tim slept in separate rooms. Windows open for the sea air. Borne on that faintest of breezes came the lulling susurration of the gentle surf breaking on the shore.

In the still and ordered cottage, I endured a dream of chaos and cacophony. Shrill screams of terror, screams of glee. Through smears of light that blur my vision, faces leer, loom, but then swoon from me. Hands pulling, pushing, plucking, slapping. Through it all the eerie tortured wail and bleat and churr and howl that might have been what passed for music in an alien world without harmony.

Although I'd never been drunk in my life, I seemed to be drunk in the dream, reeling across ground that yawed like the deck of a storm-tossed ship. Wrapped in my arms, held to my chest: an urn, a mortuary urn. I heard myself calling Stormy's name, but this was not the urn that held her ashes. Somehow, I knew this urn contained the remains of dead people beyond counting.

Ribbons of darkness suddenly wound through the whirl of blurring light, so that I feared that blindness would overcome me. The booming of my heart grew louder, louder, until it exceeded in volume the hundred other sources of dissonance combined.

Out of the seething crowd, out of the light and the darkness, came Blossom Rosedale, the one and only Happy Monster, which was a name that she had given herself, not because she loathed the way she looked but because she was truly happy in spite of all her suffering.

Without realizing that I had staggered to a genuflection, I was on one knee when her left hand—scarred by fire, lacking all digits other than the thumb and forefinger—cupped my chin and lifted my bowed head, bringing me face-to-face with her. She said with great emotion, "Oddie, no. Oh, no, no."

I had met her in Magic Beach, back in January; we had quickly become fast friends, each of us a different kind of outsider. Forty-five years earlier, when she'd been only six, her drunken father had in a fit of rage dropped her headfirst into a barrel of trash that he had set afire with a little kerosene. She toppled the barrel and crawled out, but by then she was aflame. Surgeons saved one ear and somewhat rebuilt her nose, reconstructed her lips. She had no hair thereafter, and her face remained seamed and puckered by terrible keloid scars that no surgeon could smooth away.

Never before had I dreamed of Blossom, but emerging from the chaos of this nightmare, she helped me to my feet and said that I should lean on her. For reasons I didn't understand, I warned her away, insisted that I would be the death of anyone near me. But she would not be dissuaded. Although she was but five feet tall and more than twice my age, she gave me the strength that I needed to lurch forward through the growing bedlam, through the blurred dream light and gyrating dream shadows, through the screaming multitude, toward what I could not guess, toward what proved to be the amaranth.

Twelve

The old but well-kept house stood on three or four acres beyond the city limits of Pico Mundo, a two-story Victorian structure with a deep front porch and lots of gingerbread, painted white with pale-blue trim. A long blacktop driveway led between colonnades of velvet ash trees, their spring growth dulled by dust, past the house, to a long horse stable that had been converted into a garage with five double-wide doors.

As I approached the stable, one of the electrically powered doors rose, and as I slowed almost to a stop, a man stepped out of the shadowy interior, into sunlight. Tall, lean, weathered, wearing boots and jeans and a checkered shirt and a cowboy hat, he would have fit right into any Western that John Ford ever directed. He waved me into the garage, and I parked the Big Dog where he indicated.

As I took off my helmet and goggles, the cowboy introduced himself. He appeared to be as trim and fit as a man in his forties, but a life outdoors had given him an older face, seamed and as tanned as saddle leather. "Name's Deacon Bullock, born and raised a Texan, lately of Pico Mundo. It's a five-star honor to meet you."

"I'm just a fry cook, sir." I put the helmet and goggles on the seat of the bike. I shook his hand. "There's no great honor in it."

Every one of the many lines in his face conspired to be part of his smile. "I know your selfsame history, son. Don't be hidin' your light under a bushel."

"I don't need a bushel," I assured him. "A paper cup will do."

"You wasn't followed?"

"No, sir."

"You'd bet an ear on that?"

"I'd bet them both."

"This here's a safe house where our folks can hide out, and we mean to keep it safe. You been given a phone we tinkered with?"

I produced my jacket from one of the saddlebags, took the smartphone from the jacket, and handed it to him.

When Mr. Bullock activated the phone, the first thing that appeared on the screen wasn't the name of a service provider or phone manufacturer, but instead a single thick exclamation mark in gold against a black background. It remained there until he entered a five-number code, and then the exclamation point was replaced by a photograph of my smiling face. He nodded, satisfied. After switching the phone off, he returned it to me.

"You understand, son, it don't transmit your location when you use it, like all them other dang phones do. And it don't identify the owner. Any call you got to make or text message you got to send, or any web surfin' you got to do while you're on this here property—or off it, for that matter—you use only this one phone."

"It's the only one I have, sir. Mrs. Fischer gave it to me."

"The head honcho herself. All right, then. I'm told you travel light as a mayfly, but you must have yourself some luggage."

"Yes, sir." From the compartment in which I'd stowed the jacket, I retrieved a zippered leather kit that contained my electric razor and toiletries, and from the other saddlebag on the Big Dog, I took a matching soft-sided overnight bag that contained a pair of jeans, a couple of T-shirts, spare underwear, socks. "Somehow they learned what I'd be riding. We had a little confrontation a few hours back. The bike is hot."

"So then we'll shred her and melt her down."

When I realized he was serious, I said, "Isn't that a little extreme?"

"Not when you're dealin' with them folks."

I looked at the beautiful Big Dog. "Sad."

"Let me help with that," Mr. Bullock said, and took the bag from me. "Nothin' I hate worse than bein' useless." As I closed the lid of the saddlebag, he said, "So I'm given to understand you don't have yourself a suitable gun."

"Neither suitable nor unsuitable, sir."

His eyes were blue, and when he narrowed them, they seemed to grow brighter, as if his squint compressed the color in them. "How come you rode through all that dangerous habitat of schemin' men and all that wasteland crawlin' with snakes and beasts, and you with no dang gun?"

"I don't like guns, Mr. Bullock."

"You don't need to like one to know you got to have it. I don't like gettin' a colonoscopy every five years, but I grit my teeth and drop my drawers and get it done just the same."

"I've never had a colonoscopy, either."

"Well, you're not of an age to need one. That there's a joyful experience you got to earn by livin' to my age. Anyways, around this here safe house, everyone's got to have themselves a firearm, not just to keep in a drawer, but to carry at all times. Once we get you settled in, I'll fix you up with the very thing you need. You had yourself some breakfast yet?"

"More than some, sir. Just need a bed. I didn't sleep last night."

"Then bring yourself on in the house and meet Maybelle. She's my missus. You'll like her. Everybody does. She's a peach. We haven't enjoyed a bit of company since that astronaut had to hide out here while we worked up a convincin' new identity for him. Maybelle's starved for better company than me."

Thirteen

Maybelle Bullock was a pretty lady of about fifty, trim and blond. She reminded me of that long-ago actress Donna Reed, the way Miss Reed had looked in *It's a Wonderful Life*. When we entered from the back porch, Maybelle was standing at the kitchen sink, peeling fresh peaches, wearing a housedress of the kind that few women wore in recent years, with saddle shoes and white socks.

She didn't at first favor me with a smile, but her handshake was firm and her manner welcoming. Her direct stare probed, as if the story of my life were written in my eyes in a few succinct lines that she could read.

To her husband, she said, "He's not fully smooth and blue, but he sure is close to it."

"I figured you'd see him that way," said Deacon Bullock.

"Don't you?"

"I'd be a fool to argue it."

In the seventh volume of these memoirs (this is the eighth), I have written about the mysterious organization into which I had been welcomed by Edie Fischer, who will appear before much longer in this book, as well. Although I'd been told by her and others that I was remarkably smoothed out and blue for someone my age, I had not been able to get from them an explanation of that apparent compliment. I was a novice among them, and evidently the full truth of who they were and what they hoped to achieve would be revealed to me only in stages, as I earned the right to more knowledge of them.

Maybelle's smile, when now it came, was as warm as any I had ever received, one of those that makes you feel like long-loved kin. She took my hand in both of hers, not to shake it again, but to squeeze it gently.

She said, "It's purest pleasure bein' a help whatsoever way we can."

"Thank you, ma'am. I don't want to be a bother."

"You couldn't be a bother if you tried." Picking up the paring knife once more, she said, "I'm makin' a peach pie to have with lunch, your favorite."

I didn't ask how she could know the variety of pie that I most enjoyed. She would tell me or she wouldn't. Among these folks, a novice had to live by their rules, even if they chose not to share some of those rules with him.

"Peach pie. That's kind of you, Mrs. Bullock."

"Please, you call me Maybelle."

"Yes, ma'am. Thank you. But I'm afraid I'll probably sleep right through lunch, not having slept last night. What I need most now is a bed."

"Then we'll have us a late lunch or early dinner."

Deacon Bullock said, "He don't got a gun."

His wife looked first astonished and then severely disapproving. "Why would a fine young man such as yourself not carry a gun?"

"I don't like them."

"Guns don't feel nothin' about you, one way or t'other. No fair reason for you to feel bad towards them."

"I guess that's one way to look at it."

She picked up a pistol that had, until now, been lying on the counter on the other side of the basket of peaches. "Had this Colt since my weddin' day."

"How long have you been married, ma'am?"

She cast a loving look at her husband. "Be twenty-eight years come August nine. And only six bad days in all that wedded bliss."

Deacon Bullock's grin went flatline. "Only five bad days by my calculation, sugar."

Picking up the paring knife to slice the peach that she had just peeled, his wife said, "Even if it was five by both counts, won't all of them be the same five for each of us."

Mr. Bullock appeared mildly stricken. "How many of your six you think don't match my five?"

"I'd guess two."

"What two days did I think we was good and you felt we wasn't? That's goin' to trouble my sleep till I figure it out."

Mrs. Bullock winked at me but spoke to her husband. "It'll do you some good to reflect on it."

Taking off his Stetson and fanning his face, her husband said, "Guess I got my assignment for the day."

To me, his wife said, "From what I heard, whether you like guns or don't, you got the skill and guts to use 'em."

"Unfortunately, it's been necessary."

"So it will be again. What gun was it you most recently used?"

"A Glock with a fifteen-round magazine."

"What caliber?" she asked.

"Forty-five ACP."

"That be model twenty-one, Deke?"

"I suspect so," her husband said.

"We got one for this young man?"

"More than one," Mr. Bullock said.

"One will do," I assured them.

"Oddie, Deke'll take you up to your room. You sleep like a bear if you can, don't worry yourself none about when is dinner. When it is will be when you're ready for us to put it on the table."

"Thank you, ma'am. You're very kind."

"The mister here has five days when he mightn't have agreed with you on that. And you call me Maybelle."

"Yes, ma'am."

Mr. Bullock led me through rooms where mohair-upholstered sofas and armchairs were graced with antimacassars, where mantel clocks—and one grandfather clock—ticked, where well-tended ferns cascaded from decorative plant stands. On the walls hung framed needlepoint scenes that seemed to have been inspired by Currier and Ives, and between panels of brocade draperies hung lacework sheers, so that I felt as though I'd been dropped backward in time one hundred years or more.

My bedroom offered more of the same, the kind of room where I might have stayed during a visit to my grandmother, if the only grandmother I'd ever known had not been a professional gambler and hard drinker who spent most of her life on the road in search of one illegal high-stakes poker game or another. I loved Pearl Sugars, my mother's mother, but Granny Sugars would have curled up like a pill bug and died rather than have to live a single day in such Victorian orderliness and calm.

I, on the other hand, could have stayed contentedly in that room for a month, because it was such a welcome relief from the chaos and violent drama of my life. Not that I would be given that much time. I would probably have to settle for eight hours.

The bed had been turned down. A drinking glass and an insulated carafe of ice water stood on a tray atop the right-hand nightstand, and beside the carafe waited a crystal decanter containing Scotch whiskey. Mr. Bullock informed me that many other libations were available on request.

The small en suite bathroom lacked a tub but had a shower.

"A relaxin' hot shower might help you sleep the sleep of the innocent," he suggested.

"I believe you're right, sir."

"You just go ahead and call me Deke. Every mother's son does."

"Thank you, sir."

"While you're showerin' up and brushin' your teeth, I'll be back here with your gun, so don't go lockin' me out. I'll put the little darlin' in the top drawer of that there nightstand."

Later, when I came out of the steamy bathroom in the robe that had been provided, I opened the nightstand drawer and found the Glock plus two loaded, fifteen-round magazines in addition to the one that was already in the pistol.

The sight of the weapon depressed me. Well, not the sight of it, but the hard fact that I would almost certainly need to use it.

Both windows provided a view of the colonnade of velvet ash trees and the driveway leading to the state route. Here beyond the city limits of Pico Mundo, there were no sidewalks, no streetlamps, only a few hardscrabble farms, an occasional ranchette where people bred one kind of horse or another, mostly quarter horses for racing, lots of dust, and a sky paled by bleaching sun and dry desert air.

I drew shut the draperies, locked the door, took off the robe, and slipped under the covers, grateful that the house was well air-conditioned. I left the nightstand drawer open to be sure that I could have the pistol in hand quickly if I woke and needed it.

Fourteen

Some dreams matter. Most don't. Often it can be hard to know which might be which. The dream that afflicted me in the bedroom of the Bullock house was more intensely real than a 3-D movie; and if it had needed a movie title, I would have called it *The Swimmer.* Both during the unfolding of the dream and after I woke from it, I had no doubt that it mattered.

I swam underwater without effort, hardly kicking my feet, never stroking with my arms, as if drawn along by a current, and either I had no need to breathe or I breathed in water and took oxygen from it as efficiently as a fish. I drifted through the flooded central historic district of Pico Mundo, which was genuinely quaint in some places and artificially quaint in others, the latter buildings having been added after downtown had become a tourist destination because it was so picturesque. Numerous specialty shops and restaurants and bakeries and art galleries lined these streets. Light from their windows and from the antique cast-iron streetlamps, each crowned with three frosted globes, radiated through the water. The jacaranda trees that lined these avenues were laden with purple flowers that stirred in the water as they might in a mild breeze. Initially the mood was magical, full of wonder, so that I glided along in a kind of ecstasy, as I had during dreams of flying when I was a boy.

Soon, however, the mood changed. I came to feel that this was not a pleasant fantasy of life underwater, that Pico Mundo would not reveal to me a population of mermaids and mermen, that instead it was drowned. Drowned and dead and lost forever. The quality of the light changed subtly at first, the warm and welcoming glow of shop windows turning cold and off-putting. Beyond those display windows, dark shapes now floated, no doubt ruined merchandise adrift in flooded rooms.

I did not yet feel suffocated, continued to breathe water for air, but felt the urgent need to know how deeply submerged the town might be, whether under lake or ocean. I worked my arms, fluttered my feet, seeking the surface, but I could not ascend, only continue to drift forward through the streets. The longer I struggled to rise but failed to gain a fraction of a fathom, the more fearful I became, until upon me settled the conviction that this submerged world was a graveyard, the home of Death himself, and that life existed only at the surface, which I must reach in order to survive.

The light grew not merely cold and uninviting but also eerie, as if the shops were not shops after all, as if they were the dwellings of sorcerers and necromancers and voodooists, as though beyond their windows much witchery and diabolism were under way. In my peripheral vision, I became aware of something floating beside me, and when I looked more directly, I met the fixed stare of a corpse. A young woman, perhaps twenty, floated past, arms limp and moved only by the feeble currents, head turned toward me. She might have been lovely in life, with raven hair and celadon eyes, but she was not lovely now. Her bloodshot eyes bulged in their sockets, and her face was clenched in an expression of stark terror, as though, in the last instant of her life, such a frenzied state of fear had overcome her that even death could not relax her features.

When she sailed past me, the currents somehow conveying her at greater speed than they moved me, I sensed a looming horror more blood-freezing than a corpse. I eeled about and discovered behind me a flotilla of dead bodies, men and women and children, hundreds and perhaps thousands of them drifting through the weirdly lit flood, none of them bloated with gas and rising toward the surface as a corpse would in the waking world.

As they came past me, to both sides and above and below, I saw that in every case the eyes were protuberant, the face frozen open-mouthed in an expression of extreme fright. A little girl of about seven, her long blond hair billowing around her like the seeking tentacles of a sea anemone, bumped against me, and I shuddered in revulsion. Her protruding eyes rolled with sudden life, and from her open mouth issued a froth of gas bubbles that broke against my lips and carried with them one word: *"Contumax."*

I thrust up from the bed, flailing at the sheets as if I were a drowning man trying desperately to throw off the arms of the sea that would drag him down. I needed a moment to understand that I'd been dreaming, that I had come awake, and another moment to remember where I had gone to bed.

Although I occasionally indulged in a beer or a glass of red wine, I wasn't much of a drinker. I had no taste for hard liquor. Nevertheless, I fished a few cubes of ice from the insulated carafe, dropped them into the glass, and poured more Scotch than I needed.

At one of the windows, I drew open the draperies with the pull cord and pushed aside the lace sheers. Drinking the Scotch, I stood looking out at the colonnades of velvet ash, the dry land, the distant purple mountains. With its fire, the whiskey gradually warmed away the chill with which the dream had left me.

A couple of months earlier, in Nevada, I had rescued children who had been kidnapped to be used as human sacrifices. The satanists who abducted them, who now planned some torment for Pico Mundo, were fond of elaborate ceremonies, rituals, secret passwords. They had a formalized greeting, the equivalent of *Heil Hitler,* which consisted of the first cultist declaring *contumax,* Latin for "defiant" or "disobedient," to which the second cultist replied *potestas,* Latin for "power." They were declaring that their power came from defying all that was good.

What did it mean—the whole town under deep water?

Malo Suerte Lake, a mecca for boating enthusiasts from all over the Southwest, covered a few thousand acres. Not far offshore, it quickly grew deep. The lake lay upland from Pico Mundo; and the town had been built in a shallow bowl in the parched terrain.

I didn't know the average depth of Malo Suerte or its exact acreage, or how to calculate the volume of water held back by the breast of the dam. But I couldn't believe a sudden failure of that structure would result in all of Pico Mundo submerged like some modern-day Atlantis.

Nearly forty thousand people lived in our town, which was a place of many neighborhoods, from rich to poor, where humanity in its infinite variety dwelt in expectation of no greater catastrophe than perhaps a major earthquake. We anticipated a temblor that one day would cast off the cornices and crack the walls of some of the oldest structures that hadn't been reinforced to meet new building codes.

Flash floods happened, sure. But they were nuisances quickly flushed away through both the municipal storm drains and the network of natural arroyos that cut through town and that were bridged by our streets.

I didn't realize that I had finished all of the Scotch in my glass until I tasted only ice melt.

When, as an aspect of my sixth sense, I had a dream that struck me as predictive, its meaning was sometimes clear, sometimes more difficult to interpret. For that reason, among others, my paranormal abilities seemed to be both a gift and a curse.

A flood caused by the purposeful destruction of the dam would cause serious destruction, and dozens—perhaps scores—might die. But I couldn't conceive of any circumstances in which the drowning deaths could mount into the hundreds and thousands.

Consequently, perhaps the nightmare had been in part symbolic, its full meaning accessible only after some analysis. A flood, yes, but something else, too, a second and simultaneous catastrophic event that multiplied the effect of a dam failure.

Such as?

Such as . . .

More Scotch would not inspire an answer. I needed more time to think. And a better brain with which to do the thinking.

Fifteen

When I ventured downstairs a few minutes before five o'clock the knotty pine table in the kitchen had been set for dinner. Mrs. Bullock was pouring iced tea into three tall glasses as I arrived, as though she must be psychic herself and therefore anticipated the precise moment of my appearance.

"You look all the way rested, fresh, and ready for anythin' short of Judgment Day," she declared. "But where's the gun my Deke give you?"

"I didn't think I needed to bring it to dinner, ma'am."

"Young man, you need to bring it everywhere your feet take you. Mrs. Fischer says you're a fella's got more common sense than any hundred folks picked random from the phone book."

Edie Fischer, who had taken me as her protégé and had assisted me in the rescue of the kidnapped children in Nevada, seemed to be the primary benefactor if not also the leader of the clandestine organization that maintained this safe house and, apparently, a vast network of committed followers and secret facilities. She was eighty-six years old, with the physique of a bird, sometimes enigmatic to the point of being incomprehensible, but she was wealthy enough and wise enough and courageous enough to have earned my respect.

"Unless you mean to make a fool and liar of Edie, the sweetest woman this side of forever," said Mrs. Bullock, "then you best hie yourself up to your room and quick fetch that pistol."

"Yes, ma'am."

As I turned to leave, she said, "And not just the gun, but them spare magazines come with it."

"Be right back," I assured her.

Two minutes later, when I returned with the Glock and the extra magazines, the back door opened, and Mr. Bullock stepped into the kitchen, carrying a shotgun. He saw my weapon and smiled broadly.

"Good to see you put your silly don't-like-'em behind you and come down packin' the way you should."

His wife said, "He come down defenseless as a fawn, so I sent him up to get himself right."

Mr. Bullock's smile faded to a look of disappointment. "This here's a war we're in, young fella, even if it's so secret most folks don't never have a clue about it."

"Yes, sir. I know. I'm sorry. I won't forget the rules again. Where should I put it?"

Mrs. Bullock indicated the pistols beside two of the plates on the table. "Quick to hand is best."

As I put the Glock and spare magazines beside the third plate, I said, "Something sure smells good."

She said, "My grandma's best-ever meatloaf in cilantro-tomato gravy, with just a tetch of inspired fiddlin' by yours truly, plus all the trimmin's." To her husband, she said, "Seein' as you're alive, must've been a false alarm like you thought."

"Dang coyote," he said as he went to a broom closet tucked into a corner of the kitchen cabinetry. "Slinkin' around, maybe hopin' for one of the chickens we don't even raise, set off a motion detector."

Indicating the sunlight at the windows, she said, "Early for one of their kind bein' on the hunt."

Instead of brooms, the broom closet contained a gun rack with another shotgun. Mr. Bullock racked his 12-gauge beside the first weapon and hung his hat on a peg in there.

"It was a bonier specimen than usual, maybe too hungry to wait out the sun."

He washed his hands as his wife served dinner family style: the meatloaf on a platter, half of it sliced; butter-rich mashed potatoes mounded in a bowl; different vegetables in each of four other serving dishes; two gravy boats to ensure no waiting; a basket of pull-apart rolls.

When we were seated, Mr. Bullock said a brief grace, and Mrs. Bullock said, "Amen," and we ate like longshoremen who'd just worked grueling overtime on the docks. Everything was delicious.

Watching me eat, Mr. Bullock said, "Maybelle, this here young fella seems to think your cookin's more out of this world than our astronaut did."

"Everything's delicious, ma'am, it's perfect."

"High praise comin' from such a renowned fry cook. I'm flattered."

I said, "Why did the astronaut need a new identity?"

They glanced at each other, and she raised her eyebrows, and he shrugged, and she said, "Edie adores him, Deke. She don't

mistake a demon for a saint. And you know what he done . . .
back then, the mall."

To me, Deke Bullock said, "The astronaut fella seen somethin'
up there, he couldn't for the life of him keep shut up about."

"Up there?" I asked.

Mrs. Bullock pointed at the ceiling. "Space."

Her husband said, "He was up there doin' science or somethin'
on the space station awhile. The thing happened, and the astronaut was told he never seen what he knew dang well he'd seen."

Mrs. Bullock said, "So when he gets back, he goes and tells
some people he thinks they should know the truth, but they're the
wrong ones to tell. Next thing, they're all chasin' him."

"Who?"

"CIA," Mr. Bullock said.

Mrs. Bullock said, "FBI, too."

"IRS," Mr. Bullock added.

"Occupational Safety and Health Administration."

"Social Security Administration."

"Library of Congress and heaven only knows who else," Mrs.
Bullock said.

I considered all of that for a moment, and then I asked, "How
did he find his way to you?"

"Never did," Mr. Bullock said. "Edie Fischer found him how
she finds so many. She took him someplace for a new face, then
brung him here, so we could paper him up with a new name."

I took a second slice of meatloaf. "What did he see up there?"

Neither of them replied.

"I mean, up there in space," I said. "What did he see up there in
space?"

Mrs. Bullock had gone pale. "Better we don't say."

"Not a bit of good can come of sayin'," her husband agreed.

"It's not we don't trust you, Oddie," she assured me.

Mr. Bullock looked grim. "It's just you don't never want it in your head. I mean, the thing that happened up there."

"Once it's in your head, there's no gettin' it out, what the astronaut described." Mrs. Bullock shuddered. "Them images," she said in a tone of voice in which she might have said, *Oh, the horror.*

"Them images," Mr. Bullock agreed, having gone whiter than the mashed potatoes.

Mrs. Bullock said, "Them images keep comin' back on you when you least expect, and your blood runs ice-cold."

"Ice-cold," her husband agreed, and nodded solemnly.

The woman nodded solemnly, too.

The three of us sat there nodding until Mr. Bullock suddenly turned his head to look at the window above the sink, as if he'd heard something that unsettled him.

Maybelle's right hand went to the pistol beside her plate, and she turned in her chair to look at the same window. "Deke?"

"Probably nothing," he said.

I was facing the window that interested them. I didn't see anything alarming. I didn't hear anything, either.

After they had been staring at the window for the better part of a minute, Mr. Bullock said, "I'm just jumpy."

"You sure?" Maybelle asked.

"As sure as a fella can ever be in a world where every dang place you set foot, there's a trap door waitin' to be sprung."

He returned to his dinner, but he ate with his left hand so that he could keep the right one on his pistol.

After we finished the meal in silence, Maybelle looked at me and broke into a smile as radiant as the one Donna Reed turned on Jimmy Stewart in the last scene of *It's a Wonderful Life*. "Oddie, time for your favorite peach pie!"

Mrs. Bullock seemed to be of good cheer again, but her husband regarded the window with a frown, as though he doubted that we would live long enough to enjoy dessert.

Sixteen

M r. Bullock provided me with a shoulder holster that held both the Glock and the spare magazines. In front of a free-standing full-length mirror in my room, I shrugged into the rig and adjusted it while he stood watching and nodding approvingly.

He owned two sport coats, two more than I did: a black one for funerals and a powder-blue one for what he referred to as "warm-weather dress-up occasions." He had worn the latter only once when, in 110-degree desert heat, a friend had held a memorial service for a beloved house cat. Although the blue number went with my white T-shirt, jeans, and white sneakers, the pastel shade of it made me feel a little bit like a dandy.

"Nothin' matters," he said, "but what it fits you loose enough to hide that there gun you're packin'. You got yourself the phone?"

"Yes, sir."

"The little flashlight I give you?"

"It's on the dresser."

"Supposin' you end up in some hugger-mugger where you got to have yourself a pencil light 'bout as bad as an innocent man in the electric chair wants a last-minute go-free call from the governor, but it's not in your pocket 'cause it's there on the dresser?"

He retrieved the little flashlight and handed it to me, and I tucked it into an inside coat pocket. He asked if I had enough money, and I assured him that I did, and he told me to be careful, and I said that I would. He tugged on the lapels of the sport coat and smoothed the shoulders, and I felt as if I were being sent off on my first date.

In the kitchen, Mrs. Bullock insisted on hugging me and kissing me on the cheek before I left, a rather different send-off from any that James Bond ever got from his handlers at MI6.

Outside, in the last hour of light, Deke Bullock used a remote control to open one of the garage doors on the converted stable. I had said that I wanted an inconspicuous set of wheels. Of the two vehicles in that stall, he gave me the keys to a fifteen-year-old Ford Explorer that was dinged, scraped, and in need of being washed.

"She looks like a worn-out old spavined mare, don't she? But under the hood, she's a spirited filly."

"I'm just going to ride around town, see what there is to see, feel it out. I don't expect I'll have to outrun a hot pursuit."

He nodded and patted me on one shoulder. "Let's hope it don't come to that. But just when a man expects he's earned the littlest bit of milk and honey, the world throws a load of horseshit at him."

"I'll keep that in mind, sir."

"Now, say you find yourself comin' back here after midnight. Then you call the number I give you earlier, so I can get out of bed and open the door for you, instead of shootin' you dead. Tell me you got the number memorized?"

"Yes, sir. But I don't want to disturb you folks."

"You couldn't if you tried, son. The missus don't sleep at all anymore, and I don't need but an hour a night."

"Because you're fully smoothed out and blue?" I asked.

When I'd first met Edie Fischer, she had claimed that she never slept anymore. In time, I had learned that she was telling the truth, though I still didn't understand *why* she didn't need sleep or what was meant by "fully smooth and blue." She promised that understanding would come to me in time. When you're given a life as bizarre as mine, you tend to be accepting of other people's strangeness and eccentricities.

"Maybelle," he said, "she's smooth and blue all through, but I got me a ways to go yet. Now, you be careful out there, son. Don't be expectin' milk and honey, and maybe then you'll get yourself some."

He watched me drive out of the converted stable and through the tunnel formed by the velvet ashes.

As I turned right on the state highway and headed into Pico Mundo, I felt not merely that I was coming home after a long time away, but also felt, stronger than ever, that I had a rendezvous with destiny somewhere in those streets, the destiny that had been promised to me by a carnival fortune-telling machine called Gypsy Mummy.

To the east, the sky had turned from blue to bishop's purple, with the gloss of satin. Like a juggled orange coming slowly down, the westering sun swelled as it settled toward the horizon, soon to be a blood orange.

West of the historic district, the first neighborhood I cruised was Jack Flats, which fifty years earlier had been called Jack Rabbit Flats. The area had undergone decline when, during city government's crusade to greatly ramp up the quaintness of the downtown streets, non-quaint enterprises like muffler shops and tire stores and pawn shops were forced to relocate to Jack Flats. More recently, the area had begun to undergo gentrification.

I can't say what vibe I was searching for, but I didn't feel it in Jack Flats. I drove out of there as the swollen sun balanced on the horizon, pouring red light through the town. Stucco walls glowed carnelian and every window glimmered like a jewel. Shadows lay long and black, silhouetted trees were as dark as masses of rising smoke, and the windshields of the passing traffic reflected a fiercely fiery sky, as though every driver must be on a journey to Armageddon.

If one kind of hell or another would soon come to this town, there should have been at least a bodach or two slinking along the streets, unseen by all but me, seeking out those soon to be dead, to savor the smell of them as they ripened toward their fate, to thrill at the imminence of their death by stroking them with hands and licking them with tongues that they could never feel. But not one of those featureless, shadowy connoisseurs of violence was in evidence.

Without consciously making my way to Marigold Lane, I found myself on that familiar street, in a neighborhood where Victorian houses seemed to have been transported, entire blocks at a time, out of the eastern cities from which many of Pico Mundo's oldest families had migrated during the early decades of the twentieth century.

In the still red but fading light, I pulled to the curb in front of the house owned by Rosalia Sanchez. For a few years, when I lived in the small studio apartment above her detached garage, she had been my landlady and my friend.

She would be sixty-five now, with that saintly face worn by so much caring for others, by loss and grief, by waiting patiently for what she would never receive in this life.

Back in 2001, she had awakened one day to the discovery that her much-loved husband, Herman, had died beside her in his sleep and lay there cold and pale, one eye closed and the other open, staring. Later that same year, still in mourning, she had bowed out of a long-planned vacation to New England that she and Herman had intended to take with her three sisters and their families. On the morning of September 11, Rosalia woke to the news that their return flight out of Boston had been hijacked and flown into one of the World Trade Center towers.

Having lost every relative in one year, while she was sleeping, without a child of her own to whom she could turn for solace, Rosalia went a little mad. Intellectually, she knew that they were all dead, but in this case, emotion trumped reason. She would never speak of terrorists or plane crashes, nor would she listen to such talk. She chose to believe instead that as a consequence of some rare natural phenomenon, everyone she loved had turned invisible. She held fast, as well, to the theory that soon this event, like a magnetic field, would be reversed, rendering her loved ones visible again.

Her madness involved no resentment or anger, and she posed no danger either to herself or to others. She continued to keep her house immaculate, to bake her marvelous cakes and cookies as gifts for friends and neighbors, to attend her church, and to be a force for good in her community. And to wait for her family to be returned to visibility.

I never knew whether I was drawn to eccentric people or if they were drawn to me. Either way, my life had been full of them—and they had enriched it. I suspected eccentricity was often if not always a response to pain, a defense mechanism against anguish and torment and sorrow. With a father who played no positive role in my life and with a mother whose behavior often made her a candidate for an asylum, I am sure that I would have been the eccentric I became even if I'd never been gifted or cursed with my sixth sense.

No bodachs were in view along Marigold Lane.

As the last light bled out of the day, less than fully aware of how I had gotten there, I found myself parked across the street from St. Bartholomew's Church, where Stormy's uncle, Sean Llewellyn, still served as the priest and rector.

Some of the happiest times that she and I shared were on the open deck of St. Bart's bell tower, to which we would sometimes climb with a picnic dinner, to dine there among the immense but silenced bells, surrounded by the best view in Pico Mundo. We felt that we were above all strife in that high redoubt, our future together no less enduring than the town we overlooked.

With the approach of night, the tower was up-lit, and a red aircraft warn-off light served as finial at the peak of the belfry roof. As I watched it winking, I recalled how spectacular the sunset had been the last time that Stormy and I had climbed up there with a picnic hamper, on what we could not know would be the final night of her life.

No bodachs crept the front stairs of the church or climbed the walls, or danced in glee upon the bell-tower roof.

Four minutes till seven o'clock. I pulled back into traffic.

Stormy had lived in one of four apartments in a house three blocks from the Pico Mundo Grille. In my not-so-random drive through town, I next parked across the street from that place.

Orphaned young, supporting herself as a counter girl and then as the manager of an ice-cream shop, she had been poor by almost any definition. She had furnished her humble rooms with items from thrift shops, and yet her apartment had been stylish and comfortable. Old silk-shaded floor lamps with beaded fringes. Upholstered Victorian footstools paired with crude imitations of Stickley-style chairs. Maxfield Parrish prints. Carnival-glass vases. Cheap bronze castings of various breeds of dogs displayed on end tables and windowsills. The eclectic mix shouldn't have worked, but it did, because she had magic in her and because she could see the magic in everyday things.

I had moved out of my studio apartment above the garage and into Stormy's place after she died. I lived there for a year, until I left town on my journey of discovery. Her things had been packed away and stored in a room at Ozzie Boone's house. I could dispose of nothing. Every item she owned, however inexpensive it might be, was to me a treasure, a store of memory and a memento of love unrivaled and undying.

How long I sat there, across the street from the house in which she had lived, I couldn't be sure. I drove away only when my tremors stopped, only when the world gradually regained its detail and ceased to be just a blur.

Now that night had fully claimed Pico Mundo, I allowed intuition to guide me and cruised to the town square, at the center of which lay Memorial Park with its handsome bronze statue of three soldiers from World War II. Unlike the other streets of the historic district, those four blocks surrounding the park were lined not with flowering jacarandas but with magnificent old phoenix palms with enormous crowns of fronds.

Couples occupied the park benches, cuddling in the light of the three-globe cast-iron lampposts. The many restaurants were open, of course, but also all of the specialty shops, which catered as much to tourists as to locals. People were window-shopping, some of them carrying cones of ice cream as they ambled from shop to shop, some sipping from Starbucks cups, some walking their dogs, some talking and laughing. Although my perception might have been distorted by melancholy, it seemed to me that most of those people were in pairs, the larger percentage of them holding hands, as if they were extras in a movie of high romance, accessorizing a scene for which the director's purpose might have been to say that life was a parade lived two-by-two, as it had been since before Noah's fabled ark and as it would be always.

No bodachs capered among the crowd. None slithered under the benches on which couples shared moments of affection.

Neither circling the town square nor cruising any of the other streets before this had I received the slightest psychic impression that one day the town would be submerged, a community of drowned and drifting cadavers. Indeed, if Pico Mundo were inundated because of the collapse of Malo Suerte Dam, the town would not stand underwater in precisely the same condition as now, which is how it had appeared in the dream; the rushing waters would do great damage, tumbling cars along the streets, uprooting trees, ripping down awnings, smashing windows. . . . No rational scenario allowed for the lights to remain aglow in the aftermath of such a disaster, as they had been when I had floated through my nightmare.

Brooding about that, I circled Memorial Park a second time and saw an enormous banner that I had somehow overlooked before. It was strung across an intersection: big red and black letters on a white background, announcing the annual spring fair at the Maravilla County Fairgrounds, currently under way. Fun for the whole family. The lowest of three lines on the banner declared FEATURING THE WORLD-FAMOUS SOMBRA BROTHERS MIDWAY SHOWS.

The carnival was back in town.

Sombra Brothers Midway Shows had occupied the fairground six years earlier, when Stormy and I found the fortune-telling machine in an arcade tent.

You might think it was a coincidence that I should return to Pico Mundo in expectation of the fulfillment of the fortune-teller's prediction just when the Sombra Brothers returned as well. So very much about our strange and deeply layered world remained mysterious to me, but my experiences had taught me, among other things, that there were no coincidences.

Seventeen

At ticket booth number four, the cashier was a plump woman with long ringlets of auburn hair. The carnival had a jackpot drawing to entice people to stay later and spend more. When she took my money and gave me an admission ticket, she said, "Honey, be sure you stay for the big drawin' at eleven-forty-five. Three nights, the winners didn't hang around to collect, so now it's up to twenty-two thousand dollars. Got to be here to win. Hang on to your ticket. You're the one tonight, honey." She had such a beatific smile that her sales pitch seemed like a sincere prediction.

My intuition—which is seldom wrong—insisted the carnival held secrets that, if revealed, would help me to discover the meaning of my nightmare and the nature of the threat hanging over Pico Mundo. Carnies are a tightly knit community and generally more law-abiding than the rest of us. But there was no reason to dismiss the notion that a few cultists might have made their home in the Sombra Brothers operation, perhaps without other carnies being aware of their demonic nature and their keen interest in terrorism.

The first thing I did after paying admission and entering the fairground was to head for the southern perimeter of the midway, where in the past there had been a long row of specialty tents, including games (not of the arcade kind) and novelty services. The offerings along that flank of the concourse were pretty much as they had been in past years, among them: Bingo Palace; Quarter Toss; an air-rifle shooting gallery; Wearable Art, where an artist with an airbrush would paint any image you wanted on a T-shirt; Face It, where you could have your face decorated with water-soluble paints in an almost infinite variety of ways.

Although I had not intended to go anywhere incognito, I had changed my mind about that when it came to the carnival. If possible, I preferred to prowl the midway without being recognized. I had not lived in Pico Mundo for the past eleven months, but I had known a lot of people there. Furthermore, after the events at Green Moon Mall almost two years earlier, photos of me had been in the newspapers; therefore, I might be recognized by many people whom I *didn't* know.

Some of them would tell me that I was a hero, which would be embarrassing. I'd never felt like any kind of hero, considering that, even with my intervention, nineteen people had died that day. Almost as disturbing, some of those who recognized me might be the cultists who currently wanted to kill me.

The front of the Face It tent was entirely open. On the interior hung blown-up photos of previous customers whose faces had served as canvases for the artists who owned this little concession.

I wondered what their true faces had looked like before they had been painted. Of course, a fresh-scrubbed face may be a lie, and the truth may be a darkness behind it.

An attractive dark-haired woman in her early forties sat on a chair beside a table on which were arranged different brushes, as well as bottles of paint and Ziploc bags of glitter in a wide variety of colors. She applied a brush and a small sponge to the face of a teenage girl who sat before her on another chair, working upward from the chin, already at the forehead, creating a floral scene, so that the girl appeared to be peering out at the world through a bouquet of wildflowers; or perhaps she was meant to be a meadow nymph with a face composed of flowers. A second teen, friend of the seated girl, stood watch, already given a leopard's visage, her face a rich golden orange with black spots and realistically rendered cat whiskers.

A second artist also worked in the tent. Currently not engaged, she smiled and raised her eyebrows quizzically and with a gesture invited me to the chair in front of her. Judging by appearance, this painter could be the daughter of the other. Attractive, with black hair and celadon eyes, she was unmistakably the dead woman from my dream, the first corpse that had drifted past me through the drowned streets of Pico Mundo.

When I sat in the chair, she said, "How do you want to look?"

"Different," I said. "Very different."

She considered me in silence for a moment and then said, "I can do all the faces you see on the walls here and almost anything else. Any character or animal. Or something abstract."

"Surprise me," I said.

She smiled again. "No one's ever asked to be surprised before. Nobody wants to risk looking foolish."

"Why would you make me look foolish?"

"Oh, I wouldn't. Why would I? But most people want to look cool, and there's a thin line between cool and foolish."

I liked her voice. It had a smoky quality. She had not spoken in the dream. The corpse of the little girl, borne along after her, was the one that said *contumax.*

"What's your name?" I asked, as she studied her bottles of paint and evidently considered what design she intended to create.

"Connie. What's yours?"

"Norman," I replied, and wondered if we both had lied. "How long have you worked in the carnival?"

"I grew up in it. What do you do, Norman?"

"I'm a librarian."

She met my eyes. "You don't look like a librarian."

"What do I look like?"

"You look like an Ethan, not a Norman, and you look like maybe a Navy SEAL or an Army Ranger, not a librarian."

"Not really. I'm no tough guy."

"Truly tough guys never say they're tough."

"Some of them do. And then they beat on you to prove it."

Opening a bottle of paint, she said, "You don't look beaten up."

"I avoid confrontation."

"By taking the other guy down before he lands a blow?"

"I prefer to run like hell away from him."

Picking up a brush, she said, "Please close your eyes and keep them closed. I don't want to get paint in them."

I closed my eyes and asked, "Why Ethan?"

"I have an older brother named Ethan. The name is from the Hebrew, meaning *permanent, assured.*"

"Does he paint faces, too?"

"He was supposed to run the Bingo Palace that my dad owns.

But he wanted to do something else. If the brush tickles, tell me, and I'll use a sponge instead, as much as I can."

"It doesn't tickle. What does your brother do?"

"He's a Navy SEAL."

I wanted to open my eyes to study hers, but I didn't. "So I must look a little like your brother."

"You don't look anything like him. But you have an Ethan quality about you."

"Is that a good thing?"

"It's the best thing."

"You're embarrassing me here."

"That's something Ethan would say."

She worked quickly, and in ten minutes or so, she told me that I could look, whereupon she gave me a large hand mirror.

Around my eyes, she had painted a harlequin's mask. Otherwise, from hairline to jawline, she'd drawn a pattern of black and white diamonds so perfectly straight-edged in spite of the contours of my face that it had the effect of making my features all but disappear into that rigid geometry. Even Stormy would not have recognized me.

"A harlequin is a clown," I said.

"More accurately, a buffoon. When I asked how you would like to look, you said, 'Different. Very different.' I can't imagine anything more different from what you are than a buffoon."

I met her stare and said, "Have you ever had a dream that came true, Connie?"

She didn't immediately reply. She took the mirror from me and put it on the table. She met my stare and held it and at last said, "Only once. I don't dream all that much."

"Was it a dream about a flood, a whole town drowned in it?"

She glanced at her mother, who had finished with the second teenager and was working on a ten-year-old girl while the child's parents watched with delight. None of them were paying attention to us, but Connie lowered her voice anyway. "No. Not a flood. It was a dream about . . . about this guy who walks in here and wants to look 'Different. Very different.' "

Her expression was so solemn that I believed her.

"Dreamed it just last night," she said.

"I told you to surprise me, and you just did."

"In the dream, I knew the guy was in trouble, he had enemies."

"I don't know what to say."

"Probably you shouldn't say anything. If you did, maybe your trouble would become mine."

I nodded, took out my wallet, and paid her.

As I turned to leave the tent, she said, "Don't worry. Your own mother wouldn't know you."

I said, "She never has."

Eighteen

Painted to deceive, I set out in search of what I did not know. The vast majority of those attending the carnival didn't sport a mask from Face It; however, there were enough of us that no one seemed to be especially interested in me.

I walked the fairground midway, where the Whip lashed its riders this way and that, where the Caterpillar enveloped screaming patrons in darkness as it slung them around a track a thousand times faster than any real caterpillar could move, where the Big Drop lifted its gondola two hundred feet into the night and then released it in what seemed to be an uncontrolled free fall, and where the Ferris wheel carried its passengers high and brought them low and raised them high and brought them low again, as if it were not merely a carnival ride but also a metaphor for the basic pattern of human experience.

It's difficult to spend time in any carnival or amusement park and not realize that a repressed fear of death may be the one emotion that is constant in the human heart even if, most of the time, it is confined to the unconscious as we go about our business.

Thrill rides offer us a chance to acknowledge our ever-present dread, to release the tension that arises from repression of it, and to subtly delude ourselves with the illusion of invulnerability that surviving the Big Drop can provide.

The carnival blazed, every ride and many other attractions decorated with low-watt bulbs, neon tubes, blinkers, and twinklers. Strings of colored lights overhung the U-shaped concourse. At the curve of the U, mounted on a flatbed truck and reliant on a chugging gasoline-powered generator, two massive swiveling spotlights threw their beams into the heavens, revealing the bellies of an armada of clouds, like dirigibles, invading silently from the southwest.

In spite of all the colorful lighting that had been crafted to attract patrons and to put them in a celebratory mood, the carnival had an air of hostility and menace that, I felt sure, was not merely my perception. Within all the dazzle and glitter and bright fake glamor, a hidden presence lurked, a watchful darkness that observed and hated and waited, a presence I had not sensed six years earlier.

Although the warm air was richly scented with the aromas of buttered popcorn, candy apples, cotton candy, the cinnamon and sugar and fried dough of churros, nevertheless, as I threaded through the colorful tapestry of people on the concourse, there were times when a delicious aroma suddenly soured. For just a moment, cinnamon had a sulfurous edge and the popcorn butter smelled rancid, as if under all its pretense of good healthy fun, the carnival was a dangerous swamp in which moldered and festered things too horrific to contemplate.

The fun house featured the giant face of an ogre, twenty feet from chin to crown, nearly that wide, a dimensional sculpture of such imaginative detail that it managed to be scary at the same time that it was pure hokum. Periodically a roar issued from its open mouth, and with the roar came a forceful blast of air that traveled about twenty feet into the promenade, surprising people who encountered it for the first time, mussing their hair and startling them so that popcorn was dropped halfway from box to mouth.

The ogre's crazed eyes rolled in their sockets, but I knew that I was being paranoid to think that it was watching me in particular.

The ballyhoo of pitchmen, the clatter and whoosh of the rides, the interlaced melodies of scores of different songs associated with various attractions, and the chatter and laughter of a few thousand voices appeared to inspire bright-eyed delight among many of the patrons. To me, it sounded like a shrill discordant symphony to which I might expect to see a horde of bodachs quivering and capering in an ecstasy of anticipated chaos—though I had not glimpsed even one of them among this multitude.

Within ten minutes I came to a large tent where flamboyant lettering emblazoned on the canvas above the entrance promised ALL THINGS FORETOLD. In smaller script under those words appeared the come-on 33 OPPORTUNITIES TO LEARN YOUR FUTURE. The words were encircled by symbols associated with soothsayers and oracles through the ages: a pentalph created with five interlaced *A*'s, an ankh, a quarter moon encircled by seven stars, the palm of a hand with a single eye gazing out from it. . . .

I hadn't needed psychic magnetism to lead me to this place. I had half convinced myself that I would discover the cultists in the carnival, but my truest reason for coming there, more unconscious than not, had been to learn if the fortune-telling machine, Gypsy Mummy, still dispensed predictions.

As on that well-remembered night six years earlier, a sawdust floor had been spread wall to wall. It lent a woodsy smell to the arcade. Thirty-three machines of prophecy were arranged in rows, some quaint contraptions dating to the 1940s, others of recent invention.

You could use two controls to operate a mechanical claw—the Hand of Fate—to fish among a collection of small painted, numbered wooden balls in a glass case. Once the claw seized a number, you could press the corresponding digit on a keyboard, whereupon your fortune would be dispensed to you on a printed card.

You could seek your future on a video screen, where for fifty cents you would be dealt seven virtual playing cards, facedown, from which you were to select three, then seven more from which you were to select two, then seven more from which you were to select another two. When all the cards you chose were then revealed, the machine printed under each its meaning and combined the seven in a single prognostication.

Or you could instead choose any of thirty-one other contraptions that would, with machinelike indifference, tell you if you would have a long life or a short one, a happy marriage or one of wedded misery. Fifteen or twenty people were sampling the various oracles, moving on to another if they didn't like what the first had prophesied.

In the center of the tent, on an elevated platform, a cashier sat within a small circular desk, changing dollar bills into quarters when she wasn't reading a Nora Roberts romance novel. Even before I went looking for it, I was certain that I would find what I sought, and so I got change for two dollars.

At the back of the tent, where it had been on that long-ago night, Gypsy Mummy stood as if she'd been waiting six years just for me.

Nineteen

Roughly the shape of an old-fashioned phone booth, the machine stood seven feet high. The lower three feet were enclosed, and the upper four featured glass on three sides. In that display case sat a female dwarf in a costume of the kind Gypsies wore only in old movies starring Lon Chaney or Bela Lugosi, or Boris Karloff. Black ballet slippers. Black silk pants. A red-and-gold scarf for a belt, a red-and-black scarf tied around the head. She evidently liked jewelry: two necklaces, a pendant, several rings with large stones, and big dangling earrings.

Gnarled and withered, her bejeweled hands rested palms-down on her thighs. Her fingernails were green, perhaps not with polish but with mold.

Her skin appeared to be as crisp as paper, wrinkled and yet stretched so tight across the skull that it seemed as though at any moment it might split open from the stress. Her eyelids and her lips were sewn shut with black thread.

According to a plaque, here before me sat the mummified corpse of a Gypsy dwarf, a renowned fortune-teller in eighteenth-century Europe, so accurate in her predictions that she'd been summoned before royalty in three kingdoms to consult with monarchs. In truth, the figure had most likely been sculpted by a low-rent artist who worked best when inebriated.

Regardless of its origins, whether mummified flesh and bones or clay and wire and latex, there might be some magic in Gypsy Mummy. The source of magic in this world is more mysterious than all the explanations that sorcerers and wizards have given for it, and it is more prevalent than can be understood by those who live according to the constricted form of reason so prevalent in our time.

On the night that Stormy and I had come here, when we were but sixteen and expected to grow old together, a man and woman in their early twenties were already consulting Gypsy Mummy. They appeared to be mystified by the predictions that they received, though the meaning seemed clear to us.

Each time they fed a quarter to the machine, the woman asked, aloud, "Gypsy Mummy, tell us, will Johnny and I have a long and happy marriage?"

Johnny read the cards as he received them. The first declared A COLD WIND BLOWS, AND EACH NIGHT SEEMS TO LAST A THOUSAND YEARS. Thereafter the machine produced THE FOOL LEAPS FROM THE CLIFF, BUT THE WINTER LAKE BELOW IS FROZEN, followed by the even more ominous THE ORCHARD OF BLIGHTED TREES PRODUCES POISONOUS FRUIT. They were not pleased with Gypsy Mummy, but by the eighth card, they were more annoyed with each other than with the mummified sage, bickering over their interpretations, which in every case failed to grasp the most obvious meaning.

With our first coin, Stormy and I received YOU ARE DESTINED TO BE TOGETHER FOREVER. We didn't spend a second quarter. There was nothing else we needed to know.

In the six years since my previous petition to Gypsy Mummy, the machine had been modified to require two quarters per fortune. When offering their divinations, even deceased Gypsies needed to account for inflation.

"How long do I have to wait," I murmured, "before your promise to me comes true?"

For fifty cents, I received a card that offered no prediction on either side.

I supposed that in any stack of pre-printed fortunes put into the machine, there might be a blank or two.

Another fifty cents got me a second card with not a word on it.

Wondering if I had been expected, if someone might be watching me right that minute, I looked around, but the other patrons were preoccupied with their claptrap prophets. The cashier had her nose in the romance novel.

I studied the stitched eyelids beyond the glass. Stormy used to insist that after we received the card so desired by Johnny and his girlfriend, the mummified dwarf had opened one eye and winked. It made no sense that sewn-shut eyes could wink, especially when the coarse black thread wasn't broken. Whether the wink might have been a moment of magic or whether it was nothing more than a little fantasy that Stormy wanted to believe, I never questioned her claim because it gave her such pleasure to think it had happened.

Again I asked, "How long do I have to wait before your promise to me comes true?"

I paid two more quarters, listened to them clink into the machine's cash box—and received a third blank card.

After a fourth of the same, I pretended interest in some of the nearby soothsaying contraptions and waited for someone to feed coins to the Gypsy.

Maybe ten minutes passed before two girls, about fourteen years old, approached the machine. Each spent fifty cents for which she got a printed card that she shared with her friend. They conferred over the meaning of their fortunes, giggled, and then swapped cards, each apparently preferring the other's future. They wandered away, sharing the popcorn.

Neither girl had spoken aloud to the Gypsy, as instructions above the coin feed directed, and I'd had no opportunity to see the messages on their cards, which they took away with them. Clearly, however, they had not received blanks.

You might say that it was just a machine, that the cards were stacked in the mechanism in no particular order, that getting four blanks for two bucks was nothing more than happenstance. All of that is rational, and certainly in the case of the two girls and others who consulted Gypsy Mummy, your point would be irrefutable. But in my life, uncanny things had happened to me with some regularity, not just related to my ability to see lingering spirits and to find my way by psychic magnetism. Because of my other experiences, I could not be shaken from the belief that the four cards without fortunes would have come to me if I'd consulted Gypsy Mummy hours earlier or hours later.

Besides, for six years, I had believed in the message on the card in my wallet, and for most of the past two years, that promise—and sometimes it alone—had sustained me. I could no more stop believing in Gypsy Mummy than I could stop believing in my own existence.

Leaving the arcade, I was able to imagine two meanings that the blank cards might have been intended to convey. First, that the promise to me would not be kept. Second, that I had so little time to live that I didn't have any future on which the mummified oracle could comment.

I much preferred interpretation number two.

Just outside of the tent, watching the people who busied along the concourse, I had a sense of time running out. I checked my watch—7:40. The crowd would keep growing for another couple of hours. Because of the jackpot drawing, the carnival wouldn't close until well after midnight, perhaps not until one in the morning. If there was something important for me to learn here, I still had plenty of time to discover it.

I concentrated on the name Wolfgang and tried to hear his whiskey-soaked voice in my mind's ear. Had I seen his face when he and his companions had pursued me through the dark mall, psychic magnetism would now be more likely to draw me to him. But because his voice had been so distinctive, perhaps it would serve nearly as well.

Turning right, I joined the crowd and headed along a length of the midway that I had not yet explored. I had taken no more than a dozen steps when I turned abruptly, colliding with a woman in a green fishnet top and red culottes. I apologized, though considering her outfit, she should have apologized as well, and I set off back the way I had come. Past the Dodgem Cars, where drivers crashed into one another with glee. Past the high-striker, where a muscular customer swung the sledgehammer and rang the bell.

Toward the flatbed truck with the two huge swiveling spotlights. Toward the major sideshows that occupied the east end of the southern concourse. Psychic magnetism had never before worked so quickly, had never drawn me with such power and urgency as this.

Twenty

I was compelled to move, move, move. The compulsion grew so strong that I almost broke into a run, but to avoid drawing attention to myself, I exercised restraint as best I could. On rare occasions, when this curious talent of mine grew especially powerful, I was to a degree at its mercy, crashing forward almost recklessly, afraid that I might plunge into some peril that I would not recognize until too late.

A hundred people had gathered in front of adjacent sideshows where two barkers ballyed their attractions. I slipped through the crowd and between the two large tents, heading off the midway, hoping that no carnies or security guards would notice me. Shadows closed in quicker than I expected. I slowed down a little, fearful of tripping over something and impaling myself on one of the steel tent stakes or garroting myself on a guy rope. Such a death was exactly the kind of end I might decisively—if unconsciously—bring upon myself to prove once and for all that I didn't deserve the unwanted label HERO, that I was only a fry cook and a clumsy one.

Behind the tents, the elevated midway withered down to a service road. I sprinted across the blacktop and checked my pace again as I found myself on another slope, this one darker and much longer than the first, covered in wild grass as high as my knees.

The hullabaloo and razzle-dazzle of the midway faded significantly. The most immediate sound became the chorus of crickets all around me. The night was warm enough that I worried about rattlesnakes, which in the right conditions liked to hunt in the dark for just such prey as crickets and grass toads.

Below lay a large graveled area that, during fair week, became a campground for the carnies, with water and electrical hookups. At least two hundred travel trailers and motor homes were parked in rows. Some were owned by concessionaires who operated independently within the carnival, on-the-road homes for them and their families. Others belonged to Sombra Brothers and were rented to those carnies who didn't have their own accommodations.

From about the age of twelve until Stormy and I became an item, every fair week I had hung out in the carnival. I had gotten some part-time work at a grab joint, flipping hamburgers and manning the deep fryer, which is where I first discovered my inner fry cook. I'd met a lot of carnies, and I'd liked most of them. In the mainstream culture, they lived as outsiders, and so did I to some extent, though by necessity rather than by choice.

Now, as I was drawn into the graveled lanes between the rows of trailers and motor homes, most of the windows were dark, because every able-bodied member of the community had gone to work. In those places where amber lamplight warmed a pane of glass, most likely an aging grandparent or a young mother with an infant looked forward to the return of the others and to the

little private family time between the post-midnight shutdown of
the midway and the show call, which was usually noon on Mon-
day through Thursday, 11:00 A.M. on Friday and Saturday.

I came to a large motor home with light in many of its windows. A curtain had been drawn across the windshield for privacy, and blinds covered the panes in both front doors. I felt
compelled to open the door on the passenger side, and I took hold
of the handle, but then I thought I heard muffled voices. I stifled
the urge to go inside, at least by that route.

After circling the big vehicle, I found a back entrance on the
port flank, and no light glowed in the small pane centered in the
upper portion of it. I tried the door. It wasn't locked.

Sometimes I thought that my paranormal gift must have come
with a measure of madness, though not insanity so fervid that I
needed to be locked up for the protection of the community. My
derangement put at jeopardy no one but myself.

Ozzie Boone said that any talent—whether to write songs or to
write novels or to track people by psychic magnetism—came with
the obligation to use it to the fullest of one's ability, with a fierce
commitment barely distinguishable from neurotic obsession. A
writer, he believed, had to stretch with every book, to explore
kinds of stories that he'd never told before, to employ narrative
techniques that tested the limits of his gift.

In fact, he said, commitment to the point of obsession wasn't
merely an obligation but a necessity, the *sine qua non* without
which the novelist might as well bite on a shotgun barrel and exit
this life as Hemingway had done.

Ozzie had a tendency toward rhetorical flamboyance that I
found charming and amusing. By his own admission, however, he

had not lived up to his ideal; and I wondered if a high-fat, six-thousand-calorie diet was for him a slow-motion shotgun.

As for my psychic magnetism, according to Ozzie's philosophy, considering that it was a talent, I had no choice but take it to the max, no acceptable moral choice other than to jump out of an airplane without a parachute if that's what it told me to do. Now it demanded that I open the back door of the motor home, which I did, and the door didn't creak, for which I was grateful, and I stepped up and inside, into a mostly dark room, and the vehicle was so large and so stable that it didn't rock in the slightest when it took on my weight.

Barely enough pale light fell through an open interior door to reveal that I had entered a bedroom.

I stood listening, and after a moment I heard low voices: two men, forward in the vehicle. I couldn't understand what they were saying. Hoping to hear them more clearly, I moved to the open door and stood beside it, my left ear past the jamb. The distance was still too great, their voices too muted, for me to hear more than one word in ten, and none of those seemed to belong in the same conversation.

Daring to lean past the jamb to scout the territory, I saw on the right an open sliding door and beyond it a bathroom. Past the bath lay a kitchen area that was open to a dining nook forward of it. On the left, opposite the bath, was the entrance to what might have been a second bedroom. From my angle, I couldn't see what lay forward of there, on the left, but I imagined a fairly spacious lounge.

Ordinarily, I wouldn't have been so bold as to go farther than the back room of the motor home, but this was no ordinary night.

Hour by hour, my sense of impending catastrophe became more urgent, and images from the dream flood kept rising unbidden in my mind. Other nightmares usually faded from recollection more rapidly with every minute that passed after I woke. But this one had tenure in my memory, growing more detailed each time that a moment from it rose in my mind's eye, as if the vividness of the nightmare increased as we drew nearer to the event that it predicted.

I drew the Glock from the shoulder holster under the powder-blue sport jacket and stepped out of the darkness, into the short hallway between the second bedroom and the bath. Just as I crossed the threshold, two men appeared toward the front of the motor home, coming from the area that I supposed must be a lounge. I froze, but when neither of them looked toward me, I sidestepped through the open door of the bathroom.

Now that their positions in relation to mine had changed, I could better hear them as they moved toward the passenger door and then stopped to settle an ongoing discussion.

"I still don't get why."

"Why? You don't get why? Because he must've seen all three of them. That's why."

"Yeah, so?"

"Bern Eckles thinks the guy knows things."

"What things?"

Bern Eckles, a former Pico Mundo cop, had also been a member of a satanic cult and, with others, he had planned the shootings at the Green Moon Mall—plus a bombing that never happened. He was serving a life sentence in prison.

"Eckles doesn't know what things."

"Cripes, Jim. Kind of extreme, don't you think?"

"What is?" Jim asked.

"This . . . this what we did here, just because this idiot Eckles doesn't know what."

"No, see, Eckles has tried to figure what happened back then when their attack on the mall went wrong."

"But you said he doesn't know what happened."

"He's got a theory. It only makes sense to him if the guy who took them down has some real mojo."

"What mojo?"

Jim said, "Eckles thinks all kinds of mojo."

"Maybe Eckles has shit for brains."

"No, Bob, he's a smart guy."

"So smart he's behind bars for life."

"Because the freak has mojo."

"What freak?" Bob asked.

"Eckles calls him a freak."

Although I look as ordinary as the next guy, I suspected that the freak under discussion was me.

Bob said, "*We're* the ones with mojo."

"*Contumax.*"

"*Potestas.*"

"Heil Hitler," I murmured from my listening post just inside the bathroom.

"We've got the dark mojo," Jim said. "Maybe the freak has the other kind."

"Well, I don't like hearing that."

"I don't like saying it. But he sure had something in Nevada, didn't he? And who's dead out there in the desert—our guys or the freak? Eckles is right. Some kind of mojo."

"Eckles have anything specific or just more blather?"

Jim said, "For one thing, maybe once this freak has met you or touched you or even just seen you, he has a way of tracking you no matter where you are."

"Tracking? Like he's a damn Tonto or something?"

"Tracking by mojo."

"Yeah, so?"

Jim said, "If he tracked Wolfgang's crew, they might lead him to us."

"Why not send them away, let him track them out to Florida or wherever the hell?"

"He'd probably know they were misleading him."

"Probably? All this because probably?"

"He'd stay here in Pico Mundo," Jim insisted. "Once he saw them, they should have killed him. They tried, but they couldn't. Anyway, there's no time to play games with him. It's happening."

With a note of wonder in his voice, Bob said, "It really is, isn't it?"

"It sure is. It's happening."

They were silent for a moment, and then Bob said, "What kind of world is it going to be after it happens?"

Jim didn't need to mull over his answer. He said at once, "Ours. It's going to be our world, brother."

"*Contumax.*"

"*Potestas.*"

"Lunatics," I murmured.

Footsteps. A door opened. It closed. Silence.

When I felt certain that I was alone, I stepped out of the bathroom, pistol in hand, and moved forward through the motor home.

In the lounge were two dead men and one dead woman.

Twenty-one

When I was no longer of the world, I would miss its extravagant beauty. I would miss the complex and charming layers of subterfuge by which the truth of the world's mysteries were withheld from us even as we were tantalized and enchanted by them. I would miss the kindness of good people who were compassionate when so many were pitiless, who made their way through so much corruption without being corrupted themselves, who eschewed envy in a world of envy, who eschewed greed in a world of greed, who valued truth and could not be drowned in a sea of lies, for they shone and, by the light they cast, they had warmed me all my life.

I would not miss the indifference in the face of suffering, the hatred, the violence, the cruelty, the lust for power that so many people brought to the pageant of humanity.

In the lounge—or living room—of the motor home, the two men and the woman had been made to kneel side by side in front of a sofa. Each had been shot, execution style, in the back of the head and slumped facedown into the hideous discharge from their exit wounds.

The murders must have occurred before I entered the vehicle, perhaps only moments before, and the guns must have been fitted with sound suppressors.

Three victims, two killers, and yet there were no signs of a struggle. I couldn't help but wonder if the dead, who were clearly compatriots of the two gunmen, had not understood what would be done to them. Supposing instead that they knew their fates as soon as Jim and Bob arrived, then could it be that strict obedience to the cult required them to acquiesce without resistance?

The latter possibility chilled me. If they were so brainwashed as to be unable to defend their lives, if they were so profoundly committed to evil that they would sacrifice themselves upon its altar, stopping their plan for the destruction of Pico Mundo might be even more difficult than I already anticipated it would.

They were, of course, the three who had pursued me in the abandoned mall barely sixteen hours earlier. Wolfgang, Jonathan, and Selene. I had not glimpsed their faces then; and I was grateful that their ruined countenances were pressed into the sofa cushions, sparing me the sight of them now.

None of their spirits had lingered, which was no surprise. I've noticed over the years that some good people linger, as do some not so good as they ought to be, but really bad people split the scene when their heart thumps out the last beat. I suspect perhaps they owe a serious debt, and the creditor wants to collect it without delay.

I holstered the Glock and, with some disgust, I fished the wallet out of one of the men's jeans. From a credit-card pocket in the wallet, I withdrew a California driver's license. His name—or at least the name under which he obtained the license—was Wolfgang Leopold Schmidt. His photo ID revealed one of those rare Neanderthals who believed that a close shave, an expensive haircut, a crisp white shirt, and a sincere smile could help him pass for human. He was wrong about that.

I dropped the wallet on the floor and took my tinkered-with, highly secure, untraceable smartphone from a jacket pocket. When I switched it on, the bright-gold exclamation point appeared against a black background.

Edie Fischer, the elderly lady who had founded whatever secret organization employed Deke and Maybelle Bullock, wore a brooch in the shape of an exclamation point formed from gold, diamonds, and rubies. In her company, when people asked her what the exclamation point meant, she had said at one time or another that it meant "Seize the day," or "Live life to the fullest," or "Sister, what a hoot it is to be me."

Later, when she had pinned the brooch to the sleeve of the sweater that I wore under a bulletproof vest, just before I went into action against the cult in Nevada, she admitted that it meant none of those things. When I asked what it did mean, she had said, "Never you mind what it means." Then she had sent me off to rescue seventeen kidnapped children. She promised the brooch would bring me through the night alive, and whether the jewelry had anything to do with it or not, I did survive.

I entered my access code in the phone. After my smiling face replaced the exclamation point, the phone didn't look as smart as it was supposed to be, but I was then able to make a call.

When Chief Wyatt Porter answered his cell on the third ring, I said, "Sir, I'm sorry if I'm about to ruin a lovely evening with Mrs. Porter."

"It wouldn't be the first time, Oddie. It's just good to have you back in town."

"Sir, I know your department does some disaster planning. What I'm wondering is if Malo Suerte Dam collapsed, do you know if maybe enough water would pour out of the lake so that Pico Mundo might be completely submerged?"

"Why would the dam collapse?"

"If maybe somebody blew it up."

"Who wants to blow it up?"

"I'm not sure anyone does." I found myself staring at the three dead people, and I turned my back to them. "But if someone does want to do it, then they're members of a satanic cult."

"This again. I was hoping you were wrong about that when you mentioned it at breakfast."

"I wish I had been."

"The bastards shot me the last time."

"I remember, sir."

"What do people get from all that devil mumbo-jumbo anyway?"

"A sense of purpose, I guess."

"They could volunteer at an animal shelter instead."

"Yes, sir. But then they wouldn't get to have group sex while wearing goat horns or kill people for fun."

"Never gave a whole lot of thought to the dam being blown up. I'd have to talk to some knowledgeable people about whether it would put us underwater. What I know for sure is it wouldn't do us any good."

"Maybe you could send someone out there to the dam to have a look at it."

"I'll be there myself at first light."

"I mean now, sir."

"It's almost eight o'clock. Can't inspect all that much in the dark, son."

"Well, you could look around and see if maybe there's a truck full of explosives parked on the dam."

"I thought this was a what-if chat."

"It's more a what-if-right-now chat."

"Seems like you must have been back more than just a day, what with all this you've already stirred up."

"I hit the ground running, sir."

"Well, all right, then, I'll get on out there to Malo Suerte and see what's what."

"You'll probably have to send deputies, sir. There's another thing you'll want to deal with yourself."

"We only have one dam. What else do these ignorant fools want to blow up?"

"They've killed three of their own, blew their brains out."

He sighed. "I should have retired after I was shot."

"You're still a young man, sir." I gave him the make and model of the motor home and described its approximate position in the carnie campground.

"Why kill their own?" he asked.

"From what I can gather, they thought I had a lead on these three and that through them maybe I'd find the others."

"Evidently you *did* have a lead on them. I'll be there with a crime-scene team, we'll talk."

"I won't be here, sir. I've got this other thing I really have to do."

"What thing?"

"I won't know until I go after it and find it. You remember how this works when I'm on the hunt."

"It's all coming back to me. You aren't getting in over your head, are you, Oddie?"

"If I am, I won't know it till I'm there."

"Karla's making you her famous apple dumplings."

"I love those dumplings."

"After she's gone to all that work, son, you better stay alive so you can eat them."

"Count on it," I said, but I didn't tell him about the four blank cards from Gypsy Mummy.

I terminated the call and switched off the phone and, without looking back at the three dead bodies, I left the motor home by the front passenger door.

The night remained warm enough for rattlesnakes, but I was less concerned about literal serpents than I was about the figurative ones like Jim and Bob. It wouldn't make much sense for them to hang around the immediate area, waiting to be linked to the murders that they had committed. On the other hand, you couldn't expect normal behavior from guys who hoped that if they committed enough mayhem in this world, they would earn for themselves a lucrative franchise selling dung sandwiches in Hell.

Moving along a darkish lane between rows of travel trailers and motor homes, acutely aware of the weight of the Glock in my shoulder holster, I kept my right hand flat against my chest, as if I were suffering a bout of acid reflux, the better to execute a quick draw if necessary.

Twenty-two

I was nearly out of the encampment, intending to return to the midway, when from between a pair of large RVs stepped two men. In the gloom, I almost drew down on them before I realized they were not Jim and Bob.

As they approached and we met in the fall of light from one of the few lampposts in the campground, one of the men proved to be a tall, muscular specimen wearing nothing but tennis shoes without socks, a pair of shorts, and a tapestry of tattoos that covered his bald head, face, and entire body. The other, a dwarf, wore a furry costume and carried the realistic-looking head of a baby bear under his right arm.

The little person said, "Hey, dude."

I said, "Hey."

They stopped in front of me, and for some reason I stopped, too, although I should have kept moving.

The moment felt surreal, but at the same time, there was about it a quality of hyper-reality. Even as I regarded those two men, I became aware of the flying beams of the spotlights, to the northeast, painting ephemeral infinity symbols across the pregnant clouds that increasingly commanded the sky, of the distant roller-coaster chain clacking through the ratchet angles of the guideway as cars full of riders climbed an incline toward the next long drop, of the dusty smell of the campground, and of the scent of rain pending. The many musics from the carnival volplaned to us, distorted by distance, tantalizing the part of us that seeks sensation as an antidote for dread, while at the same time triggering a vague alarm. I thought this would have been akin to the music that had played throughout Prince Prospero's castle in Poe's "The Masque of the Red Death," during the final horrific hours when the thousand revelers, certain that the plague could be denied entrance by the abbey's battlements, discovered the angel of death in costume among them, when blood then issued from their every pore. I was aware of the faint thrum of wings, as unseen night birds or bats traveled the darkness overhead, of snowflake moths that swooped in seeming ecstasy around the light atop the lamppost, of exaggerated moth shadows sliding-quivering down the walls of a nearby motor home and rippling across the graveled ground. The rush of detail conveyed by my inexplicably heightened senses served to emphasize the surreal pair before me, so that they seemed to have stepped through a tear in reality from someplace beyond.

This is A Moment, stay with it, I told myself, though at the time I could not have explained what *A Moment* meant.

The illustrated man said, "Cool face."

I had all but forgotten my harlequin disguise. "Connie did it."

"You know Connie?"

"Only because she painted my face."

"Yeah," the little person said, "but that's her real name."

Suspicion scrunched up the big guy's colorful ink-festooned countenance. "What're you?"

"Excuse me?"

"Are you a carnie? I don't get a carnie vibe from you."

"No, sir. I'm just a guy."

"Connie wouldn't give her real name to a mark," he said, by which he meant a patron of the carnival, someone not part of their tightly knit clan.

"I reminded Connie of her brother, Ethan."

That revelation astonished both men, and the little person said to his companion, "What do you think, Ollie?"

Ollie didn't know. "What do you think, Lou?"

"She talked family with him, like he was one of us." They returned their attention to me.

After a silence, I said, "I need to get going."

Ollie scowled again. "Wait, wait, wait."

His small friend said, "I want to shake your hand, dude, but not in this bear suit, and it takes a while for me to skin out of this damn thing."

"I'll shake your paw," I said, holding out my hand.

"No, that won't work," Lou said.

"That won't do any good at all," Ollie agreed.

"Put your hand on my head," Lou said.

"Why?"

"I won't bite it, I swear. Ever since the little person in that reality-TV show, people think we've all got an edge. I don't have an edge."

"He doesn't," the tattooed strongman agreed. "He's every bit as gentle as he looks."

"What's your name, dude?"

"Norman," I lied.

"Listen, Norman, I wouldn't hurt a rattlesnake if it was wrapped around my leg."

Ollie said, "He wouldn't even hurt his own mother, and that mean bitch sure as hell deserved it."

Lou shrugged his furry shoulders as if to say that your mom was your mom regardless of what atrocities she committed, a philosophical position with which I had some sympathy.

"Norman, listen, please just put your hand on my head so I can see something. It won't take but a few seconds."

When I hesitated, Ollie said, "Pretend you're checking him to see if he has a fever."

I wanted to be out of there before Chief Porter and his CSI team showed up; however, I was intrigued by Lou's request, and intuition kept assuring me that this was A Moment. Besides, in spite of Ollie's size, these two weren't the least threatening. They might have been a vaudeville act that had been transported through time from Broadway circa 1920 to this lamplit, graveled stage, where they only wanted to amuse.

I pretended to be checking Lou for a fever, maybe related to the ursine flu. When the palm of my hand met his forehead, I felt a weird tingle, not unpleasant, but it passed at once. The little guy closed his eyes and swayed as if his knees might fold him to the ground in his bear suit.

After perhaps ten seconds, he looked at me again, and tears spilled down his cheeks.

Startled, I took my hand off his forehead.

He said, "I wish I could help you, mister. I really do. I truly wish it. But you're far beyond me. Way far beyond me. You're the true deal. The truest. Whatever it is you've got to do, only you can do it."

Then he did the strangest thing but made it seem as natural as the words—*Hey, dude*—with which he had first greeted me. He took my hand in his two bear-suit paws and kissed it.

When he let go and raised his head, the tears on his cheeks glistened, and those yet unshed sparkled like galaxies in his large dark eyes.

I didn't know what to say, and he had evidently said all that he would. With the bear head still held under his right arm, he turned away from me.

Seemingly stunned by his companion's words and deeds, Ollie encircled me with his massive arms, hugged me to him, let me go, and said, "You take care of yourself, Norman."

Shuffling away, Lou said, "His name isn't Norman."

Ollie returned to his companion's side and put a hand on his shoulder to halt him. Glancing at me, the strongman said, "What is his name?"

"Truth," Lou said.

"That's a funny name."

"Mercy," Lou said.

"Truth Mercy—that's his name?"

"There's no right name for him."

"What did you see when he touched you?"

The little guy looked at me one last time and shook his head. "Too much. I saw too much."

Evidently the illustrated man knew his friend well enough to realize that those were his final words on the subject. They walked away from me and did not glance back again.

Shaken, I hurried out of the campground, up the long incline through knee-high grass, and across the service road to the shorter slope. When I reached the top, returning to the midway behind the sideshow tents, I looked down on the trailers and motor homes arrayed far below just in time to see two police cruisers and a morgue van enter the campground with emergency lights flashing but without sirens.

Standing there, rerunning in memory the encounter with Lou and Ollie, I thought that if there were others in the world with wild talents similar to mine, they would surely find it as difficult to live like ordinary people as I did. Perhaps for some of them, merely simplifying their lives, living in one-room apartments, wearing only jeans and T-shirts or another minimalist wardrobe, resolving not to complicate things by planning for the future, working in undemanding jobs such as fry cookery or tire sales was not enough to keep them sane and give them hope. Maybe some of them needed to withdraw from society more than I did. Burdened with one kind of psychic perception or another—or several—some might find stability and a degree of peace in the carnival, where outcasts and nonviolent misfits had long been welcome, where odd ducks were accepted, and where no one sought to know the secrets of others in the show.

Whatever Lou had seen when I touched him, his gift—or curse—obviously must be different from mine. He probably could not see the lingering spirits of the dead, but he might now know that I could. I suspected that he had learned other things about me, too, perhaps including the nature of the suffering that I might have to endure in the hours ahead. Dwarf in a bear suit, comic figure in whatever show he performed, the little guy had no doubt known his share of bullies and tormentors. And yet it was a good bet that he had more foresight and more wisdom than the thirty-three mechanical oracles housed in ALL THINGS FORETOLD.

I passed between two sideshow tents, back to the bright, loud, busy midway, no longer using psychic magnetism to seek out Wolfgang, Jonathan, and Selene, but focusing instead on the executioners, Jim and Bob.

Twenty-three

Through the open bedroom window of the seaside cottage came the pleasantly cool breath of the sea, but I sweated in twisted sheets. Perspiration streamed from me also in my turbulent nightmare, as the Happy Monster, Blossom Rosedale, led me toward what would prove to be the amaranth.

No sounds existed now except those that I made, as if the outer world had ceased to exist, as though I had become the world entire, isolated and adrift in a void. The furious knocking of my heart, the gasping for breath, each inhalation inadequate to my need, and a hard chattering sound, something rattling, that I could not identify.

There were light and shadow but no longer faces or mysterious shapes, only currents of color washing across my eyes, color and at times a rippling darkness, and I was very afraid. Sometimes Blossom seemed to manifest beside me, like a spirit, but at other times I was not aware of her.

Moving, moving forward, moving with great effort, moving, but to what, to where?

As the physicists tell us, time was created in the big bang, *a necessary condition for the expansion and maturation of the universe. All that exists outside the universe exists also outside of time, where no experience is measured in minutes. In dreams, time exists, though not as we know it in the waking world, strangely distorted and unreliable, as if on a subconscious level we're aware that time isn't enduring, that it is not a required condition of our existence, that there comes a point when we will have no need of it.*

With or without Blossom, I seemed to travel for hours, crossing a considerable distance, though it might also have been mere seconds before again I heard a sound not made by me. A voice cried out, and again a face appeared on which I could concentrate.

The face was Wyatt Porter's, and the voice was his, too, and he shouted my name: "Oddie!"

Blossom was with me again, supporting me. I struggled forward, gripping the urn of ashes with both hands. When the chief called my name again, my vision cleared further, and I stared down the muzzle of his pistol, which swelled in dimension until it was the diameter of a cannon barrel. He fired.

Twenty-four

When seeking Wolfgang, I'd had no face to associate with the name, but I'd had his singular gravelly voice to conjure in memory, which helped me to focus my mind, my gift, and home in on him. In the case of Jim and Bob, I had glimpsed them from the back of the motor home, but I hadn't seen their faces, and neither of them possessed a memorable voice. Having their first names only, I wasn't hopeful of being the Tonto that they feared.

I still believed that the key to unlocking the cultist's plan and the means to thwart it could be found in the carnival, but the longer I stalked the midway, the more discouraged I became about my prospects of finding my quarry. I tried to navigate the surging crowd on the concourse, but the people repeatedly turned like a tide and resisted me, their faces either glassy with excitement or weary with a surfeit of joyless "fun," but always indifferent to me, as the sea would be indifferent as it drowned me in a treacherous current.

Each time I passed the carousel, the wild-eyed horses pumped up and down more frantically with each rotation, and the calliope seemed to pipe with greater frenzy, growing ever more off-key. The Dodgem Cars crashed into one another with great—and then greater—abandon, their trolley poles striking ever-brighter showers of sparks from the overhead electric-wire grid. The shrieking of the shrouded riders in the Caterpillar and the screaming of those who stood in cages on the rapidly spinning and then up-tilting Roulette Wheel sounded not like expressions of delight, but instead like the death cries of terrified people pierced by the pain of mortal wounds. As they stumbled and tumbled through the giant revolving barrel that expelled them from the fun house, their shrill laughter was, to my ear, like the insane cackling in the deepest cells of an asylum, and all the while, the giant face of the ogre growled and blew out a fierce breath that took strollers by surprise.

If I concentrated too intently on Jim and Bob, if I sought them too insistently, too urgently, through the strobing lights and flung shadows of the spinning rides, I risked becoming the hunted instead of the hunter in a moment of *reverse* psychic magnetism. Sometimes, when I tried too long or too ardently to be drawn to my quarry, they were instead drawn to me. On those occasions, I saw them only after I had been seen and recognized, which was a dangerous situation when those I sought were ruthless murderers.

At last, the mélange of odors (frying burgers, diesel fumes from a generator, the reek of steam rising from grab-joint wells in which too many hot dogs had been boiled in the same water, cigarette smoke, cloying perfumes, human sweat, the stink of ripe manure wafting over from the animal exhibits in the part of the fair that was off the midway) and the whistling-honking-clattering-banging-hissing-ringing hoopla of the ten-thousand-voice Sombra Brothers extravaganza became too much for me to endure when my senses were dialed wide open as they had to be when I practiced psychic magnetism.

I decided to take a brief break from the midway. I intended to return after a calming visit to the exhibition hall, where many county artists and craftsmen and homemakers exhibited their wares and participated in judged competitions for the coveted best-of-the-year blue ribbon in categories ranging from quilts and needlepoint pillows to kiln-fired pottery, from homemade cookies and chili to elegant bentwood rocking chairs.

When I passed the exhibition hall and kept going toward the main parking lot, where I had left the dinged and dirty Ford Explorer, I realized that by shifting off the midway, I had shifted into gear. I was on the trail of Jim and Bob, after all.

Approaching the Explorer, I grew cautious. I half expected the two executioners to rise from the bed of a pickup truck in which they had been reclining in anticipation of me, or to step from behind one SUV or another. The parking lot was more brightly lighted than the carnies' campground. Before boarding the Explorer, I circled it, peering through the dust-filmed windows into the backseat and the cargo area, to be certain that when I climbed into the driver's seat, I wouldn't be surprised by an unwanted passenger with a penchant for shooting people in the back of the head, though I was likewise averse to having my throat slit.

By the time I piloted the Ford along the exit lane, I felt sure Jim and Bob had departed the fairgrounds. Even with as little as I knew about them, I seemed to be raveling toward them, spooling up an invisible ribbon that they had unspooled in their wake. I accelerated onto Maricopa Lane, which led first through the outskirts of town and then toward the center of it. Soon I began to make a series of turns from street to street, turns that seemed to be meaningful . . . until I began to feel that I'd lost my quarry.

In a residential neighborhood, I pulled to the curb, switched off the engine, and got out of the Explorer. I had parked under a grandly spreading *Ficus nitida,* which most everyone called an Indian laurel, though it wasn't a laurel and had no connection to any Indian tribe. I stood with my back to the tree and to the SUV, watching the nearby houses.

A stillness lay upon the street. The torpid air stirred not a rustle from the dense foliage of the ficus. The front porches were deserted, and no one appeared on the sidewalk with or without a dog. Although lights glowed in a number of windows, I heard no muffled TVs or even the faintest strains of music.

Perhaps because the dense clouds had erased the moon and stars, because they had lowered in what appeared to be preparation for an unseasonable storm, the town felt as though a pressure weighed upon it. I might not have been surprised if this reality and my dream had suddenly become one, if dead bodies floated into the street, drifting through the thick air as through water, their eyes protuberant and their faces contorted in terror.

Intending to call Chief Porter, I switched on my phone. But then at the end of the block, a car rounded the corner that I had recently turned, and it started toward me, and the fine hairs prickled along the back of my neck.

I wasn't near a streetlamp. Cloaked in shadows, pressed against the ancient ficus, I doubted that they could have seen me yet. I slid down until I was sitting on the sidewalk, the massive trunk of the tree and then the Explorer between me and them. They probably weren't assassins. More likely, they were a couple of harmless elderly citizens coming home from a church supper, talking about hemorrhoid creams or whatever elderly couples talked about.

The vehicle approached slowly, or so it seemed to me, and for sure it slowed somewhat as it passed the Explorer. But then it picked up speed and continued on its way. I dared to look after it and saw a white Mercedes SUV. No one leaned out a window to empty a .357 Magnum in my direction.

I had not seen a face or even a form in the car, as if it had been driven by something other than the living or the dead, both of whom I can see.

My eventful life is conducive to paranoia, but I am generally able to avoid imagining that there's a bogeyman under my bed. This cult was tying knots in my nerves. The memory of that collection of severed heads in glass jars, back in Nevada, did kind of linger.

I got to my feet, leaned against the tree as before, and phoned Chief Porter. He answered on the second ring, and I said, "You're in the motor home, sir?"

"The CSI team has it for a little while yet. We'll search it as soon as they're done, when we don't have to worry about contaminating the scene."

"Meanwhile, you're talking to other carnies in the campground?"

"They're not the most talkative folks."

"Ask them if they know a Jim and a Bob."

"Jim what, Bob who?"

"That's all I know. They're the executioners."

"Everyone knows a bunch of Jims and Bobs. Must be a million Jims and Bobs in California alone."

"This Jim and Bob hang out together."

"That narrows it down to nine hundred ninety thousand. Are they carnies?"

"I don't know. But there's somebody in the campground you might get something from. He's kind of like me, but you should pretend not to know that."

"He's what—a fry cook?"

"No, sir. I ran into him after I called you about the murders and left the motor home. He's a carnie. He's got a sixth sense of some kind. For real. I'm not sure about the scope of it."

"What's his name?"

"Oh, sorry. His name's Lou. He has a friend there named Ollie."

"Lou what, Ollie who?"

"I didn't get last names, sir. But they'll be easy to find. Lou is a dwarf in a bear suit. Ollie's a huge guy tattooed head to foot."

"In a bear suit?"

"Not Ollie, no, just Lou. And he's probably taken it off by now. Lou might open up to you more if you tell him you know me and you know about my gift. By the way, he knows me as Norman."

Two houses to my right, a man came out of the front door and stood on the dark porch. I was so tense, it seemed to me that a guy standing on a porch was the most suspicious thing I'd ever seen.

The chief said, "Well, Norman, I've never told anyone about your gift except Karla."

I couldn't be sure if the man on the porch saw me. I lowered my voice. "I appreciate you keeping my secret, Chief. I really do. But if we don't find these guys and stop them, things are going to get very desperate, very fast."

"Why're you whispering?"

"Some guy came out on a porch."

"Is it Jim or Bob?"

"No, sir. It's just some guy. I think."

A lighter flared. Porch guy had stepped outside to smoke a cigarette. Or so it appeared.

Chief Porter said, "Where are you, son?"

"Standing under a *Ficus nitida,* waiting for inspiration."

"What's a *Ficus nitida?*"

I looked up into the web of dark branches. "You probably call it an Indian laurel. Did you send someone out to the dam?"

"Sonny Wexler and Billy Mundy should be there by now."

"Your two best. I'm glad you're taking this seriously, sir."

"I always take you seriously, son. Even when there's a dwarf in a bear suit."

"He's a nice little person, by the way. He doesn't have an edge like that guy in the reality-TV show."

"There's another thing happened," Chief Porter said. "Just a few minutes ago. An alert came over the wire from Homeland Security. Three armed guards were transporting a truckload of C-4 between the manufacturer and a weapons depot at an Army base."

"Plastic explosives."

"That's right. One of the guards killed the other two and hijacked the shipment."

"How much C-4?"

"It might have been a thousand kilos."

I shivered in the warm night. "Enough to blow up the dam."

"Twice over," the chief said.

"When did this happen?"

"About three hours ago, but we just got word on the wire."

"Where did it happen?"

"They think about thirty miles from here. The feds say not to worry, they're all over it. They just found the truck. The C-4 had been off-loaded into another vehicle."

"What vehicle?"

"That seems to be anyone's guess. When the feds say they're all over it, that doesn't mean they're all over it."

"I better get my mojo working," I said.

"I sure hope you can, son. We need you on this. So why did you call it a *Ficus didida*?"

"*Nitida.* That's the correct botanical name, sir. Ozzie Boone insists that even if a writer uses the common name of a tree or other plant, he ought to know the correct botanical name. He says that no matter what you're writing about, you need to know a whole lot more on the subject than what you put on the page, or otherwise the work won't have any depth."

"So you're still writing your memoirs."

"Yes, sir. As I get the chance."

"I guess you know a lot about Indian laurels, then."

"I could go on for hours."

"I just realized I don't have your phone number."

I gave it to him.

"Things are moving fast," he said. "I'll be back to you soon."

I terminated the call.

A faint trace of cigarette smoke scented the still air. In the darkness of the porch, the smoker took a deep drag, and the end of his cigarette glowed hot orange.

Watching the man, I thought of a fuse on a stick of dynamite.

Plastic explosives were detonated with an electric current, not with a fuse, not with a flame, but I thought of a fuse anyway.

Twenty-five

Driving around, odd as I've always been, thinking: *Jim. Bob. Jim. Bob. Jim, Bob. Jim, Bob. Jim Bob, Jim Bob, Jim Bob, Jim Bob* . . .

Although neither of the executioners had spoken with a southern accent, I sounded to myself as though I must be trying to track down some good old boy with a red neck and a tattoo of the Confederate flag somewhere on his body, good old Jim Bob, with a juicy wad of chewin' tobacco tucked up in his cheek and Merle Haggard playing on the radio of his pickup, while he drove around with a loaded rifle, looking for a possum to shoot so that he could bring it home to the little woman and have her make her mighty fine stew that she served over buttered grits with collard greens on the side.

Psychic magnetism doesn't work if I'm distracted, and I was so distracted that the word *distracted* wasn't strong enough to describe my state of mind. Spinning Jim and Bob into a fantasized good old boy wasn't the only thing that kept me from focusing my paranormal gift for tracking people. I kept thinking about my dream, too, chewing it over like Jim Bob with his chaw. My mind also kept bouncing back to *Ficus nitida* versus Indian laurel, which had nothing to do with this crisis except that the chief happened to ask me about it. When it wasn't *Ficus nitida,* it was the plump woman with the masses of curly auburn hair, giving me the admission ticket and assuring me that I would be a big winner at 11:45 if I remained on the midway. And when the plump cashier stayed out of my head for a minute, her place was taken by bear-suited Lou and mega-tattooed Ollie. Or by Gypsy Mummy spitting out blank cards. Or by the coyote that had stood in the street and stared boldly at me as I'd climbed onto the Big Dog bike early that morning, after leaving the abandoned mall to the bats and carnivorous beetles that now called it home.

I also began to feel that I was being tailed. I couldn't stop glancing at the rearview mirror. Three times, when a vehicle behind struck me as suspicious, I turned at the first intersection, but none of them followed me.

Only fifteen minutes after terminating the phone call with Wyatt Porter, I realized that I was cruising the state route to Malo Suerte Lake, doing eighty miles per hour, twenty over the limit. Considering that my psychic magnetism currently functioned even less well than a ten-billion-dollar government computer system, I had no expectation of finding Bob and Jim at the dam. Either I was hurtling toward Malo Suerte out of desperation, hoping for a new lead now that those two men without faces and surnames had proved elusive, or my usually reliable intuition had kicked in once more.

Suddenly I remembered that although Jim and Bob were without faces, I had two—the one I was born with and the one Connie had given me at the carnival. The cops guarding the dam would be edgy already, on the lookout for armed-to-the-teeth cultists with over a ton of C-4. If I showed up painted like the most recent theatrical psychopath to terrorize Gotham City, a tragic mistake might be made. This was a world, after all, of tragic mistakes.

I didn't want to waste time driving back across town to the farther outskirts where the Bullocks maintained the safe house, just to scrub off my mask. If I stopped at a service station to use their facilities, I'd have to ask for the key, at which point there would probably be some tedious back-and-forth about my painted face, which would seem as bizarre outside the carnival as it had seemed ordinary on the midway.

Instead of going directly to the dam, I drove to the park on the north shore, where I'd had breakfast that morning with Ozzie Boone and Chief Porter. The park was closed for the night. I left the Explorer on the shoulder of the highway, scaled the gate, and walked about thirty yards through darkness to the buff-brick building that housed the public restrooms.

Two security lights, two doors. Both were locked.

Fortunately the desert-style landscaping around the premises offered cacti and succulents and mostly decorative rocks. Because Maravilla County wasn't so prosperous that it could afford night patrols of gated parks, I picked up two rocks the size of oranges, hesitated because of a lifelong tendency toward good citizenship, and then pitched the first one through a window. After using the second rock to break out the jagged shards that remained around the edges of the frame, I boosted myself over the sill and into the building.

I had never before broken into a bathroom. It wasn't one of those firsts that you include on a résumé.

Using the little flashlight that hadn't been left on the dresser in the safe house, glass snapping and crunching underfoot, I went to the paper-towel dispenser and yanked several sheets from it. At the middle sink in a bank of five, I regarded myself in the mirror and confirmed the wisdom of a thorough face washing. When not in the context of the carnival, the harlequin mask and the black-and-white diamond pattern looked sinister in the extreme.

For the task at hand, the flashlight wasn't as bright as I would have liked, but both common sense and paranoia argued against switching on the overhead fluorescent panels.

When finished, I leaned close to the mirror. As far as I could tell, I'd scrubbed off all the paint. Yet something was wrong with my face.

I'd never had a high opinion of my looks. I had always felt that I was ordinary, which was all right, because a girl as beautiful as Stormy Llewellyn had still found reasons to love me.

But now something about my face unsettled me, and the longer that I looked at myself, the more disturbed I became. I told myself that the quality of the light distorted my reflection, because no matter how I angled the beam of the flashlight, stark shadows carved my face into a more fierce countenance than I actually possessed.

But it wasn't just the light. This was not the face of the fry cook I had been, not the face of the boy who had walked hand-in-hand with Stormy into an arcade to pose an important question to Gypsy Mummy. I found my eyes distressing. I turned from the mirror.

I had not seen any of my current adversaries' faces, except for that of Wolfgang on his driver's license. In mirrors, did they see the wickedness behind their masks, and was there a point past which they avoided mirrors?

I thought I would leave by the door, but it could be neither locked nor unlocked from inside. When I climbed out of the window, flashlight in hand, the first thing that caught my attention was my Explorer out along the road, beyond the gate, illuminated by the headlights of the SUV that was now parked behind it.

A white Mercedes SUV. Like the one that had cruised slowly by while I'd hidden behind the *Ficus nitida.* The vehicle that I had assured myself was driven by an elderly couple coming home from a church supper.

If there had been retirees in it back then, they must have been carjacked in the meantime. Two men, neither of them elderly, were looking over the Explorer, clearly visible even at thirty yards, because the headlights of their vehicle revealed them.

Reverse psychic magnetism. Jim and Bob. I had thought too intently about them, had sought them too insistently. Because I didn't have faces to go with their names, not even a distinctive voice for either one, I had been unable to find them. But they had been drawn, and here they were.

One of them happened to be looking toward me. When I came out of the shattered window, he pointed, and at once the second man turned his attention to me as well. The security lamps over the comfort-station entrances betrayed me, as did the feeble beam of my small flashlight, but that wasn't why I had caught their attention. They could not have missed me, for I was to them what a magnet is to iron filings.

Twenty-six

I could run from them. But to what end? I needed the Explorer. The chief had been right when he'd said that things were moving fast. Whatever catastrophe might make Pico Mundo the biggest story of the year, it would unfold within the next several hours, surely before dawn. If I had any hope of discovering what the cult intended and putting a stop to it, I had to be mobile. I couldn't chase down the truth on foot or by hoping to thumb a ride every time I needed one.

If I had an advantage, it was that people who were drawn to me by reverse psychic magnetism were not aware of what had brought them into my presence. They felt no compulsion to find me, no attracting power. They made excuses to themselves for why they deviated from their plans and set off to places that they had no intention of visiting. Maybe they told themselves that they needed time to think about what they intended to do next. Maybe they convinced themselves that just cruising around would free their minds to consider their options more clearly. Whatever the case, they were always surprised to see me.

Without hesitation, I started toward the gate at the entrance, as if I had no concern about these men's intentions, as if I assumed that people who drove Mercedes SUVs were all upstanding citizens who wanted only the best for their fellow men, an end to all hunger, and world peace.

They probably didn't even know who I was. They hadn't seen me with the Explorer when they had cruised past it in town. Here the Ford was again, yes, and they would be puzzled as to why they had been interested in it earlier and why they should stumble upon it now when they were just cruising around at random, miles from where it had been parked before.

Whether they had tumbled to my identity or not, they would know me when I drew closer to them. The cult had been searching for me, and they surely had old newspaper photographs to go by, if nothing else. By the time I reached the fence, they would recognize me, and they would for a moment be surprised. A moment. Three seconds, four.

For another moment, they would wonder what I was doing out there at that hour, if I knew about the nearby dam and the C-4, and if I might have told anyone what I knew. Two seconds, three.

For another moment, they would look at each other, consulting on a course of action with or without words. They would want to kill me, yes, but they might also want to capture me, so that they could first torture me into revealing anything I knew about Edie Fischer and her organization, which was as secret as theirs and opposed to them at every turn. Four seconds, five.

Those three moments gave me a fearfully narrow path to survival. In fact, it wasn't even a path, but a tightrope, a high wire across which I had to run, not walk.

I pretended no suspicion, calling out, "Hello," as I approached them through the darkness. Pretending the kind of inebriation that can be detected not so much by the drunk's slurred words as by his too-loud and too-hearty speech, pretending also that I assumed they were park employees, I said, "Needed a damn toilet! Why'd you lock up, God's sake? Had to bust out a window, 'cause you *locked it up!*"

I couldn't shoot at them through a chain-link fence with any hope of scoring a hit. I had to climb it before they drew on me.

As I came out of the darkness into the backwash of their SUV's headlights, I faked a stumble and cursed and ducked my head to hide my face. I believe I started climbing the chain-link before they realized who I was. I reached the top by the time they were getting to the end of the second of those three moments.

Instead of coming down the other side of the gate, I froze at the top, drew the Glock from my shoulder rig, thought for an instant it was going to snag on the powder-blue sport coat, and as they went for their weapons too late, I fired down on them. The first round took one of them in the gut, and he began to scream, his gun slipping out of his grip even as he drew it. The second round took the other man point-blank in the face, blowing out the back of his skull, and he was no doubt dead before he hit the ground.

The belly-shot man lay on his back, clutching his abdomen with both hands, so racked by pain that he squirmed like a broken bug. The terror and agony that twisted his face were ghastly, and yet when I approached him, he begged for his life, which would be for him only more terror and greater agony. Instead of granting his plea, I shot him twice again, and he fell silent.

A voice behind me said, "Murderer." When I pivoted to confront a new threat, no one was there but the dead man whom I had shot in the face. I waited, but if he had spoken, he did not speak again.

Although rock-steady to that point, I began to tremble so badly that I feared accidentally firing another round, and I holstered the pistol. I shook as if with palsy, and I didn't know what to do with my hands, whether to put them in my pockets or smooth back my hair with them or tuck them into my armpits to press the tremors out of them, and so I stood there making meaningless gestures, gagging on each breath I tried to take.

In the cause of saving children and other innocents, I had killed before. I had even shot women, three of them, two who tried to shoot me and one who would have cut me to ribbons given half a chance. Killing was never easy. Regardless of the viciousness and palpable evil of the target, killing was never easy. But this time the necessity had shaken and distressed me more violently than ever.

These men didn't deserve the slightest measure of pity. They had ruthlessly executed Wolfgang, Jonathan, and Selene. They surely had killed many others, perhaps including some of the children that the cult was so fond of sacrificing on their blood-stained altars.

Their particular deaths were not what rocked me so profoundly. I was shaken instead by the *cumulative* killing that I had done, as if I'd committed the act often enough that, here tonight, I crossed some moral boundary beyond which I would be forever changed, some boundary that I could not retreat behind and find again the person I had once been.

No matter what I had become, I could not say *enough of this*, could not walk away from the fight. That choice was forbidden to me, as it had been most of my life. Something big and bad would happen to Pico Mundo if the cult wasn't stopped. My horror, guilt, and sorrow mattered not at all when compared to the deaths of thousands that I had foreseen. This task would not be lifted from me, and to refuse it would be to refuse the desired destiny that I'd been promised: Stormy.

I had to get out of there before someone drove by and saw the carnage. Because of the threat to the dam, a patrol car might cruise along that lonely road, in which case my friendship with Wyatt Porter and even my unwanted reputation as a hero would not guarantee me the freedom of movement that I must have for the rest of the night.

First I needed their wallets. No. I didn't need them. I wanted them. Not for the money. To prove something to myself.

I stepped carefully, grateful for the Mercedes's headlights, loath to step on a fragment of skull bone, a twist of hair and flesh, a spattering of brains.

Behind the wheel of the Explorer, I searched the pockets of my jeans for the keys, then my jacket pockets, panicking, wondering if I had dropped them somewhere between there and the public restrooms in the park. In the last pocket, my fingers closed on the coiled plastic ring, and then on the key itself.

I hung a U-turn and drove west. A mile from the park entrance, I pulled to a stop on the shoulder of the road.

The two billfolds I had taken lay on the passenger seat. My hands still trembled as I went through one wallet and then the other, searching for ID.

This is a world where tragic mistakes are common. The white Mercedes SUV might not have been the same one that I'd seen earlier. Perhaps the men whom I'd shot would prove to be not who I thought they were. I had killed them without hearing a word of what they had to say, without asking a question of them. They had pulled their guns only after I'd drawn mine. Maybe they had licenses to carry concealed weapons, which I did not, and maybe they were authorities of some kind, with legitimate reasons to ask me what I had been doing in the park when it was closed for the night.

Both men possessed current Nevada driver's licenses. James Morton Sterling. Robert Foster Cokeberry. Jim and Bob.

My relief wasn't as complete as I might have anticipated. They were indeed the men I suspected they were; but if I had not made a tragic mistake back at the park gate, I might well make one the next time.

Headlights appeared in the distance, and a vehicle approached from the west.

I drove onto the state route once more, and a moment later, a Dodge pickup swept past me in the eastbound lane.

In a minute or so, the dead men would be found.

In California, hardened criminals were often turned loose after serving a mere fraction of their sentences, because prison crowding was considered cruel and unusual punishment. But if you drove while talking on a handheld phone, you would be shown no mercy. I risked the pitiless brute force of the law by calling Chief Porter without pulling off the highway.

"Sir, you're going to get a call soon about a white Mercedes SUV and two dead men at the gate to Malo Suerte Park."

"It's not been half an hour since we last talked."

"Yes, sir. I've got a wristwatch. Their names are James Morton Sterling and Robert Foster Cokeberry."

"Jim and Bob."

"The two and only."

"Let me get a pen. There. Okay. Repeat their names."

I repeated them. "They both have Nevada driver's licenses."

"Are you okay, Oddie?"

"Yeah. Sure. I'm okay."

"Because you don't sound okay."

"Not a scratch," I assured him.

After a silence, because he knew me well, he said, "Not all wounds are the bleeding kind."

I didn't want to talk about it. "I've got their driver's licenses, Chief. I'm going to the dam now, so I'll leave them with Sonny and Billy."

"By the way, I talked to Mr. Donatella."

"Who?"

"Lou Donatella, you know, in the bear suit. Though he wasn't wearing it by the time I got to him. He and Ollie were drinking coffee, eating brown-sugar pavlovas. They're delicious. Have you ever had one?"

"No, sir. I don't even know what a pavlova is."

"They're delicious is what they are. Lou made them himself. He's a nice little guy. He gave me some useful stuff about this Wolfgang Schmidt."

Ahead on the left loomed a sign rimmed with pentagons of highly reflective plastic: MALO SUERTE DAM.

"Schmidt claimed to come from a carnie family when he bought out one of the concessionaires, but Lou says the guy was no more a carnie than Mozart was a carnie. Lou's into classical music."

"I'm turning on to the service road to the dam, sir. I'll call you back in a little while."

"What do you expect to find there, son?"

"I don't know. I'm just . . . drawn to it."

"You sure you're all right?"

"I'm fine."

"Call me when you get a chance. I'll be here. This is looking like an all-nighter."

"No, sir. My hunch is . . . this thing is going to blow before midnight."

"Let's hope you're right," he said.

I thought, *Let's hope I'm wrong.*

Twenty-seven

The service road led through land so parched that you wouldn't expect to find a dam and a large body of water at the end of it. To both sides, my headlights showed bare earth, scatterings of stones, an occasional bristle of nameless weeds, no mesquite, no cactus.

Far to the south, along the horizon, heat lightning pulsed through the clouds, smooth radiant waves rather than jagged spears. Forty or fifty miles away, perhaps a downpour washed the desert. Rain didn't always travel as far as heat lightning could be seen, and Pico Mundo might not receive a drop all night.

The breast of the dam didn't in scale match that engineering wonder Boulder Dam, over in Nevada. Pico Mundians prided themselves on being "the smallest town of forty thousand anywhere in the world." That slogan, created by the chamber of commerce, meant to convey to tourists that we were big enough to offer a wide range of activities and accommodations, and that nevertheless we remained simple people with homespun wisdom, down-home manners, and a tradition of welcoming strangers as we would our own kin. You could go to Boulder, Nevada, and do your boating on Lake Mead, behind the ostentatiously massive breastworks of *their* dam, if you didn't mind the greedy casinos, all owned by humongous corporations, luring you to nearby Vegas, trying every minute of the day to get their hands in your pockets. Or you could come to Pico Mundo and enjoy boating on Malo Suerte Lake, behind a dam that was practical and human in scale, nothing like that Hitlerian structure across the border, only one hundred and two feet across and thirty-eight feet from crest to sill.

Our dam had no hydroelectric powerhouse, because it had been constructed with the modest intention of creating a pristine lake for recreational use and, in times of drought, a lake that could also serve as a source of water for a few major Maravilla County reservoirs downstream from it. There were sluice gates toward the north end of the dam and a squat concrete outlet-control structure about twenty feet square. The building looked like a miniature fortress, with a crenellated parapet around its flat roof and windows hardly larger than arrow loops.

When I braked to a stop at the end of the service road, Sonny Wexler and Billy Mundy were standing by their squad car. One of them held a shotgun. The other had what might have been a fully automatic carbine, like maybe an Uzi, which indicated the seriousness with which they took the threat.

They must have had a way to operate the headlights remotely, because as I approached, the high beams from their black-and-white nearly blinded me. The officers eased behind the squad car—one near the rear, the other at the front—using it as cover, leveling their weapons, as if they thought Dr. Evil had just arrived on the first step of a crusade for world domination.

I switched off my headlights, put down the side window, and

leaned my head out, so they could see who had come calling. They knew I was close with the chief. In fact, after the business at Green Moon Mall a couple of years earlier, they were among the officers who had insisted that I be given a citation for bravery, which was now packed away with Stormy's belongings in a room in Ozzie Boone's house.

Shotgun at the ready, Sonny Wexler, big and tough and as soft-spoken as a monk, with forearms as thick as a sumo wrestler's calves, cautiously approached the Explorer. He stayed wide of it, so that Billy could have a clear shot if someone in addition to me came out of the vehicle. "You alone in there, Odd?"

Haunted by the shootings at the park, I worried that my voice or a recurrence of the shakes would give them reason to wonder about me, but when I spoke, I sounded normal, which may not speak well of me.

"Yes, sir, I am. I'm alone."

"The chief said you were back."

"Good. 'Cause I am. I'm back."

"It's good to have you back," he said, but he didn't lower the shotgun.

"It's good to be back," I assured him.

"You know what's happening?"

"I do, sir. I put the chief on to it."

"Why don't you get out," Sonny said, "and walk around your vehicle, open all the doors and the tailgate, so I can see straight through."

"All right, sir." I got out of the driver's door.

"It's not that I don't trust you, Odd."

"I understand, sir."

"I trust you like a brother."

"That's good to hear, sir."

"It's just you might have come here under duress."

"No problem," I said, opening the back door on the driver's side.

"It's not every night of the week somebody wants to blow up the dam."

I said, "Boring old Pico Mundo," as I raised the tailgate.

After I opened all the doors and after Sonny circled the Ford, looking straight through it from every angle, I closed up what I had opened.

Tension reduced, the three of us gathered by the back of their cruiser as they remoted the headlights off. Billy Mundy wasn't a titan like Sonny Wexler, but he had a few inches and thirty pounds of muscle on me. Standing with them, I felt like Lou the bear with two Ollies.

The lights were on for the length of the single-lane road that crossed the crest of the dam, and a series of spotlights lit the breast from the top. It really looked pathetic compared to Boulder Dam.

More heat lightning throbbed through the clouds far to the south, too far away for the trailing thunder to reach us, and for some reason the sight of it made me shudder.

"You hear about the C-4?" Sonny asked.

"Yeah."

"That is major wicked stuff, ruinous. Who would want to do this?"

"People who know Bern Eckles."

That surprised them. They had been on the force with him, and he was an embarrassment to them. Billy said, "Eckles, that sonofabitch, he's away for life."

"You could say these people go to the same church."

Sonny shook his head. "Wackos. The world is full of wackos these days. All these wackos, it's not going to end well."

"Nothing like this ever happens with Baptists," Billy said.

"Or even with Presbyterians," Sonny said. "What can we do for you, Odd? What brought you all the way out here?"

That was an excellent question. I wished I had an answer. "The chief just asked if I'd come to the dam and, you know, sort of have a look around, you know, maybe walk across the service road there on the crest, just in general kind of see whatever there is to see, if there's anything at all, which probably there isn't, but it won't hurt to give it a try."

I sounded so lame, rambling toward incoherence, that I wouldn't have been surprised if they'd wanted to test my blood-alcohol level.

Maybe the only good thing about people thinking you were a hero once long ago is that they treat you seriously no matter how idiotic you might sound. Sonny and Billy nodded solemnly as I babbled, hearing more sense in my speech than I put into it.

"Sure," Sonny Wexler said. "That's a good idea. Go on out there and have a look."

"Fresh eyes," Billy Mundy said. "Always a good idea to get fresh eyes on a problem."

"There were some prairie wolves around when we got here," Sonny said, "bolder than usual. Give us a holler if they bother you."

Some people in Maravilla County referred to them as prairie wolves, but most just called them coyotes.

"Yes, sir, I'll keep a lookout," I said. "But a coyote pack doesn't worry me half as much as the lunatics who stole the C-4."

"What we've been waiting to hear," Sonny said, "is an incoming plane."

Billy said, "If they load the C-4 in a plane and time it just right so it detonates as they crash the plane into the breast of the dam, there isn't a thing we could do to stop them."

"If you hear a plane," Sonny advised me, "best do what we'll do, which is run like hell."

"I wouldn't have thought of a plane," I said.

Billy nodded. "We wish we hadn't."

Twenty-eight

Entering from the north, I walked more than halfway across the crest of the dam before I leaned against the guardrail and looked down the lighted spillway that sloped to the plunge pool. In a planned outflow, water would collect in the pool before brimming over the sill into the stilling basin, and in controlled volume it would pour from there into the dry riverbed.

I didn't see anything suspicious. But of course I didn't know whether the scene before me was as it should be; I had no idea what I was looking for.

Often it seemed to me that my psychic gifts ought to have been bestowed upon someone with a higher IQ than mine.

On the lake side of the road, the regularly spaced lamps built into the guardrail cast some light upon the water that lapped gently at the tainter gates. But only ten or fifteen feet out, the lake went black, an inky immensity in this moonless, starless night.

In certain old movies set in World War II, Navy frogmen would approach a target underwater—bridge supports, ships in harbor—and surface just long enough to plant explosives. I didn't know how many well-trained scuba divers would be required to attach more than a ton of C-4 to the dam, though probably at least fifty, each of them burdened with forty pounds of the stuff, schooling like fish. No. Impractical.

A boat was more likely than frogmen. Anyone guarding the dam would hear the boat coming, especially in this quiet. But they most likely wouldn't be able to stop it in time, not just by hoping to pick off the pilot with sniper fire. If the boat had an electric motor, it could approach silently, raising no alarm.

Sonny and Billy hadn't mentioned an attack from the water, but if they had considered an airplane loaded with C-4, they must have thought of a boat.

When I turned from the lake, I saw movement past the south end of the dam, beyond the last lights, a lesser darkness in the deeper dark. Squinting brought no further clarity, only the same impression of restless motion.

Reaching beneath my sport coat, keeping one hand on the Glock in its holster, I walked south to have a closer look. When I was about twenty feet from the end of the dam, the visitors' shining eyes turned on me, three pairs mirroring the crest lamps, intently staring. As I came to a halt, they ventured a few steps out of the shadows.

During the past twenty-one months, coyotes had been a recurring presence in my life, beginning on the night before Stormy's death, when three of them had stalked me outside a rusting Quonset hut on the abandoned grounds of a commune where once had lived people who believed that extraterrestrials had created human beings and that the ETs would soon return. Just four months before I found myself on the crest of the Malo Suerte Dam, I'd been through hard and desperate times in Magic Beach,

California, during which I had been threatened by coyotes in packs.

On one such occasion, Annamaria had been with me, walking the wild rim of Hecate's Canyon in Magic Beach, when a pack approached with such an obvious intention to make dinner of us that they should have been wearing bibs. Usually coyotes fear humans and keep their distance from us. A loud noise will frighten them off, as will a tossed stone that doesn't even hit them. But the pack that came out of Hecate's Canyon had exhibited no fear whatsoever.

I'd had no gun that night, because I'd loathed guns then as I did now. And we were on a greensward where I couldn't find any of the impromptu weapons to which I often resorted: buckets, brooms, garden rakes, Granny Smith apples, cats that when thrown will reliably take out their fury not on the thrower but instead on the person at whom they're thrown. I didn't like throwing cats or animals of any kind, as far as that goes, but every once in a while, in a life-and-death situation, there was nothing to be done but grab a cat and throw it, or an angry ferret.

Anyway, as it turned out, I wasn't without a weapon, after all, because Annamaria proved to be a weapon herself. She had said that the coyotes were not only what they appeared to be, and she'd stepped toward them instead of cowering, unfazed by their threatening demeanor. She spoke to them not as if they were bloodthirsty beasts, but rather as if they were naughty children who had gone astray and needed to be put on the right path again.

Now, months later, as the lantern-eyed pack crept onto the crest of Malo Suerte Dam, daring to stalk me, I didn't want to shoot them. I didn't shout for help from Sonny and Billy, who were beyond the outlet-control building and not in my line of sight, because I didn't want the coyotes to be shot by *anyone*. I'd had enough of killing to last me a lifetime. I might have to do it again, maybe more than once, but I didn't have to do it here and now.

Ears flattened close to their skulls, teeth bared, hackles raised, tails tucked, they tentatively approached me, every muscle in their lean bodies taut. They were bony specimens, in need of a good meal; but it would be a mistake to conclude that they were weak. Were I not to use my pistol, just one coyote would be enough to finish me if it could not be frightened away.

I spoke to them as Annamaria had spoken to the toothy crew on the greensward near Hecate's Canyon. "You aren't only what you appear to be. You do not belong here."

The leader of the pack halted, and the other two drew nearer to it, closing up what had been a three-prong attack pattern. Their pointy ears were no longer back against their heads, but were instead pricked, as though they were interested in what I said.

Their mouths cracked wider, however, and they regarded me with malevolent grins.

Again echoing Annamaria's admonition to that other pack, I said, "The rest of the world is yours . . . but not this place at this moment."

Back in the day, I hadn't understood what she had meant by those words. Now I thought perhaps I did.

Far to the south, pulses of heat lightning billowed deep within the heavy clouds, again too distant for the associated thunder to reach us.

Although their backs were to the southern sky, and though the celestial flare was too faint to cast even a wan reflection upon our immediate surroundings, the three coyotes shivered, as if aware of the storm light and affected by it.

"I am not yours. You will leave now."

They didn't depart, didn't move so much as an inch, but neither did they growl.

The coyotes in Magic Beach had not at once obeyed Annamaria. They had been stubborn, or maybe whatever wished to use them had been stubborn.

And so I repeated, "You will leave now."

The predatory trio looked around as though confused, as though unsure how they had gotten where they were. Their hackles smoothed, and although they nervously licked their chops, they no longer bared their fearsome teeth. Ears pricked, regarding me not with hostility or hunger, only with curiosity, they warily backed away.

"Leave now," I repeated.

They turned and slunk off the crest of the dam, toward the darkness out of which they had appeared.

When they paused in the pale light of the narrow shadowland that separated the brightness of the dam crest from the blackest night, I watched them watching me, and I knew they were now only what they appeared to be: coyotes or prairie wolves, whichever you preferred. Briefly, some vicious twisted spirit had entered them and had overridden their fear of me. But for all its malice, it was a weak entity that obeyed a simple order to leave once its presence had been recognized and resisted.

The coyotes moved away into the blinding dark, gone as if they'd never existed. I felt again the mysterious nature of the world, its deeply layered and profound strangeness.

I wondered at my inability, until now, to understand what Annamaria had recognized in the coyotes in Magic Beach and why she had felt that she could command them to leave us alone. Considering that I saw the spirits of the lingering dead and bodachs—whatever they might be—it troubled me that I had not realized she could perhaps see other entities unknown to me, such as spirits that were not and never had been human, that sprang from origins even darker than the worst specimens of humanity.

I'd long known Annamaria possessed some power of her own, that she had well-guarded secrets. She, too, was more than she appeared to be. I had come to believe that her powers, whatever their nature, were greater than mine. But now I was chagrined to realize that I had failed to grasp how we were at least in one way alike: Some things visible to us were invisible to the vast majority of human beings, even if perhaps each of us saw *different* things from what the other perceived.

At the railing once more, I peered toward the farther reaches of Malo Suerte Lake, which were cast in such perfect blackness that I couldn't discern either those waters or anything of the shore that embraced them. When I turned my attention down to the water lapping against the dam, I couldn't see it, either, not really see it, for it was black, as well, and I could know that it slopped against the tainter gates below me only because reflections of the crest lights undulated upon its surface.

Standing there, I was overcome by the certainty that, since returning home to Pico Mundo, I had failed to see much more than just the malicious entity that had sought to use the three coyotes against me. A monstrous act of terrorism would soon be perpetrated. The truth of it, the approximate place and the general nature of the threat, had been revealed to me in a prophetic dream; or if they had not been fully revealed, they had at least been strongly suggested.

Yes, I could see what others could not, but seeing wasn't the same as understanding. I had been given perceptions that Sherlock Holmes would have envied; but I didn't have Sherlockian wit to make the most of what I saw. With fewer clues than I possessed, Holmes routinely puzzled his way to the mystery's solution, with little or no violence. In spite of my hatred of violence, I more often than not had to bludgeon and shoot my way to a resolution.

When last Pico Mundo was threatened, I had put the pieces together a few minutes too late, saving some potential victims, but not nineteen. And not *her.*

I looked at my wristwatch. Nine o'clock. Not only minutes were slipping through my fingers, but also the lives of those I might fail to save.

When I returned from the dam, Sonny Wexler said, "Anything?"

"You must've thought of a boat, sir. An electric boat?"

Billy Mundy shook his head. "It couldn't get close enough. A hundred yards out from the dam, there's a loose-woven net of steel cables shore to shore. Starts about two feet above the highwater line and goes almost all the way to the bottom."

"One-inch-diameter cable," Sonny added. "You'd need acetylene torches and a few hours to get through it—and either night or day, you'd draw a lot of attention to yourself."

"The net's to keep recreational boats and jet skis from getting too near the dam," Billy explained. "If a swimmer was in the water when tainter gates were opened, he might be pulled in and over the spillway. Or dragged under by a current and drowned."

"Can the net be raised and lowered mechanically?" I asked.

"Sure. From the outlet-control building. But no one's getting in there as long as we're guarding the place."

Sonny Wexler said, "And the chief's sending backup. Two more guys will be here soon."

I knew why Chief Porter made that decision, and I was reminded of Jim's and Bob's driver's licenses. I fished the plastic rectangles from a jacket pocket and handed them to Sonny.

"I told the chief I'd give you these. They're conspirators in all this. Very bad guys."

As he and his partner examined the licenses, Billy Mundy said, "Memorable faces. We'll know 'em if we see 'em."

"You won't be seeing them," I said. "Those are just for you to give to the chief."

Sonny frowned. "We won't be seeing them? How'd you get their licenses, anyway?"

I said only, "The chief knows all about it, sir."

Their stares were of the kind that make the most law-abiding citizens feel as if there's a crime to which they should confess.

I didn't look away from them, met the eyes of one and then the eyes of the other. They didn't look away from me, either.

Peripherally, I was aware of heat lightning to the south, as if an alien spaceship or a colossal creature of light passed through the shrouding clouds along the horizon, but the storm wasn't here, wasn't now.

At last Sonny tucked the licenses in the breast pocket of his uniform shirt. "I thought you came home just to come home, but I guess there's more to it than that."

"Well, sir, I'm sure glad to be home, it's where I belong, but there's always more to everything than there seems to be."

"That's as true as it gets," said Billy Mundy.

Sonny put one of his enormous hands on my shoulder. "You be careful out there, Odd."

"Yes, sir. I want to be."

I drove the Explorer all the way along the service road to the state highway before the connection occurred to me. It wasn't one I wanted to make, but I knew immediately that it was *right*.

For the time during which they had stalked me, the coyotes at the dam had been more than they appeared to be. Some dark spirit had taken possession of them.

Earlier in the day, shortly after dawn, when I'd encountered the coyote on the street where I'd parked the Big Dog motorcycle, it must have been more than it appeared to be, as well.

And at the safe house, when I'd come downstairs to the kitchen for dinner, Deacon Bullock had at that moment entered through the back door, carrying a shotgun. His wife, Maybelle, had said to him, *Seein' as you're alive, must've been a false alarm like you thought.*

Dang coyote, Deke had said. *Slinkin' around, maybe hopin' for one of the chickens we don't even raise, set off a motion detector.*

Indicating the sunlight at the windows, she had said, *Early for one of their kind bein' on the hunt.*

It was a bonier specimen than usual, he'd replied, *maybe too hungry to wait out the sun.*

That coyote, like the others in my day, must have been more than it appeared to be.

The four who had been the only members of the cult that shot up Green Moon Mall—Eckles, Varner, Gosset, Robertson—had been pretend satanists, men with a taste for murder, cruel sadists who dressed up their barbarism with occult nonsense that had nothing to do with real devil worship.

As I'd told Chief Porter earlier in the day, the cult that had owned the isolated estate in Nevada was serious about its satanism. It had been established in England, in 1580, and among its founding members had been clergymen and nobility. Over the generations, the cultists accumulated enormous wealth, which bought them political influence, but not only wealth. During the centuries, they also acquired genuine supernatural power, not so much that they could stop me from rescuing the kidnapped children and bringing about the destruction of that estate, but power nonetheless. I had spied upon a ceremony for which they conjured demonic entities to witness their human sacrifices. Using animals as their remote eyes and ears might be well within their abilities.

The coyote that had triggered the motion detectors outside the safe house might have been a proxy for the cultists, a proxy through which the property's perimeter alarm system could be explored and its weak points discovered.

I phoned the number that Mr. Bullock had asked me to memorize. He'd said that he would be available whenever I called, even after midnight. Following four rings, I was sent to voice mail.

Dreading that I had called too late, I left a brief message.

"This is me, this is Odd Thomas. Get out of the house. Get out *now!*"

Twenty-nine

Driving back to town, I repeatedly checked my rearview mirror. Apparently I had no tail.

I didn't drive directly to the safe house or cruise past it. I concluded that would be suicide. I wasn't ready to die, not until I had stopped—or had done my best to stop—whatever catastrophe might be planned for Pico Mundo.

I knew my hometown well, even here in its rural outskirts. In an area of horse farms and ranchettes and undeveloped land, I pulled off the two-lane blacktop and parked among a stand of cottonwoods, far enough from the road that the headlights of passing vehicles wouldn't reveal the Explorer.

After switching off the engine, I called Deke Bullock again, and as before, he didn't answer. Which most likely meant he was dead. Maybelle Bullock had probably been killed, too.

Perhaps the safe house had been discovered and invaded, its caretakers murdered, because of the astronaut who had seen something shocking in space and had been running for his life ever since, or because of some other hapless fugitive who had been given shelter there for a while. Maybe. But I was convinced that the responsibility lay with me, that unknowingly I'd led someone to it when I arrived that morning on the Big Dog bike.

Maybelle had made my favorite peach pie. She had hugged me and kissed my cheek before I'd left. She and Deacon had been so sweet together, bantering about whether they'd endured five or, instead, six bad days in twenty-eight years of marriage. My anger might serve me well in the hours ahead, but it came with a gray despair that I had to resist.

If the Bullocks were dead, there could be no good reason for me to return to the house—and no wisdom in doing so. If my only purpose was to confirm their deaths, I would most likely ensure my own.

Supposing they were not dead, however, I had an obligation to assist them. Perhaps they were under siege and needed reinforcements. Or one of them, wounded and left for dead, might still be saved.

Our world was a battleground on which good and evil clashed, and many of the combatants on the dark side were known to everyone. Terrorists, dictators, politicians who were merchants of lies and hate, crooked businessmen in league with them, power-mad bureaucrats, corrupted policemen, embezzlers, street thugs, rapists, and their ilk waged part of the war, and their actions were what made the evening news so colorful and depressing.

But those fighting in that dark army had their secret schemes, too, intentions and desires and goals that would make their public villainy seem almost innocent by comparison. They were assisted by other politicians who concealed their hatred and envy, by judges who secretly had no respect for the law, by clergymen who in private worshipped nothing but money or the tender bodies of children, by celebrities who trumpeted their concern for the com-

mon man while in their off-screen lives assiduously hobnobbing
with and advancing the interests of the elite of elites. . . .

The war *unseen* by most people was one of clandestine militias, unincorporated businesses, unchartered organizations, philosophical movements that could not survive fresh air and
sunlight, secretive coalitions of lunatics who didn't recognize
their own lunacy, nature cults and science cults and religious
cults. And, as I knew too well, there was supernatural evil partic-
ipating in this secret war against order, good, and innocence;
however, the supernatural was only one regiment of that army
and, you might be surprised to hear, numbered far fewer troops
than the flesh-and-blood human beings who fought in the countless other battalions.

Until I had met Mrs. Edie Fischer two months earlier, on the
Pacific Coast Highway, when she'd come cruising along in a humongous limousine, I hadn't realized that my side in this secret
war had its own clandestine militias and unchartered organizations determined to defeat all the aforementioned malevolent individuals and forces. I now had companions-at-arms, like Mr.
and Mrs. Bullock, with resources to match those of the enemy.

On our side of this war, one didn't leave a friend unsupported.
You never, *never* left a friend to die alone.

I walked out of the grove of cottonwoods and crossed the quiet
country lane, marveling at how ordinary the night seemed, as
every night and day seemed if you saw only the surface of things.
I climbed a split-rail fence into a pasture where, during the day,
horses grazed on sweet grass.

Remaining properly oriented in a night so deeply overcast,
with nothing to illuminate my way except the glow of downtown
Pico Mundo reflected dimly off the low clouds, I would have

stumbled or fallen, or stepped in a pile of horse product more than once, if not for my psychic magnetism. Focusing on a mental image of the Victorian house at the end of the driveway that led between colonnades of velvet ashes, I followed the fence to a corner, turned right, and followed it farther before my sixth sense told me to climb it again and to cross a graveled lane into an unfenced field.

I stayed away from stables and outbuildings, and avoided the occasional house with lighted windows. In ten minutes, I came to the ground behind the stable that had been converted into the long garage where my Big Dog Bulldog Bagger awaited deconstruction. I drew the Glock from my shoulder rig and crept along the back wall of the garage to a corner from which I could see the safe house.

Lamplight, none of it very bright, filtered by curtains and draperies, shone at some windows, and others were dark. The back door stood open, which I interpreted as meaning either that Mr. and Mrs. Bullock had fled an assault or that the assassins had done their dirty work and gone away.

I considered both those possibilities, but my usually reliable intuition wouldn't endorse either of them.

Although I stood listening for a minute or two, I heard nothing that warned me off. The night was so quiet that it almost seemed to be already submerged under fathoms of water.

I left the cover of the garage and crossed the yard. Warily I climbed four brick steps to the back porch.

When we'd sat down for dinner, the kitchen windows had been open to the late-spring light. Now they were covered by blinds.

Surprisingly, the porch floor didn't creak underfoot. Although it appeared to be painted wood, it felt as solid as concrete.

At the open door, I hesitated, but then went inside quick and low, with the Glock in a two-hand grip.

A light above the sink and another under the cooktop hood kept darkness at bay, but the kitchen was large, and shadows draped a few corners. Rounding the dinette table, I almost stepped into a pool of some liquid that was difficult to see on the dark floor. Judging by the more obvious scarlet spatters on the nearby doors of the glossy-white cabinetry, the pool must be blood.

Thirty

The pantry door stood open on darkness. I assumed that if anyone had been waiting in there, he would already have shot me.

The swinging door between the kitchen and the downstairs hallway was blocked half open by a large dead man—not Deacon Bullock—lying facedown across the threshold, dressed in black sneakers, black jeans, and a long-sleeved black T-shirt.

Ordinarily I wouldn't describe what a dead man was wearing any more than I would describe the design on a ten-dollar bill that I used to buy a burger and fries. But in this case, the hombre's outfit was important because he was clearly dressed like an assassin. And then there were the ski mask and the latex gloves.

Professional killers, sent to clean out one of their enemy's safe houses, would expect resistance. This guy wouldn't have come alone to do such dangerous work, and in fact his team probably would have numbered three or four.

Two interior doors led out of the kitchen, and the second opened into the dining room. To avoid the dead man and the soup of bodily fluids in which he sprawled, I preferred to stay out of the bright hallway. I eased open the swinging door to a dining room that was dimly revealed by the crystal chandelier hanging in the center of that space. The fixture had been adjusted to a low setting, and in the faint light, the table appeared to be intended not for serving a meal, but for conducting a séance.

Earlier, during my stay in this house, I hadn't noticed the uncanny silence with which doors moved on hinges and with which the floors received each footstep. For all the noise I made, I might as well have been a ghost.

A half-open door on the left led to the hallway. Another at the far end connected to the parlor, which I knew because Deacon Bullock had brought me this way from the kitchen when he had first taken me upstairs to see my room.

Another sizable dead man lay across the threshold between the dining room and parlor. He and the first stiff were dressed alike in every detail. He hadn't purged bowels and bladder in his death throes, as had the other guy, but he still lay in a bit of a mess. His head was turned sideways. Through one of the holes in the ski mask, a fixed eye stared into another world. Just beyond his reaching hand, on the floor of the next room, lay a pistol fitted with a sound suppressor.

I had seen so few of these people's faces that I was tempted to pull off the dead man's ski mask. I resisted the urge when I thought, irrationally, *What will you do if the face is yours?*

I didn't want to step in blood or on a corpse, but the latter was unavoidable because of the dead man's size and the limitations of my stride. The heel of my right shoe came down on the fingers of his right hand. Fortunately, the contact produced little sound— the faintest squeak of the latex glove stretching under my shoe—

and I didn't stumble, although I almost revealed my presence by saying, *Sorry, sir.*

Doorways were the worst. When you're on the hunt, you must clear them properly, low and fast, weapon in a two-hand grip, tracking the muzzle left to right or right to left, depending on the situation, seeking a target. Even fry cooks know that. The two men who had stopped bullets were dressed and armed like professionals who were trained and experienced in making such transitions, and yet they were dead in doorways.

The parlor was poorly lighted by a single lamp with a pleated blue-silk shade, and crowded with heavy Victorian furniture. A pair of chesterfields, wing-back armchairs: things to crouch behind for concealment. No one popped out of hiding to blast away at me, though the metronomic *tock-tock-tock* of the pendulum in the grandfather clock seemed to be counting off my last seconds.

As in the dining room, the draperies had been drawn shut at all the windows, perhaps to prevent anyone outside from determining the location of the residents.

A wide archway, instead of a door, connected the parlor to the foyer. I found it refreshing to see that no one lay dead on that threshold.

The foyer. Deserted. To the right, the front door was closed. To the left of the archway lay the brightly lighted hall. Opposite the dining room and parlor were three other rooms that I hadn't explored.

My sense of things was that the action had moved on from the ground floor after the first two men had been shot. I regarded the stairs, hesitating to climb them and leave unsearched rooms behind me.

Overhead, someone said, *"Ahwk,"* as though violently clearing his throat, and immediately thereafter something thudded to the floor in an upstairs room.

If, as I had every reason to expect, a third dead man had just given up his ghost, the thud wasn't as loud as it ought to have been. The floors allowed me to walk as quietly as a cat, and they soaked up most of the sound of dead men falling, which suggested that silence favored the Bullocks and that the place had been constructed as both a safe house and a trap.

Cautioning myself that a trap can sometimes spring unexpectedly and catch not the prey but instead the one who set it, I went to the stairs and climbed warily, silently. I glanced back now and then, prepared to discover that I was looking down the barrel of a gun, but I remained alone.

Thirty-one

At the top of the stairs, I looked along a hallway with large paintings on the walls between doorways, of which there were four on each side. No dead guys were tumbled across any of the thresholds.

The first door on the left stood half open, and a lamp glowed in there, but I couldn't see the entire space, just the foot of a bed and a dresser and a small armchair in a corner. I cleared the doorway and discovered the room unoccupied.

There were an attached bath and a closet, but I didn't want to investigate them. A hit team didn't enter a house to hide in closets and behind bathroom doors. An assault required speed and continuous movement—even if, as seemed to be the case here, it started to go wrong.

In the hall again, on my right, the first door stood open wide. Another bedroom. A third large man, dressed like the two downstairs, lying on his back, leaked enough to require that the carpet be replaced. The uniformity of their dress began to seem like stage clothes, costumes, as though they must be members of a weird punk band, musicians who moonlighted as killers.

I won't go on about how my heart was pounding and my mouth was dry. Been there, described that.

Because there were no shattered mirrors or bullet holes in the walls, no visible damage from any misspent rounds, it appeared that none of the assassins had gotten off a shot. But such incompetence seemed unlikely. I thought I must be missing something, the kind of missed something that would get me shot in the head.

Nevertheless, I moved silently along the hall, toward the second door on the right. A large painting of mountains towering above a lake and splashed through with spectacular light, maybe a print of something by Albert Bierstadt, abruptly disappeared soundlessly up into the wall as if on pneumatic tracks, leaving only the ornate frame. Where the painting had been was now an opening into the room toward which I had been headed. Standing there, aiming a silencer-equipped pistol at my face, Mr. Bullock managed to check himself before he blew me away. He raised his eyebrows and whispered, *"Get in here!"*

As the painting slid quietly back into place, I stepped to the door, went into another bedroom, and found that Maybelle Bullock was alive, too. She eased the door almost shut, and her husband put a finger to his lips.

I saw that a different painting, perhaps a print of another Bierstadt, hung here, directly behind the one in the hall, and it evidently retracted simultaneously with the other.

Mrs. Bullock held a device I'd never seen before, about the same width as a cell phone and twice as long. A screen occupied the top half, and two rows of buttons were positioned under it. Nothing on the screen but a field of cool blue. She swung it away from the wall that this room shared with the hallway, toward the wall between this room and the next room, as a fairy godmother might gesture with a magic wand and leave the air sparkling in its wake.

On the blue screen, a red form shaped itself out of pixels. Not anything identifiable. Just a shimmering horizontal mass on a field of blue. It twinkled, constantly adjusting around the edges. My guess: We were watching the heat signature of assassin number four as he moved cautiously through the room adjacent to this one.

As Maybelle moved her hand slowly, from right to left, keeping the red form in the center of the blue screen, tracking it, Deacon stepped to a large painting hung to the left of the bed. This one looked as if it might be a print of something by John Singer Sargent. Deacon aimed the gun at the painting, as if he were an art critic with violent tendencies. His wife pressed a button on the device she held. The artwork vanished up into the wall, leaving only the frame, in which a fourth assassin stood no more than three feet from the muzzle of Mr. Bullock's pistol. Mr. Bullock fired twice, point-blank, and the hit man dropped out of sight, as if he had stepped through a trap door.

I started to speak, but Mr. Bullock frowned and put a finger to his lips again. Then he put the same finger to his right ear and pressed on something that resembled a hearing aid. I hadn't noticed it before. A wire ran behind his ear and down his side to an object about the size of a walkie-talkie that was clipped to his belt. He listened for half a minute, pulled the microphone from his ear, and said, "House says no more damn fools inside or out."

"Who's House?" I asked, assuming it was a name.

"This here house, son."

Mrs. Bullock said, "House computer, Oddie. It's got itself eyes and ears everywhere."

"Weight sensors, heat sensors, a whole gaggle of sensors," her husband added.

"So you knew when I got here?"

"We knew," Mrs. Bullock said, "but we was too busy stayin' alive to check video and see who you was."

"Had to figure you for another of them bastards," Mr. Bullock said. "Sorry if maybe I just about killed you dead."

"That's all right, sir."

"Call me Deke, why don't you?"

"Yes, sir."

Thirty-two

While we waited for the clean-up crew, Maybelle Bullock insisted that we have coffee spiked with Bailey's. We took it in mugs, in the dining room rather than the kitchen, because the dead man lying half in the dining room hadn't soiled himself while dying, as had the dead man lying half in the kitchen. The air smelled nicer in the dining room. The Bullocks sat side by side, frequently exchanging little smiles that I presumed to be expressions of approval about how each had performed in the crisis. I sat across the table from them.

Mrs. Bullock said, "Well, Oddie, we didn't figure you'd be back till late."

"I put a few things together and realized the safe house was going to be attacked. I'm sorry I brought them down on you."

She looked surprised. "Oh, shush, wasn't nothin' you did or even you bein' here that caused this darn foolishness."

"This here kind of squabble happens once't in a while," her husband assured me.

"Squabble?"

"Tussle, scrap, whatever you feel like callin' it."

"Every now and then," said Maybelle, "their kind gets a bead on one of our safe houses, so they show up all full of mayhem."

"An operation like this here tonight," Mr. Bullock said, "takes these bastards some plannin'. For sure they been on to us some weeks now, long before you come around."

Maybelle said, "Maybe it was 'cause of the astronaut they got on the scent of this lovely place."

"Or that cute-as-a-button ballerina girl," said Mr. Bullock.

His wife grimaced and shook her head. "Oh, they wanted that dear girl so bad, a thousand of their kind would've slit their own throats if maybe it would gain 'em just a thin chance to slit hers."

"Do these squabbles always end like this?" I asked.

"Gracious, no," Maybelle said. She smiled at her husband and then looked at me again. "Was it that easy, then this war would be done before it ever did start."

"Sometimes, it's our folks end up dead as dirt." Deacon winked at his wife. "But not here and now."

"Not here and now," she said.

Mentally, I was wobbling a little from thinking about the scope of the secret conflict that all of this implied. "I didn't realize the cult was so big."

"Them cultists that want to sink their teeth in you, dear? Why, they aren't big at all. Them and others like 'em wasn't the ones would've killed our astronaut had they got their hands on him."

"Or that little ballerina," her husband said.

"Or that Army lieutenant, he won the big medal."

"Or that comedian, years ago, we had to fake his death and do him a new face."

"It's not one cult," Maybelle said, "it's a way of thinkin'.'"

Mr. Bullock agreed. "Thinkin', *What is it I want, and how can I take it from someone that has it.*"

"Thinkin', *Who is it I hate or envy most, and how can they be got rid of,*" Maybelle said.

"Thinkin', *Can't be me made a mess of my life, must be your fault, so you're gonna pay.*"

"A way of thinking," I said. "But it's a way that an awful lot of people think."

"But not anywheres near the most of 'em," Maybelle said. "Not the most, and that's one reason why doin' what we do is worth doin'.'"

"I hope you're right, ma'am."

"Call me Maybelle."

"Yes, ma'am. What happens to you now?"

"Me and Deke? We move on wherever."

"Wherever?"

"Wherever Edie Fischer thinks best. Most often some far place from where we was last."

"So the clean-up crew you mentioned deals with the dead bodies?"

"Well, it's partly what keeps 'em busy."

"What happens to this house?"

Mr. Bullock said, "Clean-up crew tears all the tricks out, puts things back like they was before us, makes it normal as normal ever can be, so it'll get sold. No safe house never can be a safe house again once't the bastards know about it."

Mrs. Bullock finished her spiked coffee and smiled. "We been here three interestin' years, made some fine memories. But it does a person good to move on from time to time, keeps you fresh."

Mr. Bullock reached into his shirt pocket. "I hate how it vibrates like a squirmin' lizard." He produced a cell phone, put it to his ear, said "yeah" three times, "dang" once, and "no" twice before he terminated the call.

His wife asked, "Clean-up?"

"Yep. Them boys got a job and a half this time around. They'll be pullin' in the driveway in about two minutes."

I said, "They got here really fast."

"This team is mostly close, a lot of the time just over in Vegas. Got themselves more cleanin' up to do there than here."

Looking at my watch, I said, "Did they teleport or something?"

"We had us three false alarms today," he said.

"One just before dinner," I remembered.

"Right after that, I called out to Vegas for clean-up, told 'em there's likely to be one mess or t'other."

"How did you know the alarms weren't false?"

"One false alarm in a day," Maybelle said, "might be nothin' but truly false. More than one, well, then you got to figure they're all as real as my own teeth."

"You've got beautiful teeth, ma'am."

"Thank you, Oddie. I always say everythin' worthwhile starts with a nice smile."

Mr. Bullock got up from his chair. "Boss lady's right behind the crew."

I rose to my feet. "You mean Mrs. Fischer?"

"About six o'clock, she come in town from the coast with them three friends of yours."

That would be Annamaria, Tim, and Blossom Rosedale, the Happy Monster.

"Edie holed up somewhere safe with 'em," Mr. Bullock said.

"We don't got to know where. Don't want to know. She's come here just herself now, with the clean-up crew, so she can chat with you, son."

The three of us stepped onto the front porch as a forty-foot box truck and a paneled van appeared out of the dark colonnades of velvet ash. Neither vehicle sported a company name. They swept past the house to park in the backyard.

A black superstretch Mercedes limousine with tinted windows followed close behind the paneled van and stopped in the driveway, near the front porch. The driver doused the headlights.

Mr. Bullock said, "Edie wants to see you in the car, son. The biggest dang snoops in the world, with all their evil electronic ears, won't never hear but even a word of what's said in that limo. Get in the front, 'cause she's drivin' herself."

Thirty-three

The night before my return to Pico Mundo. The sea. The shore. The cottage. Annamaria and the boy, Tim, asleep in their rooms. And I in mine. The bedsheets damp with sweat.

The nightmare of chaos and cacophony.

In a place without detail, where luminous smears of red and blue and gold and white and green whirled and pulsed, swooped toward me and soared as if they were shapeless birds of light. A place of harsh sound, music too shrill and tortured to be called music, voices that spoke what I knew to be English but could not understand, screams and panicked shouting. There had been faces all around me, swelling and receding and swelling again, but now there were only parts of faces, eyes looming out of the blur of light, a mouth wide and howling, a nose with cavernous nostrils, a rouged cheek, and an ear with a silver loop dangling from the lobe.

At my side, supporting me as if I were drunk, Blossom Rosedale maneuvered me through the bedlam as I clutched an urn to my chest. Chief Wyatt Porter had appeared out of the tumult, calling my name. He had pointed his pistol at me, and the muzzle had *grown until it was as large as the mouth of a cannon. He had fired the gun, and with the crack of the shot, he had disappeared into the pandemonium once more. Blossom led me onward.*

As scenes in dreams often transition one into the other without logic, I found myself lying on my back on a hard surface, holding fast to the urn, the mysterious urn that held the ashes of countless dead. All the strident noise had faded, the music without harmony and the shrill voices and the screams. The kaleidoscopic play of light in smears of brilliant color had given way to a warm golden glow and a soft surrounding grayness.

Standing around me, three lovely women with white-and-gold feathered faces regarded me with solemn brown eyes. They had noses and mouths, not beaks. Although I tried desperately to hold on to the urn, strong hands took it from me, and I lacked the strength to resist. I could see that the bird women were speaking, whether to one another or to me, but I couldn't hear what they said. Another face appeared, the beautiful fire-scarred and broken face of Miss Blossom Rosedale. Beside Blossom materialized Terri Stambaugh, the woman who owned the Pico Mundo Grille, who had given me a job when I was sixteen and helped me to master my natural talent as a hash-slinger, refining me into a griddle master.

I tried to speak to Blossom and to Terri, but I had no voice. I could neither hear nor be heard. The spirits of the lingering dead can't talk, but they can hear; therefore, my current deafness proved that I was not dead.

For a moment I closed my eyes, and when I opened them, I seemed to be alone. I tried to look around, but I couldn't lift my head. I couldn't sit up. I couldn't move as much as one finger. Panic took me. I thought that I must be paralyzed. But then An-

namaria spoke to me, and her voice at once calmed me, though I couldn't see her.

"Well, young man, you have had quite a day."

Another of those dream transitions left me sitting in a chair, across a table from Annamaria. Between us stood a wide shallow bowl containing an inch of water, and in the water rested an exquisite white flower larger than a cantaloupe, thick white petals spiraling from a loose perimeter to a tight center.

During our four months of friendship, this flower graced rooms where Annamaria lived. In the cottage by the sea, there were always bowls of these enormous blooms. She claimed that she cut them from a tree in the neighborhood. Although I went on long walks for blocks in every direction, I never saw a tree laden with such flowers.

Back in January, in the town of Magic Beach, using the flower, Annamaria had performed a magic trick of some kind for Blossom Rosedale, but I hadn't been present to see it. The Happy Monster had been amazed, astonished, exhilarated by the illusion with the flower. Annamaria promised that she would perform it for me, too, when the time was right. In her ever-mysterious way, she had never felt the right time had arrived— until now, here in a dream.

"The flower," she said, "is the amaranth."

Around my neck, upon a chain, the thimble-size bell given to me by this woman, on the occasion when she asked if I would die for her, began tinkling sweetly, although I did not move. The tiny silver clapper beat against the silver strike and silver lip, perhaps to call me to some task, perhaps to celebrate some pending triumph—perhaps to warn me of a mortal threat.

Annamaria began to pluck loose the largest of the petals, those *around the perimeter of the bloom, and drop them on the table. They were as thick as if they had been peeled from a wax flower. At first they glowed snow-white against the wood, then began to yellow, turn brown. Soon they withered even as they fluttered from her fingers. (The silver bell rang faster, louder.) Fear welled again as the petals began to discolor and shrivel before she could pluck them. The deterioration of the bloom accelerated, racing from one petal to the next, around the spiral pattern, rapidly toward the center. (Louder, the silver bell, louder, faster.) I tried to tell her to stop. She was killing not the flower, she was killing me. I could not speak. The large petals fell out of the flower of their own accord, as if they were puzzle pieces from a picture of a beaten and bruised man, quickly curling, cupping, now as crisp as the skin from a desiccated corpse.*

I thrust straight up, out of the dream, sweating and gasping, damp sheets clinging to me as if they were a shroud, as if I had sat up not in bed, but from a granite slab in a morgue, where an autopsy was about to be performed on me.

At the end of the silver chain around my neck, the tiny bell rang three times. Each time it sounded less insistent than in the nightmare. Then it fell silent.

I had awakened late. Annamaria and young Tim had finished their breakfast. They were off somewhere together.

After a shower, I packed what little I needed in my toiletries case and in a soft-sided overnight bag. I loaded them in the Big Dog motorcycle's saddlebags.

Annamaria and Tim returned on foot at 1:30, having eaten a light lunch at a restaurant in town. The boy had not been much like a boy, emotionally and intellectually, when we rescued him *from horrific circumstances in that Montecito estate. He had been old beyond his years. But day by day, he seemed to forget what he had endured. Soon he became an ordinary, energetic boy of nine. This change had been wrought by Annamaria, but she had declined to explain how she could have done what an entire corps of psychiatrists and a pharmacy of the latest antidepressants would surely have failed to achieve.*

Now Tim wanted to change into swim trunks and search the shore for seashells, go wading, swim a little. Annamaria preferred to keep him in sight when he was on the beach. She said she'd been pregnant a long time and would be pregnant longer still, but she declined to say if this child she carried was her first. As she was eighteen, it most likely would be her first. Yet, as she had shown with Tim, she had about her the wisdom and the manner of someone well experienced in mothering.

As the boy entertained himself along the breaking surf, plucking up half-buried shells to add to his collection, we stood seaward of the picket fence that separated yard grass from sand.

Between the clear sky and the blue rolling sea, brown pelicans glided northward in formation.

She said, "So, odd one, you had a dream, and the bell rang you to action last night."

"How could you know?"

"The way things are known," she said with an enigmatic smile. "A dream but not just a dream."

"Not just a dream," I agreed. "Chief Porter was in it, so I must have been in Pico Mundo. But I don't know exactly where."

"You've known since Nevada, the cult will strike in Pico Mundo."

"You were in the dream," I said. "Will you be there for real?"

"I phoned Edie Fischer this morning. Tim and I will go out there with her. I wouldn't miss it, young man."

"What is it you wouldn't miss?"

"Whatever is to be."

"There you go again."

"Where do I go?"

"In clouds of mystery. By the way, you frightened me in the dream."

She put a hand on my shoulder. "I will endeavor not to frighten you for real."

I watched Tim dancing jubilantly in the foaming surf. "Should I be afraid?"

"Not of anything in Pico Mundo," she said.

"Of what comes after Pico Mundo?"

"Don't lay out an entire itinerary, Oddie. Take one destination at a time."

Thirty-four

When I got into the front passenger seat of the limousine and closed the door behind me, Mrs. Fischer grabbed one of my hands in both of hers, pulled me toward her, and kissed me on the cheek.

"Child," she said, "even the sweetest baby in a cradle isn't more kissable than you."

She was a pixie, an inch short of five feet, perched on a pillow to see over the steering wheel. At eighty-six, she had more energy and considerably more gumption than the average thirty-something corporate hotshot.

"I've missed you, Mrs. Fischer."

"And I've missed you, too, my dear chauffeur."

As I've detailed in the next-to-last volume of these memoirs, I had been employed as her chauffeur for an event-packed day or so, during which she had done most of the driving.

"But of course," she continued in her lilting voice and cheery manner, "I've been busy helping our little network of like souls to neuter as many rotten scum as we have time to confront. I'm sorry to say, there are so many rotten scum in these perilous times that some days I fear we're falling behind. But then . . ." She looked toward the front porch, where the clean-up crew had joined Mr. and Mrs. Bullock and were following them into the house. "But then sometimes the rotten scum come to us, which saves us the trouble of finding them." She looked at me again and frowned. "What is it, dear? You don't appear to be having as much fun as you should be having after all your success in Nevada."

"A lot of people died there, ma'am."

"Yes, many of those kidnappers and would-be child-killers died, but the children all lived, thanks to you. Don't mourn the death of monsters, dear. Celebrate the saving of the innocents."

"You're right. I know you're right. I guess what disturbs me isn't so much killing the killers. It's the *necessity* of killing them, that they push us to that."

"We're not engaged in police work, child. This is war. A secret war at our level of the action, but a war nonetheless. There are fewer shades of gray in a war than in police work."

She had one of those faces—fine-boned and symmetrical—that not only weathered the years well but also pushed the GRAND-MOTHER LOVE button deep in your psyche, so that you took seriously whatever she said and felt it to be wise. Her soft skin hadn't wrinkled randomly, hadn't puckered her face in unflattering ways; every line seemed to have been designed to maintain a gentle and genteel countenance and to have been executed by a seamstress to royalty.

"Ma'am, as totally impressive as your network was when we worked together back in March, I'm only now beginning to realize its true scope. You and Heathcliff must have built quite a fortune."

Heathcliff, her husband, apparently had been many things, including a magician. No. What she had told me, exactly, was that he could "appear to be a magician," that he could appear to be anything he wished, and convincingly.

"Oh, dear, don't give me too much credit. Heathcliff already had a Scrooge McDuck fortune when he met me and saved me from a life as a mediocre actress. Over the years, my little ideas added only a couple of hundred million to the pot. Anyway, I'm not the only one who funds the resistance. Now tell me, what should we be afraid might happen to your darling little Pico Mundo?"

She had left the engine running, so that we could have air-conditioning in the warm desert night. Although the instrument panel in the dashboard had been dialed up to its brightest level, the limo was softly illuminated. I felt cocooned and, as I always did in her company, quite safe in a dangerous world.

I told her about the dream of the flood, about Malo Suerte Dam and the stolen thousand kilos of C-4. "But you see, ma'am, I never know about my dreams. Sometimes they're literal, other times only symbolic. If I have to live with this gift, I don't understand why things can't always be clearer to me."

Patting my cheek affectionately, she said, "Because, dear boy, then you would be just another silly superhero who's never really at risk."

"I could live with that."

"But you might then grow too certain of yourself, cocksure and arrogant. Even you. And then you might become one of the very people that my network of friends must thwart. Isn't that a lovely word—*thwart*?"

"*Thwart*? I've never thought about it, ma'am."

"Well, do think about it, dear. Please do. It's a lovely word. *Thwart*. To obstruct is as noble an act as to facilitate, if what you are obstructing is the facilitation of evil. Anyway, to maintain the right perspective, sweetie, we always should be at risk of failure, the possibility of making wrong choices."

"Free will, you mean."

Pinching my cheek this time, Mrs. Fischer said, "Now, there's the lovely fry cook who could save this town. You're very nearly fully smooth and blue."

"Fully smooth and blue. I still don't know what that means, ma'am."

"Oh, don't puzzle yourself. You'll know what it means when you know. Meanwhile, there isn't going to be a test about it."

She was dressed in a pink pantsuit with a frilly white blouse. On the lapel of her jacket glimmered the exclamation point crafted of gold, diamonds, and rubies.

"I don't know what that means, either. A version of it turns up on the phone you sent me."

"It's a kind of logo," Mrs. Fischer said. "It's like that Pepsi circle with the red-white-and-blue waves in it. Or the smiling cow on a can of Lucerne whipped cream."

"Cows and cream. Okay, *that* I understand."

"Of course you do. A smiling cow makes everyone feel good. A smiling cow is a delightful thing, and whipped cream is delightful."

"But the exclamation point . . ."

"Well, it's also a promise."

"A promise of what?"

"And a statement of conviction. It's many things, dear, just as anything you can point at in this world is many things."

I pointed at *her.*

She pointed at *me.*

I couldn't help but laugh. "I wish Stormy could have known you, ma'am. She'd think you were a hoot."

"She was a lovely girl. She still used the name Bronwen then, hadn't quite started calling herself Stormy. We got along famously."

Mrs. Fischer could draw upon a greater variety of smiles than anyone I'd ever known, perhaps because the life that she'd lived had given her so many different kinds and degrees of happiness. The smile with which she favored me now was one I'd seen several times before: what I might call the Smile of Pleasurable Expectation, with her head cocked to one side and her blue eyes bright with curiosity regarding my response to her revelation, also with an impish pleasure in having astonished me.

"You knew Stormy? How did you? When did you?"

Mrs. Fischer took one of my hands in both of hers again and pressed it firmly. "After she was adopted by that dreadful couple, after that horrible thing happened, our little organization got her out of the situation."

Stormy was seven years old when her parents died in a plane crash, seven and a half when she was adopted by a wealthy, childless couple in Beverly Hills. During the second week in her magnificent new home, her adoptive father came into her room after midnight, exposed himself to her, and touched her in ways no grown man should ever touch a child.

She had still been intensely grieving for her lost parents. Humiliated, ashamed, frightened, alone, confused, she endured the man's depraved behavior for three months before desperately seeking help.

"But," I said, "she reported it to a social worker who was making a house call for the adoption agency."

"Yes, dear. She did."

"So she was taken out of that place. And then . . . then she lived in Saint Bart's Orphanage till she graduated high school."

"Yes, but she wasn't removed for a week. Your lovely girl never realized that the first social worker wasn't the one who helped her. In fact, never would have helped her."

Having to discuss this, having to consider again what Stormy had told me about the abuse she suffered, I found that the memory came braided with heartache.

Mrs. Fischer said, "The couple who adopted Stormy—"

"She called them Mr. and Mrs. Hellborn. Not their real names, obviously."

"But apt," Mrs. Fischer said. "Mr. and Mrs. Hellborn weren't just corrupt. They were also corrupting of so many people who came into contact with them. And the first social worker was corruptible. Another caseworker in the same child-welfare agency heard a few things and became suspicious. She was one of us."

By the gentle tenor of her voice, by the compassion in her eyes, by the hands with which she held my hand, she made it clear that what she had to tell me might leave me shaken, but that she would be my anchor through it all.

"The Hellborns thought of themselves as citizens of the world. Which in their case meant they felt above the laws of any one city or state, or country. They had lived in several exotic places where life is accorded less value than it is here. Tragic places where children of the slums are vulnerable, often regarded as a commodity. The crooked authorities let the Hellborns pursue their desires unobstructed. But they had a reputation among locals."

Stormy and I had never made love. She wanted to know beyond any doubt that I loved her for herself, not merely for the physical pleasure that she could give me. Considering what happened to her, considering that she had triumphed over what would have destroyed many others, considering that she became such a self-sufficient joyful person, I would have been a world-class jerk if I pressured her. Stormy wanted to wait for marriage; I wanted whatever Stormy wanted.

Mrs. Fischer said, "The Hellborns were making plans to take little Bronwen out of the country aboard their hundred-sixty-foot yacht. The Beverly Hills estate was owned by their corporation in the Cayman Islands. The corporation quietly listed it for sale. Those people would never have brought your girl back. Never. And God knows what might have happened to her."

At first it seemed to me that there was no good reason for Mrs. Fischer to tell me all of this. Stormy was gone. What might have happened to her didn't matter. What mattered was only what *did* happen to her both at the hands of the Hellborns and years later on a day of evil at the Green Moon Mall. Why dwell on horrors that *might* have occurred?

"She was," said Mrs. Fischer, "the sweetest child, orphaned and abused and traumatized, but already determined not to be a victim. Not ever again. I spent only two days with her, but they were days I will never forget, Oddie. There she was, this precious little person, forty-some pounds, hardly taller than a lawn gnome, but determined to take on the world and win."

I said, "Nothing scared her, not really. She was afraid for me sometimes but never for herself."

Mrs. Fischer squeezed my hand. "The dear girl said her name, Bronwen, sounded like an elf or a fairy, and she wasn't either one.

She decided to find a strong name for herself. The second day we were together, there was a terrible storm. Such bright bolts of lightning. Wind and thunder that shook the building. She stood at the window, watching it all, fazed by none of it, and that's where she found her new name."

I realized that I was squeezing one of Mrs. Fischer's hands so tightly that I must have been hurting her, though she didn't so much as wince, let alone try to pull away. I relaxed my grip.

"I never . . . never knew why she chose Stormy. It fit her so well, you know, 'cause she had such power, such a strong presence. But there was no destruction in her, like there can be in a storm, none at all."

Cocooned in the limo, with the purr of the engine and the soft light and the coolness issuing from the dashboard vents, I almost felt that we weren't in a mere car. We might instead have been aboard a more significant conveyance, perhaps outbound in space or traveling in time, seeking a world more peaceful than this one or a future when, by some great grace, humanity had recovered its innocence and its birthright.

The exclamation-point brooch on Mrs. Fischer's lapel sparkled in the dashboard light when I looked at her again. I said, "At first I couldn't understand why you told me all this. But now I get it."

"I knew you would, child."

"Sometimes, when I'm feeling sorry for myself, it seems that I'm made to carry this impossibly heavy weight, the crushing weight of losing her. I have moments of bitterness and doubt. You know? But the weight is a blessing, really, and I shouldn't be bitter about it. The weight is on my heart because I knew her and loved her. The weight is the accumulation of all we had together, all the hopes and worries, all the laughs, the picnics in Saint Bart's bell tower, the adventures we shared because of my gift. . . . If they had taken her away on their yacht, if I had never met her, there would be no weight to carry—and no memories to sustain me."

Mrs. Fischer smiled at me and nodded. "Fully blue and so very, very near to being fully smooth."

Thirty-five

Minutes before the cultists found me, Mrs. Fischer drove off the two-lane blacktop and parked on the shoulder of the road, near the grove of cottonwoods in which I had left the Ford Explorer. She shut off the engine, switched off the lights, got out of the limo, and came around to my side, so that we could have a proper hug.

She was birdlike, tiny. And yet I suspected that anyone who tried to mug her or hijack her would discover that being petite and eighty-six did not guarantee that she would be an easy target.

Walking with me through the dark, toward the trees, she said, "I want you to know that Tim will be fine. Set your mind at rest about him. Some of our people are taking him into their family. They'll take the dog, too, Raphael. They have a golden retriever of their own and a twelve-year-old boy, so Tim will have two dogs and an older brother."

"What if his past starts coming back to him, who he was and all he went through?"

"It won't come back to him, dear. Annamaria tells me that she has spared him those memories. And he has new memories that give him a good foundation for a happy future."

"I know he remembers a different past from what he actually lived. I just don't understand how it could be done. Not hypnosis. Not drugs."

"No, no, no. Good gracious, nothing as crude as that."

"Then what?"

"Well, it's all a little mystical, isn't it? Don't worry your lovely head about it."

"Back in March," I reminded her, "you told me I would eventually understand the true and hidden nature of the world. It's still hidden to me, ma'am."

"That doesn't mean it's any less true, sweetie."

I had come to love Mrs. Fischer, to trust her entirely. But at times, our conversations seemed to have come straight from the Mad Hatter's tea party.

I said, "Am I right to think you've known Annamaria a long time? Much longer than I've known her?"

"Oh, yes, I've known her for ages."

"She's only eighteen."

"Yes, dear, she's been eighteen for ages."

"How does that work?"

"It works splendidly for her."

I was silent for a moment. Then I said, "I could be inscrutable, too, you know."

"Actually, you couldn't be, dear."

"Who is she?"

"It's not for me to tell you, Oddie."

"So who *will* tell me?"

"She will, when the time has come for you to know."

"When will the time come?"

"You'll know the time has come when it comes, of course. You're so full of questions, you should be the host of a game show."

I sighed and stopped at the trees.

We had neither moon nor stars. Her face was ghostly in the gloom. Her white hair veiled her head, all but her face, as if she were of some holy order. I didn't resort to my flashlight, because under her talk of game-show hosts, I heard a repressed sadness and sensed that she might be struggling to hold back tears. If this might be my last encounter with, my last memory of, Mrs. Edie Fischer, I didn't want it to be one in which she wept.

"Will I see you again?" I asked.

"Of course you will, dear. You'll see everyone again. Let me have a question now. What is your next move?"

"You'll know my next move when it's time for you to know it."

"You simply are not charming when you try inscrutability, dear. It's most unbecoming on you."

"I'm sorry."

"Is your little rebellion over now?"

"Yes, ma'am. My next move is . . . I've got to talk with Chief Porter and find out if he's gotten any new info on this Wolfgang Schmidt, one of the cultists."

"Yes, one of the three that were shot in the back of the head by others of their ilk."

"How do you know that?"

She pinched my cheek. "How could I *not* know, dear?"

"If you don't mind my asking, ma'am—and I'm sure you do— what's *your* next move?"

"As always, I'm an open book. I intend to pick up Annamaria and Blossom Rosedale where we're staying together, and go over to the fairgrounds for a couple of hours."

"Hey, whoa. That's a bad idea, ma'am. I'm heading back there myself, 'cause I think that's where something pretty serious might happen. Not necessarily the big thing. Not the whole town drowned. But something not good."

She clapped her hands together with girlish enthusiasm. "Well, isn't that where it's always the most fun to be—where things are happening?"

I hugged her again. "Heathcliff must have been some guy, ma'am." I let her go. "Tell me straight now. Do you know what's going to happen tonight?"

"No, Oddie. For all you may think differently, I'm only human. Annamaria's human, too, though she's more than that, as you no doubt suspect. But human nonetheless. We don't know. Whatever happens will happen because you—and others—make it happen."

"Free will," I said.

"Free will," she agreed, "our greatest gift, the thing that makes life worth living, in spite of all the anguish it brings."

"Got to be going. I'm running out of time. I think we all are."

I could see her nod only because her cap of white hair moved up and down.

"Good-bye, Mrs. Fischer."

"Until we meet again, dear."

She made her way back to the limousine as if guided by some lamp that I could not see.

I watched her get in the enormous car and drive away. She

drove well. Back in March, her best friend and chauffeur of twenty-two years, Oscar Dunningham, had died of a massive heart attack at the age of ninety-two. They had been at dinner in a superb restaurant in Moonlight Bay. As Oscar finished his last spoon of an excellent crème brûlée, his eyes widened, and he said, "Oh, I think the time has come to say good-bye," and he slumped dead in his chair. According to Mrs. Fischer, although she usually tipped twenty-five percent, she tipped seventy-five because the waiter was kind enough to wipe a dribble of crème brûlée off dead Oscar's chin. She was also pleased that the busboy, the waiter, and the maître d' all continued to refer to the deceased as "the guest" even as they assisted in his quiet removal from the dining room, leaving most of the other customers unaware that a death had occurred, and presenting Mrs. Fischer with a small box of chocolate mints accompanied by a sympathy card.

I would have liked to be her chauffeur. I'm sure the pay was good. And the benefits would have been unique.

I switched on my flashlight. Walked among the cottonwoods to the Explorer. Behind the wheel, I inserted the key in the ignition. As the engine turned over, I looked up, through the dusty windshield and between the trunks of the trees, toward the two-lane backroad. Distant headlights flared.

I would have driven from the cover of the trees if the vehicle hadn't been approaching so fast. On that narrow, curved, and potholed blacktop, such high speed was reckless, almost suicidal. The driver evidently needed to get someplace yesterday. Or maybe he needed to get to *someone*.

Sometimes intuition tickled like a spider crawling along the back of my neck. At other times, it was a cold robot hand that clamped around my throat for a moment and wouldn't allow me to breathe. This time: robot hand.

The oncoming vehicle closed on me so fast that I had no hope of getting to the road and away before it blocked access. I could tell now that the headlights were high off the pavement, as if it must be either a jacked-up SUV on big tires or a truck. Probably a truck.

I switched off the engine. Got out of the Explorer. Hurried around to the passenger side, to put the Ford between me and the road. Drew the Glock from my shoulder rig.

I was not—and never had been—a man of action. I only pretended to be one. I remained always aware that I was pretending, desperately trying to be Mr. Daniel Craig or Mr. Vin Diesel in one of their more assured performances. Consequently, I frequently felt foolish while doing all the jumping and running and brandishing guns that a man of action is called upon to do.

Now I felt like a self-delusional fry cook as I crouched beside the Explorer, Glock in hand, when it should have been a spatula, watching the truck rocket along the roadway. I told myself, *Don't be paranoid. It's just someone in a hurry. His wife's in labor or his little boy swallowed an entire package of laxatives and he doesn't want to wait for an ambulance. They're not looking for me. They're not worried I'll upend their plans. They have no way of locating me.*

The truck shifted gears. Brakes shrieked. The vehicle departed the pavement, angled toward the grove of cottonwoods, and jolted to a halt in a cloud of dust, the headlights slashing through the trees, cutting away some of the shadows, possibly revealing the Explorer. I heard what might have been a segmented steel door rolling up on the back of the truck, and, peering through the many trees, I glimpsed men spilling out of the cargo box.

Not being bulletproof, as is the average man of action in the movies, I holstered the Glock, turned from the Explorer, and ran deeper into the cottonwood grove, trying not to think about trees, lest my psychic magnetism lead me face-first into one.

Thirty-six

Never before had I relied on my gift to guide me through a dark woods by concentrating on the idea of open land. Not until that very morning, of course, had I used it to find my way through a pitch-black shopping mall, and that had worked out all right. Perhaps this was a day of firsts. The day one dies, of course, is a first in any life.

I held my right arm in front of my face, hoping to avoid having an eye poked out by a branch. With my left hand, I felt from tree to tree, hurrying because enough thin blades of light from the truck's headlamps sliced through the grove to suggest where the cottonwoods relented a little. No undergrowth inhibited progress, but a thick carpet of dry leaves crunched noisily underfoot, so that if my pursuers stopped now and then to listen, they would have a pretty good idea of where I was headed.

Instead of pausing to listen, however, they opened fire. For an instant, I thought they must see me. Within a few steps I would be riddled. But then the Explorer's windows shattered, sheet metal cried out *pock* and *pong* as bullets tore into it, a couple of tires popped, and there could be no doubt that they were trashing the

SUV with the expectation that I might be inside. The barrage was so ferocious that I couldn't tell if they were using fully automatic weapons or if there were so many gunmen firing with such enthusiasm that it only sounded as though they were spraying the Ford with a couple of Uzis.

Inevitably there were ricochets and wild shots, and I heard a round *thwack* into a tree. If I could discern that particular sound separate from the crackle and roar of gunfire, the hit had to be nearby, mere inches away. Another bullet tunneled through sprays of leaves, spitting bits of bark and vegetation onto my head, into my face, and a third round impacted with a sound like an axe blade biting wood, which probably meant it was a high-velocity round and perhaps a hollow-point.

The land sloped slightly, and if I remembered the neighborhood, there was an aquifer not too deep underground, so that the soil grew damp again each night, no matter what heat the Mojave sun blistered down on the land during the day. The aquifer slaked the thirst of the cottonwoods and made it possible for farms in this area to draw enough water from wells to grow crops. The assault on the Explorer ended, and although my ears were ringing, I could hear that the dead leaves underfoot had lost most of their crunch. Surface roots became more prominent, and the air grew moist and thickened with the smell of moldering forest mast. I rushed off the slope into a wide swale, where the trees opened a little and where the detritus underfoot squished.

Voices echoed through the woods. Although I couldn't make out their words over my own hard breathing, I imagined that the cultists—for who else could they be?—were calling to one another, probably one of them giving directions to subordinates, each of those then answering, everyone getting on the same page.

They would come through the woods in a search line, maybe ten feet between them, depending on how many there were.

After weaving through twenty or thirty yards of trees, through the swale, to where the land began to rise, I stopped and looked back and saw that they had switched off the truck's headlights. I waited to see flashlight beams, hoping to estimate their numbers, but the woods remained dark. They no longer called to one another. The entire crew couldn't have gotten back into the truck and driven away, not that quickly. Besides, I would have heard the engine starting. And they hadn't come after me so aggressively only to retreat when they didn't nail me in the Explorer.

They were still out there among the cottonwoods. In the dark. Being quiet.

What were they doing?

Listening? Reloading after their exuberant reenactment of the D-Day landing? Taking a collective leak?

The loud attack on the Explorer seemed crazy to me, even if they thought that I was inside that vehicle. We were in a rural area, but it wasn't on the dark side of the moon. There were woodlets and large fields, some weedy and some cultivated, but there were also a few ranchettes where horses were bred and raised, not Thoroughbreds but quarter horses and various special breeds for sale to enthusiasts, which meant people were living in these parts. People who didn't usually hear barrages of gunfire in the night. If even one of them called the police, the Odd Thomas hunt would be interrupted by the authorities before I could be properly shot in the head and ritually dismembered.

I knew it was dangerous to stand there listening, that I was wasting time, but I stood there listening, anyway, because I didn't understand what they were doing, what was happening. In a life-

or-death struggle with a formidable enemy, you had to make de-
cisions based on accurate information. You couldn't always rely
on intuition even if your intuition, like mine, would probably
make you a fortune at a roulette wheel or a blackjack table.

Half a minute passed before one of the hunters put a foot
wrong, thrashed through foliage, and cursed. Another voice ordered, *"Quiet!"* Somehow they were coming without lights to
guide them.

There was no accurate information to be gotten, no explanation for their stealth that wouldn't have to be puzzled out, and the
only kind of analysis I had time for was the simple kind that could
be done on the fly. Striving to focus my attention on the concept
of open land—*open land*—I wove among the cottonwoods, as-
cending the slope that rose out of the moist swale. Moving quickly.
As fast as I dared. Not as blind as I was in the mall that morning,
but definitely hampered by the gloom.

Immediately above me, maybe a double score of birds exploded
from their night roost, racketing through the trees and skyward.
If my pursuers were experienced trackers who could get a direc-
tional bead on a sound in this environment, the flock erupting
into flight would confirm for them my approximate position in
the woods. At once I turned sharply to the left, which I thought
must be east, angling up the easy incline, hoping that their search
line would re-form to center on the place where the birds had
spooked away from me. If I could get past the last man at the east
end of their formation, while they were adjusting their hunt toward the southwest, I might be able to put some ground between
me and them, maybe escape them entirely, but at least gain time
to think.

Open land, open land, open land. I wanted out of the trees as badly as any swimmer might want to get out of the water when spying the fins of a dozen schooling sharks. Even with psychic magnetism, however, even though I was not entirely blind in the night woods, I couldn't proceed as quickly as I had at moments in the pitch-black mall. Tree trunks complicated this darkness. Low-hanging branches. Exposed roots. I kept moving, aware of crisp dead leaves crunching underfoot again, hoping that the men behind me were making their own noises that masked mine.

Maybe it would prove to be paranoia, maybe it would prove to be true, but I sensed that my pursuers weren't nearly as hampered by the cottonwoods as I was. Maybe they had military night-vision gear. One explanation. Logical. The cult's resources, a treasury built up over four and a quarter centuries, since their early days in Oxford, would enable them to acquire pretty much anything they wanted. Or they could steal it, as they had stolen the C-4. I didn't know much about night-vision goggles. In fact, nothing. I *thought* such devices needed at least starshine, a minimum of ambient light to magnify into an enhanced field of vision, but I could be wrong.

More worrisome was the possibility that they could track me with the assistance of a supernatural power beyond my comprehension. No other quarry in my circumstances would have leapt to that suspicion. But because of my experiences, I had an open mind. Some might say that it was as open—and empty—as a wind tunnel. Nevertheless, in Nevada, the past March, I'd seen that the cultists could conjure entities not born of this world. In the court of Odd, even the most preposterous suspicion was admissible.

Concentrating on open land while trying to evade the searchers probably established a conflict of needs. The emotional need for more light—more hope—versus the base animal need for cover, camouflage, a bolt-hole. In the open, I might be more easily spotted, therefore less safe than if I remained in the woods. Such a conflict could explain why I stumbled, clipped one tree trunk with my left shoulder, another with my right, slipped and fell to one knee, thrust up and took only a dozen steps before foundering against a projection of rock, over which I clambered as gracefully as if I had been wearing clown shoes.

In spite of this increasingly slapstick performance, I angled eastward until I staggered out of the cottonwoods, near the crest of the slope. Breathing too noisily. I strove to quiet myself. More but shallower inhalations. Draw air and exhale through the mouth only. Heart hammering, but they couldn't hear that. I ascended the last of the rise to a flat width of dirt and wild grass, beyond which a white-plank-and-chicken-wire fence ran east-west, barring my way.

Under the unrelenting low cloud cover, the rural landscape offered better visibility than the woods, although it, too, was dim. And more than dim. I felt as if the night and the place held within them some recondite meaning that my eyes could not quite resolve out of the gloom, that my mind could not interpret.

I peered west along the fence, toward where the posse might emerge from the trees if I had indeed angled past the outermost man on the search line. No one. In case they had not re-formed their line toward the eruption of birds that I had caused, if they were instead close behind me, I needed to get off this open strip of land, where I would be an easy target. I scaled the five-foot-high board fence, snagged Mr. Bullock's sport coat on a twist of wire, tore the fabric getting free, and dropped into whatever might wait on the other side.

Thirty-seven

Although I hadn't remembered what I would find when I put the cottonwoods behind me, I knew at once where I was: Maravilla Valley Orchards. Row after long row of almond trees running north-south, precisely spaced to accommodate the harvesting equipment that would shake the ripe nuts from the branches. The alleys between the rows were likewise calculated, not merely to allow tractor-drawn harvest bins to pass but to ensure that one rank of trees did not shadow the next for too much of the day, so that every side of every tree received a wealth of light as the sun traveled from dawn to dusk. Like dutiful sentinels standing watch, the trees dwindled into the dark, across a couple of hundred acres.

Eager to put more distance between myself and the searchers before they might climb into the orchard to scope it out, I ran east along the barrier of boards and chicken wire. I had gone only thirty or forty feet when I saw black-clad figures scaling the fence perhaps sixty feet ahead of me, far from where I'd thought they would be. In the woods, the posse had not re-formed in the direction of the flock of birds that scattered skyward. Instead, as though anticipating my actions, they had angled east.

No one called out. I hadn't been seen.

In a crouch, I scurried six feet to the south, to the first tree in the nearest row, and took cover there, frantically trying to think what to do next, which way to go, according to what strategy.

Peering east, around the tree, I attempted to count them as they gathered by the fence. All in black, they were darker than the night, contrasted with it, but they milled around, making it difficult for me to tally them. There were at least six. Maybe eight. Either number was too many, bad odds for me.

We were in a kind of forest again, but one that was regimented, geometric, offering less cover than the wildwood. They could spread out more here, maintaining a longer search line, yet each man would still be within sight of those to either side of him. Not yet one flashlight. With night-vision gear, they wouldn't be foiled by the density of the trees, as they had been among the cotton-woods. They would have clean lines of sight. If I raced along one of the open alleys, I would be quickly spotted. Even crossing an alley from one rank of trees to another, I would draw attention to myself, because from their perspective, I would be the only mov-ing thing in the warm stillness of the almond grove.

I had to stay to a single row of trees, close to the trunks, head down to avoid taking a low branch in the face or across my throat. *And I had to get moving.* They were already forming a line, get-ting ready to come into the grove on a north-south hunt. I set out to the south, keeping to my single-row tactic. I moved fast but not nearly at a sprint, not at first. This close to them, my pounding footfalls would locate me in seconds. I needed to put some dis-tance between us before I could run flat-out. Taking short quick

strides, almost gliding across the ground, I tried to recall how far
it was to the southern end of the orchard. The grove was much
longer from north to south than from east to west. Hundreds of
acres. A mortal distance under the circumstances.

Birds worried me, the possibility of another mass exodus from
branches overhead, a flare of sound that would declare, *Here he
is!* After I had gone thirty yards or so, an owl loudly questioned
the night. From elsewhere in the grove, another owl replied, and
almost at once yet another. Every orchard attracted field mice
and sometimes rats, depending on the crop, and owls considered
rodents of any size to be delectable. Wherever owls stood night
watch, other birds tended not to roost, because owls also had an
appetite for their smaller feathered brethren.

Moving quickly, light-footed, moving, moving, anticipating
shouts and gunfire, I tried to remember what I'd find at the end
of the orchard. I couldn't recall a farmhouse or trailer, not any
kind of living quarters. The operation was owned by a large corporation, not a family, and as far as I knew, no one lived on the
property at night. There was an immense processing building in
which the green fruit of the trees would be stripped away from
the pits, and the smooth almond seeds from their hard, fibrous
jackets. Maybe three or four additional structures. Garages for
the harvesting equipment and other machinery. Product storage.
Offices. If I could survive the orchard and get a few buildings
between me and the posse, night-vision goggles wouldn't be of as
much use to them. When the search involved land around buildings, they couldn't hold to a rigid line. They would have to split
up to some extent, and my options would multiply.

There might be a security guard or two at night, not to patrol
the orchard, but to prevent thieves from stealing valuable ma-

chinery and vehicles. Problematic. Not that a security guard
might be rash enough to shoot me first and ask questions in the
afterlife. But if the cultists on my trail would be so bold as to chop
the Explorer to pieces with automatic-weapons fire in an area
where the noise could trigger calls to 911, they might answer a
guard's challenge with bullets. I didn't want to be responsible for
leading them to a victim. I hoped the orchard buildings were pro-
tected only by good steel doors and state-of-the-art alarm systems.

The owls, perhaps as many as half a dozen roosting across the
length of the orchard, were hooting regularly to one another, their
voices echoing eerily among the trees, as if they were urging me
on—or cheering those who pursued me. The time had come to
run full tilt, without regard to the noise I would make. Remaining
close to the same row of trees, I bolted, taking longer strides, feet
slamming against the ground, gasping for breath, making enough
noises that I could now hear only the closest owl.

I thought they couldn't run and fire their weapons at the same
time. Not effectively. Not even if they caught sight of me. Afraid
of losing me unless they matched my pace, they would have to
forgo shooting in order to stay close on my trail. Wrong. If they
had Uzis or other fully automatic carbines, they could flick a
switch from single-fire to burst-fire, which at least one of them
did. The hard stutter of a machine gun rattled through the almond grove, no doubt chasing even the fearless owls from their
perches. Full-metal-jacket rounds snapped into the trunks with
terrible power, louder than a nail gun driving steel spikes into a
four-by-six, loud enough for me to hear those impacts separate
from the gunfire.

Dirt and pebbles sprayed across my shoulders and the back of
my head, as a low round must have kicked the ground behind me.

I dodged from one side of the row to the other, better using the trees for cover, slaloming among them, which increased the chances of being taken down by a branch harder than my head.

A scream. Loud, shrill, prolonged. As the gunfire abruptly ceased, I thought that maybe one of the searchers, hurrying forward too eagerly, had gotten ahead of the gunner and had taken a round or two.

As the hideous screams seemed to slither through the grove with corporal substance, I stopped dodging around the trees and ran only along the west side of the row. My legs on fire. Chest aching. Each exhalation hot as furnace air. I couldn't keep up that pace much longer. I was no more a marathon runner than I was a man of action.

I thought the need to tend to one of their own injured would bring a couple of them to a halt, improving my odds of survival. I saw a pale geometry in the darkness ahead, the white boards of the southern fence. If they were delaying ten seconds, twenty, I could be up the fence and over, at least temporarily out of sight. A shot rang out, and the screaming stopped. Another single shot perhaps made certain that the screamer had been permanently silenced. They weren't the type to leave a wounded comrade behind. They were the type who would finish him off and be done with the distraction. I shouldn't have expected anything else, considering that Jim and Bob executed Wolfgang, Jonathan, and Selene merely because I might have seen their faces. True believers. Fanatics. They didn't fear death. In their view, death came with a reward. They probably thought they would be royalty in Hell. The execution of their own had set them back no more than five seconds, if at all, but the fence loomed immediately in front of me.

Thirty-eight

I slammed into the fence, grappled for handholds, toed up from the base rail, went monkey-fast over the top, and fell to the ground on the farther side just as a hail of man-stoppers cracked the top rail and the cross-boards. Bullet-plucked chicken wire twanged and plinked as I went flat and squirmed away.

The land sloped down to a wall of boulders stacked as they might be in a breakwater at the entrance to a harbor. I scrambled down them to a flash-flood channel about twelve feet wide and at least ten feet below the elevated orchard. Crane-placed boulders formed the farther wall, as well.

Maybe the cultists knew what lay beyond the fence, knew that I could stand upright and still be well below their line of fire. The guns fell silent again. In seconds, they would be climbing the fence.

We didn't get a lot of rain in the Mojave, but from time to time we were hit by a storm of such power that everyone made lame jokes about building an ark. In town, a well-planned and exten-sive drainage system could handle all but the most intense, pro-tracted downpours. But where there were no city streets and storm drains, the rushing torrents either created temporary lakes or raced through the arroyos that had been carved in the land by centuries of such deluges. This was one such arroyo, fortified for the length of this property to protect the orchard and to prevent further erosion.

If I went to the right, west, I'd eventually reach a two-lane county road. There wouldn't be much traffic at that hour. Even if I could flag down a vehicle, I would be less likely to escape than to be shot along with whoever stopped to give me a ride.

I hurried to the east, toward the array of buildings that served the orchard. If you're running for your life, a drainage channel of that kind is no safer than a long hallway, which itself has much in common with a target lane in a shooting range. When my pursuers caught up with me, I wouldn't have anywhere to hide, because the sloped walls of boulders weren't as nature might have tumbled them, but were instead stacked tightly and with calculation, to ensure stability.

Far away in the night, a siren wailed. It didn't give me any hope. The police might have been responding to 911 calls related to the barrage that destroyed the Explorer, but they surely weren't already aware of events at the orchard.

Delaying a few seconds longer than seemed wise, I finally darted to my right and scrambled up the massive rocks. Maybe the assassins' weapons, which were more cumbersome than pistols, and whatever other gear they might be carrying slowed them down a little when they had to scale the fence. Or maybe they needed a few seconds to spot me after they reached the channel. Whatever the reason, I made it to the top of the boulders and started toward the nearest building before gunfire rattled again. One brief burst. The keening of a few spent rounds ricocheting off stone. The subsequent silence suggested that I must have gotten ahead of them to an extent that persuaded them not to waste ammunition.

Here the ground was heavily graveled to keep down workday dust, and it crunched underfoot as I approached the first building, which appeared barnlike but massive. Perhaps two hundred feet long and sixty wide. Two stories. Small windows high on the long wall, maybe thirty of them in a row, a few feet under the eave of the curved roof. All were dark. The narrow end of the structure featured two large roll-up doors and a man door between them. Above each truck-size entrance, a security lamp poured forth a pool of light, and a camera gazed down from higher still.

I feared being an easy target in that brightness, but I didn't want to waste time running wide of it. I sprinted onto that well-lit stage and hoped that we had not arrived at the death scene. Past the first big door. Past the second. Turned right at the corner. For the next several seconds, they would not have me in sight, with or without night-vision goggles.

Twenty or twenty-five yards beyond the first building stood three others, smaller but still large, each a different size, a different shape. This one wood, that one concrete block skinned with stucco. I ventured among them, putting more walls between me and the cultists. The security lights here were dimmer, regular bulbs, not floodlights like the first two. Shadows were plentiful.

Gravel had been spread in a thinner layer here than elsewhere, but silent movement remained impossible. On the upside, I couldn't leave footprints in a carpet of small loose stones.

I'd had about enough of running, whether under fire or not. The air temperature was seventy-five degrees or a little higher. I was sweating like you would think a pig would sweat; actually, however, pigs don't sweat, another fact that I learned from Ozzie Boone, who wrote a novel in which an expert on hogs trained three of them to kill an enemy of his. Anyway, my mouth was dry. Throat scratchy. Eyes burning from sweat salt. I needed to get out of the chase, find a hidey-hole.

Acutely aware that I had mere seconds to disappear from sight before the search team streamed among the buildings, rejecting one possible hiding place after another, I came to the back of the two-story block-and-stucco building. Ladder rungs embedded in the wall led to the flat roof. I almost didn't see them in the dim light from a caged security lamp at the farther end of the structure. They were painted to match the stucco.

When you think of hiding places, you imagine crawling under something or behind something, or into a hole, but you can be easily trapped in such places. I could be trapped on a roof, too, but they would not be able to get me in their sights if I stayed below the parapet wall. And the only way to get to me would be by the ladder. Any fool who climbed it, even mildly suspicious that I might have taken refuge up there, would lose the top of his head when he came into view.

I climbed quickly. The parapet wall, encircling the flat roof, was about three feet high, maybe higher. On my hands and knees, I crawled across the forty-foot-wide roof, intending to take a position directly opposite the ladder.

Halfway across the roof, I realized my mistake. Forty feet would be too far from the ladder. In spite of my aversion to guns, I had learned to use them, but I was not a skilled sniper. And the Glock wouldn't be as reliable at forty feet as it would be from a distance of, say, six inches.

As I crawled back the way that I'd come, I heard the rattle and crunch of footsteps on gravel. I kept moving, making a lot less noise than the hunters were. Sitting with my back pressed to the parapet wall, immediately to the right of the ladder, I drew the Glock.

As dark as it was on the roof, I could nevertheless see the pale-white stucco of the parapet, the clean sweep of it. If I had been sitting directly opposite the ladder, I would have been spotted the instant the climber's eyes cleared the top. I would have been the only dark shape silhouetted against the stucco, except for a few low vent stacks.

On the ground, the cultists didn't like the gravel. Moving among the buildings, they tried to place their feet cautiously, but the loose stones defeated them. After taking several careful steps, each of them made the same decision: to bull forward, clattering through the pebbles without regard to the noise, evidently convinced that too much caution was more dangerous than advancing boldly.

The distant siren had faded to silence. Either the patrol car had been responding to a call about the shooting at the Explorer or to something else altogether that had nothing to do with me and the posse on my trail.

As I waited for the sound of feet on the ladder rungs, I tried to figure out how these people kept finding me. After the events in Nevada, they had revenge on their minds. They were using all of their considerable resources, all their corrupt contacts in everything from the political establishment to law enforcement, to get their hands on me. If they had known about the beach cottage where I'd been living for a couple of months, they would have tried to kill me there. They knew about the Big Dog Bulldog Bagger, but apparently didn't know that it had been garaged at the cottage.

With my left hand, through my T-shirt, I felt the tiny silver bell at the end of the chain. I pulled it out from under the T-shirt and held it between thumb and forefinger. My racing heart slowed, and my fear diminished.

If my enemy with a million eyes remained blind to the cottage, if they were unable to locate it, their failure had something to do with Annamaria. The more I thought about it, the more it seemed as though I was not only safe from them but also *invisible* to them while in Annamaria's company. Almost from the day I met her, I had known that she was more than she appeared to be, that the eccentric things she often said would in fact prove to be the plainest truth if only I knew who and what she was and could consider her words in the context of her identity. I remembered what Mrs. Fischer said: *For all you may think differently, I'm only human. Annamaria's human, too, though she's more than that, as you no doubt suspect.* Human but more than human—and with curious powers that, if fully known, would probably make my paranormal abilities seem pathetic by comparison.

Below, the searchers were still crunching through the gravel, but not with as much enthusiasm. Not as many of them, either. From over near the largest building, the one I'd first come upon, I heard voices, but I couldn't make out the words.

I turned the miniature bell back and forth between thumb and forefinger, pleased by the smoothness of it. It remained pleasantly cool. Neither the warm night nor my body heat nor the friction of my fingers rubbing the smooth, smooth silver could steal the coolness from it.

Okay, the Big Dog motorcycle. I had known since March, since Nevada, that sooner or later I would be returning to Pico Mundo, that the cultists had plans for my hometown. I knew, as well, I must make the trip alone. This threat was mine to thwart or fail to thwart. My fate, whether or not the promise of the fortune-teller's card would be kept, depended on my success or failure. Mrs. Fischer insisted on buying a car for me, but I worried that Tim and Annamaria would be determined to make the trip with me if I had a car. I would not put them so directly at risk. Furthermore, Blossom Rosedale had sold her house in Magic Beach and had been intending to join us as soon as her affairs there were concluded; I couldn't put her in jeopardy, either. Finally, and most important, I didn't want to rely on whatever protection Annamaria's immediate presence might afford me. This battle was mine to win or lose, by my best efforts, by my choices, by the right or wrong exercise of my free will. And so Mrs. Fischer had bought for me instead the Big Dog bike.

The cultists found me as I'd driven home to Pico Mundo, found me more than once thereafter; and not all of their success in that regard could be attributed to reverse psychic magnetism. If you believed the condition of humanity to be what they believed it to be, then their patron was the prince of this world, and at least some of his dark power was theirs to draw upon. The quest to find and kill a fry cook with a few marginal psychic talents that he couldn't fully control might not be a war to them, might be instead a pleasant game. For all of Mrs. Fischer's wealth and cleverness and loyal friends and courage, she and I might be hopelessly outmatched by the cult.

Two floors below, the sound of gravel scattering underfoot had ceased. I listened, wondering if they had gone or were only standing still, waiting for me to emerge from hiding. The voices over by the main building had fallen silent a couple of minutes earlier.

Although I continued to rub it, the bell remained cool, cool and smooth. I was still sheathed in sweat, dripping—except for the thumb and forefinger on my left hand, which were perfectly dry as they held the tiny silver bell.

I strained to hear the stealthy tread of shoes on ladder rungs. Nothing. There was no climber. No one could ascend that ladder in absolute silence.

I felt the night moving like a sea toward some shore, a great wave of darkness swelling under me, a tsunami under Pico Mundo, under Maravilla County, rising toward a terrible height from which it would fall in upon us, smash us, and sweep us away. And not just the town and county but the state, too, and the country. The feeling grew so strong that I was tempted to rise to my feet and survey the land in all directions, as if the darkness itself might in fact have acquired real mass and the power to wash destruction across a continent.

Just then the largest building in the orchard complex was torn by a massive explosion.

Thirty-nine

The blast rocked the ground, the building under me shuddered, and I nearly bit my tongue as my teeth clacked together. The flash left my eyes less adapted to the dark than they
had been an instant earlier. Louder than any crack of thunder
that I'd ever heard, the detonation rolled away through the orchard, but in the aftermath a solemn tolling continued in my ears,
as if I were not atop a two-story building but were inside the bell
tower of a cathedral.

A sudden downpour clattered onto the roof. Not rain. Debris.
Splinters of wood. Slabs of wood as long as my arm. Dirt and
gravel. Scraps of metal, twisted and hot and smoking. I closed my
eyes and averted my face and covered my head with both arms
until the stuff stopped peppering me.

Torn and burning, the massive edifice, the almond-processing
plant, groaned as if it were a living leviathan, groaned and torqued
out of true. At the sight of that structural torment, a woman below
let out a wild rebel yell of exaltation, her voice shrill with glee.
Another cultist answered her. A second. A third. A fourth. The
curved metal roof of the tortured structure bulged and buckled,

rivets popping like corn, welded joints shrieking as they separated, widths of sheet metal peeling up to claw like robot hands at
the night sky, where the low clouds reflected the sudden rush of
fire.

Two hundred feet away, at the farther end of the same building, a second explosion equaled the first. Because it was more
distant, the flash seemed less bright. The bang split the night with
cleaver-sharp sound. Although the stucco building quaked less
violently under me than before, the effect on the processing plant
was greater than that of the first explosion. Lit by fire, the immense structure rippled from the farther end to the nearer, as if I
were not looking at it directly but were seeing its reflection in the
surface of a breeze-ruffled lake. Wood rafters and joists and studs
cracked like the whips of the gods, structural metal squealed as it
was deformed by the initial shock wave, and what window glass
had not shattered in the first blast shattered now.

The behavior of the cultists, when they shot the Explorer to
pieces and when they opened fire on me in the almond orchard,
had been reckless, but this was *insanity.* They had not come here
with the intention of blowing up that building; they had come
here only because they were chasing me. The doors were locked,
the windows high. I couldn't be hiding inside the place. The destruction of the processing plant seemed to be a pointless crime of
opportunity. Worse, it seemed to have been done on a *whim.* They
probably thought that I had gotten away clean, and they were
frustrated, disappointed, badly in need of a mood boost. Nothing
could elevate your spirits more than blowing the crap out of a
large building, a point of view that half the lunatics in the world
would enthusiastically endorse—if, when you asked their opinion, they weren't busy beheading people.

I figured we could be certain now that the ton of C-4 hadn't been hijacked by some other group of maniacs, that these apostles of the demon Meridian were indeed the culprits. The amount detonated in this instance was at most a few pounds, which left them with more than enough to break the Malo Suerte Dam if that happened to be their intention. Maybe C-4 was the least of it.

But if they *did* intend some epic act of evil, destruction on a scale so enormous that it would assure this night a place in the history books, wasn't it stupid to waste their time and risk compromising their main objective by blowing up a nut-processing plant in an almond orchard? Just because I'd given them the slip and they were miffed? They were probably fist-pumping when they let out those rebel yells, maybe doing an end-zone dance of triumph. They appeared to be spiraling out of control. The discipline that had marked their scheming in the past seemed to be dissolving.

Great tongues of flame seethed from the roof of the stricken building, licked through every crack in its walls, spewed out of the small high windows. Huddled against the parapet, I was at most eighty or ninety feet from the blaze. The heat began to wring more sweat from me than had the long run through the cotton-woods and the almond grove. Smoke, thus far churning into the night sky, suddenly rushed in thick gray masses from the side of the structure and plumed toward me as a portion of the wall collapsed.

I couldn't stay on the roof. If smoke inhalation didn't kill me, it would cause fits of coughing, which would locate me for the cultists. If they didn't want to brave the climb and come after me, they could just wait for me to suffocate. Or they could blow this place up, with me atop it. In fact, maybe they had already placed more packages of C-4. Maybe they were going to destroy every building at the orchard.

I rose, turned to the ladder, and looked down, pretty sure that I would see a grinning face and a gun muzzle. No one waited below. Although some shadows danced here and there, the graveled ground between this building and the other two was largely well revealed by throbbing reflections of firelight. I hoped that the cultists were either gathered elsewhere to watch the fiery spectacle or had gone away altogether.

Holstering the Glock, I swung onto the ladder and started down just as a tide of smoke washed across the roof. Even though I was under the worst of the fumes for the moment, the air smelled wicked, a bath of toxic chemicals. At the bottom of the ladder, I drew the pistol, surveyed my surroundings, saw no one.

Holding my breath, I ran toward the last two buildings, toward the space between them. No one would hear footsteps in gravel above the roar of the flames and the thousand sounds of distress issuing from the doomed building.

As big as silver dollars, ashes like enormous gray snowflakes spiraled to the ground around me. A storm of burning embers rained down, too, carried by thermal currents from the ferocious blaze, dropping out as the currents weakened with distance. Each ember was a potential new fire if by chance it fell upon fuel. I winced as one of them glanced off my face, shook another off my jacket sleeve, and brushed yet another out of my hair, blistering my left thumb in the process.

Behind the last two buildings, at the east end of the complex, the gravel gave way to bare earth. Here, the night lay in deeper darkness than the territory that I'd just left, although still somewhat revealed by firelight. I could see just well enough to discern a series of large troughs, maybe twelve feet long, six feet wide, four deep, elevated on concrete pads, each with a swan-neck spout and a spigot at one end. I couldn't imagine a purpose for them, but they looked as if they were public baths for a race of giants.

Beyond the troughs and the board-and-wire fence lay twenty feet of bare ground and then, to the east, a shadowy vista of chaparral. On a warm evening like this, it was the kind of land that teemed with nightlife, though not the kind that required a dance band and adult beverages. Tarantulas as big as my fist. Lizards and rabbits that wouldn't hurt you, rattlesnakes that would. Coyotes. A bobcat or three.

I needed to get back to the fairgrounds. I *still* believed that the cultists had some intention there, other than to use the Sombra Brothers carnival as their cover and headquarters for this operation.

As something inside the burning building exploded and shrapnel banged and thudded off all manner of surfaces in the conflagration, I headed south, using the line of troughs for cover until there were no more of them. Low and bent-backed. Hurrying but not running. I hastened into a secondary orchard much smaller than the first.

The heat of the fire and the flurries of ashes and smoke were far behind me. In the distance I heard sirens once more, sirens combined with stentorian horn blasts that identified the vehicles as fire engines.

As before, I stayed close to one row of trees, pausing at the sixth, the twelfth, the eighteenth, to scope the orchard ahead and to keep my breathing as slow and quiet as possible. I was too far from the burning building for the racket of its piecemeal collapse to provide much cover now.

I resisted the temptation to glance back at the blaze. My eyes were not yet fully dark-adapted again, and I needed them to adjust to the gloom as quickly as possible.

Although lacking headstones and monuments, the orchard at night reminded me of a graveyard, perhaps because of the regimented rows, perhaps because I believed that black-clad figures, as faceless as Death, would at any moment step out of cover and loom before me.

At the twenty-fourth tree, six from the end of the orchard, I stood with my back to the trunk, held my breath, listened. I thought I heard a voice. Two voices. I drew a breath or two, listened again, but heard nothing except a tree rat or a raccoon scratching its way along a branch overhead. Then the voices again. They were speaking low, but they weren't as quiet as they should have been if they were cultists on the lookout for me.

I needed to locate them. In as low a crouch as I could get without proceeding in a duck-walk, I moved from the twenty-fourth tree to the twenty-fifth, leaning to the left, to the right, trying to tune in to their conversation.

They fell silent. Back pressed to the almond tree, I waited, hoping that they hadn't gone quiet because they'd seen or heard me.

My eyes were well adjusted to the dark again, which meant only that now I was merely *half* blind. If money could buy anything, I would have called Mrs. Fischer and asked her to buy off the cloud cover and bring back the moon.

Judging by the tone of their voices, when they spoke again, the unseen men were irritated.

I eased forward to the twenty-sixth tree, to the twenty-seventh.

Halfway to the twenty-eighth, I saw them. On the right. Two figures dressed in black. Ahead of me, at the end of the alley between this row and the next. So close.

They evidently were supposed to be scanning the ten feet of open ground that separated the almond trees from the fence that marked the southern perimeter of Maravilla Valley Orchards. They didn't seem to be deeply committed to the task.

I kept moving, afraid one of them would look toward me at any moment. I put my back to the twenty-eighth tree, two from the end, and found that I was now close enough to hear what they said.

"Damn it, Emory, that freak never come this way."

"Yeah," Emory said, "but this is where they want us."

"You'd break your own neck tryin' to kiss your own ass if one of the inner circle said so."

"I'm not afraid of the inner circle."

"Hell you ain't. Come on. I wanna be where the *action* is."

"Me, too, Carl. Who doesn't?"

"Well," Carl said, "it ain't here."

Emory didn't respond.

"Five or six minutes till maybe they blow that church."

"They'll blow whatever they find."

"If it's the church, I gotta see it."

"You don't care about the church."

"Don't tell me what I don't care about."

Emory said, "It's the farmhouse that has you hot."

"You, too. You seen the pictures—them two girls, their mother."

"They aren't for us, anyway."

"But we can watch it bein' done."

"I've already seen it done. Lots of times."

"This is bullshit, man."

"We don't want to get in trouble."

"All we *do* want is trouble."

"You know what I mean."

"Yeah, you're a chickenshit."

Emory didn't reply.

Frustrated, Carl said, "Ain't we anarchyists?"

"It's pronounced *an-are-kists*. And no, we aren't."

"I thought we was."

"We rule through chaos. That's different."

Carl sounded like a pouting child. "We need to be doin' some anarchyism."

Intellectual arguments between satanists were less witty than I had expected.

"You hear them sirens?" Carl asked.

"Of course I hear them. Fire trucks."

"And cops close behind."

"Shouldn't be here for the cops," Emory said.

"Finally you said a smart thing."

"It's maybe ten minutes before the farmhouse."

"So let's go, let's get in the *action*."

"All right. You're right."

"Bet your ass I'm right."

I heard footsteps, the rustle of clothing. Looking past the tree behind which I sheltered, I saw them moving away, toward the fence.

Prudence suggested that I should let them go. There were two of them, and they were heavily armed. The element of surprise might not be sufficient to get me into a confrontation and out the other side alive.

This was the night of nights, however, and too much prudence might result in the forfeiture of the game.

Forty

I stepped away from the line of trees that I had been following, into the alley between this row and the next, directly behind Emory and Carl as they approached the fence.

One of them had some kind of combat rifle strap-slung over his shoulder. The other, carrying a rifle of his own, shouldered it, too, as they drew near the fence.

My stomach seemed as if it were full of cocoons from which a flock of butterflies were emerging with still-wet wings: the fluttery feeling of nervous anticipation combined with nausea.

I moved with them, wanting a point-blank situation. They didn't hear anything. I was so close, they should have smelled me.

With the Glock in a two-hand grip, arms thrust forward, taking an isosceles stance, I waited until the first man started to climb before I said, "Freeze."

They froze, for a moment, anyway, and then the guy with two feet on the ground started to pivot, sliding the rifle off his shoulder as he turned, and I saw that he was indeed wearing goggles as I shot him twice.

At the crack of the pistol, the guy on the fence looked in my direction, and after the second shot, as his companion dropped, I said, "I only want information."

In his black clothes and ski mask and goggles, he looked like an extraterrestrial geared up for Earth's hostile atmosphere.

"Information," I repeated. "Don't want to have to kill you."

"Shit you don't." He turned away from me, clinging to the fence.

"What farmhouse?" I asked. "What's happening there?"

The fool went for it, tried for the top of the fence, because he could not unsling the rifle in his position and would rather die than tell me about their intentions with the dam or anything else.

I couldn't let him get away. I shot him in the back. It didn't feel like the worst thing I'd ever had to do, but it felt like one of the worst and equal to many others.

He fell off the fence, onto his back, not dead yet, gazing up at me through his goggles as I stepped forward and stood over him. Between clenched teeth, a thick guttural expression of pain escaped him, as if he didn't want to give me the satisfaction of hearing him suffer.

There was no satisfaction in it for me.

"Just tell me what's going to happen tonight. What's all this about?" My solid-state digital watch didn't tick. And yet I heard it ticking.

Instead, he told me to perform a sexual act with myself that no one with a basic understanding of human anatomy would have believed possible.

He was no longer able to bite off his pain. A squeal of agony escaped him.

I shot him in the head and put an end to it.

Closing my eyes, shuddering, I asked for a sign that what I had done was necessary. Just one small sign. Nothing big. One small but incontestable sign. I opened my eyes. There was no sign. It doesn't work that way and never did.

I knelt beside the first dead man and removed his goggles. A rubber-sheathed wire connected them to a power pack clipped to his utility belt. I hooked the pack to my belt and put on the goggles.

The night glowed green. There was darkness in the green night, plenty of it, but not as much as before this vision assist. Getting used to the eerie color and distorted perceptions arising from it would take a few minutes.

The sirens weren't distant anymore. The fire trucks sounded as if they were near the orchard, perhaps already turning off the county road. Police might be following close in the wake of the trucks. The firemen and cops would know within two minutes that the explosions hadn't been related to gas-line problems or to any other accidental causes. The blast evidence could be easily read. Chief Porter would ask the state highway patrol to lend some manpower. Soon this usually quiet rural area of Pico Mundo would be swarming with police, perhaps some of them manning roadblocks. Not all of them would be officers who knew me and would vouch for me.

From the man who failed to climb the fence, I took a centerfire combat rifle. I had never used any weapon like it.

I had been raised by a mother who was mentally ill but never institutionalized. She pretended to have suicidal tendencies, though she used her pistol only to intimidate her child. As a consequence, I disliked guns, but I learned to use them. I had come to understand guns, that they were tools and that they were no more evil, in their essence, than pliers and wrenches. At times, they were a necessity. In a world of evil, they were often also a blessing. Now and then, as I've said, I was able to fight off a thug with my encyclopedia of unconventional weapons, such as a clarinet, an oboe, and a trombone (a confrontation in a musical-instrument shop), three buckets full of pig slops (*not* in a musical-instrument shop), a wet mop, coconuts, wasp spray, and once in fact with a twelve-volume encyclopedia. But often firearms saved my life and the lives of others who depended on me.

From personal experience in the orchard, I knew that these fully automatic rifles, as illegal as briefcase nukes, were capable of firing a single round or a deadly burst of bullets. I didn't know how this one was set or how to change the way it was set. I assumed it was still on fully automatic fire. These lunatics were unlikely to practice gun safety.

From the dead man's utility belt hung four spare magazines. They appeared to hold perhaps thirty rounds each. On the rifle, I found the release button and ejected the current magazine, slapped a full one in its place. I found the bolt catch. Made sure the bolt was not locked. I recognized the trigger. That was the extent of my knowledge of this kind of weapon. It was going to be a learn-as-you-go event.

I took a spare magazine from the dead man. Put it in an inside sport-coat pocket, tearing the lining in the process. Mr. Bullock would never lend me another garment. I put a second spare magazine in an exterior pocket.

With the rifle slung over my shoulder, I went up and over the fence. How ironic it would have been if someone had shot me in the back as I climbed.

In my mind's ear, I heard Emory and Carl.

Five or six minutes till maybe they blow that church. . . .

They'll blow whatever they find.

The next explosion would be only two or three minutes away now, not five. I didn't know which church and had no time to go looking for one.

Although math had never been my strongest subject, I could put two and two together. The crew that pursued me through the orchard might or might not be the only one at work this night. They weren't using all the C-4 to break the dam. They didn't need all of it for that. They were blowing up anything they encountered.

Ain't we anarchyists?

It's pronounced an-are-kists. *And no, we aren't.*

I thought we was.

We rule through chaos. That's different.

The behavior of these cultists wasn't as insane as I had first thought. They had a strategy and tactics to support it. The almond-processing plant and the church were distractions. Whatever else they blew up in the next hour would also be meant to distract the police, overwhelm them, and leave them with insufficient resources to deal with the true threat when it came.

I needed to call Chief Porter, but I didn't have time just then. I thought I knew where the farmhouse was, the identity of the woman and her two daughters who were in imminent peril. With all the chaos erupting, the police would never get there in time.

It's the farmhouse that has you hot.

You, too. You seen the pictures—them two girls, their mother.

They aren't for us, anyway.

But we can watch it bein' done.

I've already seen it done. Lots of times.

In the midst of sowing chaos, and before the main event of the night, the cultists were intending to take time for a quick religious ceremony. They were going to make an offering to ensure that the prince of this world, his satanic majesty, would look with approval upon the catastrophe that they hoped to bring down upon my beloved Pico Mundo.

Three human sacrifices.

Beyond the orchard fence lay a much-patched single-lane blacktop driveway, dating back decades, cracked and crumbling at the edges, tufts of grass and withered weeds growing through it in places, overhung by California live oaks as old as any trees in Maravilla County. This picturesque lane connected the nearby county road to Blue Sky Ranch, a place with a great deal of history both triumphant and tragic.

I turned at once eastward, into the green night, away from the county road, and I ran for my life, as well as for the lives of the mother and her two daughters who lived on the ranch. If Emory and Carl had their facts straight, I no longer had ten minutes. Maybe seven.

Or six.

Not even half a minute after coming off the fence and setting out for Blue Sky Ranch, I halted when it sounded as though God, in disgust, had slammed his big door on the world. I felt the explosion tremble the ground underfoot, and scores of dead leaves rattled down through the live oaks, falling upon me and around me, as if Death himself, in a mood to mock, were sprinkling me with his equivalent of the holy water that a priest shook upon the faithful from an aspergillum.

I pivoted, searching the night. Stepped between two of the live oaks on the south side of the lane. The brightness overwhelmed my goggles, and I slipped them up onto my forehead. Perhaps a mile away, to the southwest, a hundred- or even two-hundred-foot tower of fire cast off gouts of flaming debris that showered down the night like fireworks out of season.

No church would burn that fiercely, that fast. They had blown up something else. Later I would learn that it was the county highway department's fuel depot, to which bulk gasoline was periodically delivered for the fueling of all county- and municipal-owned vehicles. A packet of C-4 with a timer had been lowered on a wire into the underground storage tank. With the blast, hundreds of gallons of burning gasoline had been at once spewed high into the night, and thousands of gallons remaining in the ruptured tank had been set ablaze.

Even as I stood awestruck by the cultists' boldness and by the terrible scope of the destruction they had committed—and must intend yet to commit—another explosion slammed the night. Nearer than the first blast. Perhaps a quarter mile this side of the raging gasoline fire. A fierce flash of white light was at once followed by an oak-shaking bang and an echoing roar, as if Thor, Scandinavian god of thunder and rain, wielding his hammer, Mjölnir, had smote the vault of heaven.

I imagined that some church had just been reduced to rubble.

Nearly two years earlier, before the mass murder at the Green Moon Mall, the lesser coven, that quartet of maniacs led by Officers Bern Eckles and Simon Varner, had distracted me and had fogged my understanding of what was soon to happen. Had they not planted a corpse in my apartment and shot Chief Porter the night before that massacre, I might have put the pieces together more quickly, might have gotten to the mall five minutes sooner. Now I had the sense, yet again, that although these more ambitious cultists had failed to kill me in the cottonwood grove and in the orchard, they had nonetheless put me on the run and distracted me, so that when they pulled the trigger on their main event, I would be crucial minutes late, as before.

I didn't wait to see the more modest flames that would build now in the wake of the blast. Turning east again, pulling the goggles over my eyes, I sprinted toward Blue Sky Ranch.

Forty-one

To the right of the driveway were acres of meadows secured by ranch fencing infilled with fine wire mesh. The same aquifer that made possible the almond orchard provided sweet grass and clover for the breed-worthy horses that, during the day, could sometimes be seen grazing there.

Blue Sky Ranch had been for two generations one of the three or four most successful quarter-horse breeding operations anywhere in California and the Southwest. As a secondary business, they bred and trained horses for sulky racing. Bing Torbold and his wife had built the ranch and the business. His son, Bing Jr., upheld the family traditions and brought even greater glory to the storied Torbold stables. When Bing Jr. fell ill and his son, Carter Torbold, took over a decade sooner than anticipated, the slide to bankruptcy began. Carter gambled. Not on horses. In Vegas. The casinos called his kind "whales," because of their fat bankrolls. Carter loved to gamble, but he had neither the discipline of a professional poker player nor any luck at all.

The valuable breeding stock was sold off to an operation in Arizona. Without the legendary Torbold horses to breed new champions, the property and buildings were worth less than they might have been had the bloodline been still an asset of the ranch.

Fourteen years ago, when they were twenty-five, Dave and Lauren Ainsworth had bought the ranch at a distressed price. They had modest capital, a deep knowledge of horses, a willingness to work hard, and the wisdom to know that delayed gratification was often the secret to success. In ten years, they built a business and a winning bloodline that Bing Torbold would have admired. Then Dave got cancer and was gone in six months. Lauren had been running the place ever since, doing the work of two and raising her twins, Veronica and Victoria, by all accounts succeeding at both tasks. She and Dave had brought the girls to the Pico Mundo Grille occasionally, and often they had sat at the counter to watch me perform with spatulas, whisk, pot fork, and draining spoon, which could be an entertaining juggling act, especially if I hammed it up for the kids.

As the driveway turned to the right, the residence came into view: a two-story Kentucky-style manor house, white with black trim. The place was smaller than it appeared to be, because the generous veranda that wrapped three sides created the illusion of grandness.

Most of the windows were bright, and the veranda lamps were aglow. The goggles magnified the light into a consuming green flare, and I pushed them onto my forehead again.

I glanced at the luminous dial of my watch. How long? Five minutes. Four? Maybe just three?

Lauren was standing in the side yard with her daughters, gazing west toward the colossal flames surging from the gasoline storage tank and the less dramatic fire at, possibly, a distant church. Their yellow Labrador retriever, Muggs, stood with them, alert. I called to them and identified myself as I hurried off the driveway onto the front lawn. The girls, almost twelve years old and marked by the easy ardency of that age, squealed with excitement and ran toward me, and Muggs came galloping after them. They hadn't seen me in nearly two years, but the events of this night so astonished them and inflamed their imagination that the suddenness of my arrival seemed ordinary by comparison.

"Mr. Thomas! What're all the fires?"

"Mr. Thomas! Did you hear the booms?"

"They were crazy loud!"

"We were watching TV!"

"The whole house shook!"

"BOOM! BOOM!"

"Muggs went Scooby Doo on us!"

"He hid under the kitchen table!"

Muggs wove among us, his tail beating against our legs, panting and grinning, having overcome his terror, now filled with the girls' enthusiasm.

They were lovely girls, with their mother's blond hair and their father's gray eyes. They would turn heads when they were grown, just as their mother had turned heads—and still did.

Lauren joined us near the veranda where it cornered from the front yard to the side yard. She had none of the girls' giddiness, and she shushed them. She was serious, and when she saw the combat rifle that I carried and then met my eyes, anxiety took possession of her face.

"Trust me," I said.

"Of course."

"You have a gun?"

"A pistol."

"Get it. Fast. Take the girls to the stables. Hide there."

She sprinted for the porch steps.

I called after her, "Leave all the house lights on."

Veronica and Victoria remained with me. They were still excited but now also anxious.

"What's wrong, Mr. Thomas?"

"What's happening?"

"Are we going to be okay?"

"You'll be fine," I said. "Does Muggs bark much?"

Veronica said, "He hardly ever barks."

"He grumbles sometimes," Victoria said. "Sometimes he farts loud."

"Hardly ever."

Veronica said, "But when he does, it's a window-rattler."

"In the stable," I warned them, "make sure he doesn't bark."

Veronica held the agitated dog by the collar.

Both girls looked toward the fires, and Victoria said, "Is someone gonna bomb us?"

I'm not sure how I knew which of them was Veronica, which Victoria, but I knew. "No one's going to bomb you, but you need to be brave."

"We can be," Veronica said.

"We have been," Victoria said.

Veronica said, "We had to be. Since we lost Daddy."

Their mother hurried out of the house, closed the door behind her, and descended the porch steps. She carried a pistol and a flashlight.

I said, "Hide as best you can. Then don't use the flashlight until I come for you."

"All right."

I thought I heard, faintly, an approaching engine.

When I glanced back at the colonnades of oaks that canopied the driveway, I saw no telltale headlights.

Nevertheless, I said, "Go. Go, go, *go!*"

The three of them and the Labrador hurried past the house, east toward the stables and the training track.

Trusting Lauren to follow my instructions, I retreated from the well-lighted house to the darkness along the perimeter of the lawn. I took up a position behind shrubbery, from which I could watch the driveway.

I thought I knew how the cultists intended to get the job done. They wouldn't drive right up to the house, wouldn't want the engine noise to announce their arrival. Besides, they'd block the driveway with their vehicle, so that no visitor could get past it. One man to stay with the car. The others—four, five, whatever—would arrive on foot. Two for the front door. Two or three for the back, to prevent Lauren and her daughters from fleeing that way. All of them with combat rifles. Kick in the front door. Maybe fire a burst into the ceiling to intimidate. Blue Sky Ranch was semi-isolated. Anyone who heard the gunfire at a distance wouldn't be able to pinpoint its origin. The invaders would move fast through the house, find Lauren and the girls. Herd them to one room. Gang-rape them within sight of one another. Humiliating them was an important element of the ritual sacrifice. Humiliate, terrify, demean, diminish, bring to despair. If this church had a community-outreach program, it would be symbolized on their stationery not as an open hand, but as a fist. There might be black candles on whatever makeshift altar they used. Tannis-root paste and a fungus called devil's pepper that those being sacrificed were forced to swallow. Most likely a quick ceremony. A couple of

Hail Satans. A sip of blood. This was a busy night for the Cult of Meridian. From the rapes, they would go directly to the ceremonial knife. None of the usual preliminary torture and disfigurement. Just the killing cut. Three times.

A cold, controlled fury had gripped me, greater than any anger I had experienced before. I felt as if there were two Odds in the same skin—the fry cook who had written poetry for the girl he loved and wept at movies like *Terms of Endearment,* but also the ruthless killer who could shoot men in the back. The darker Odd Thomas thought his violence must be righteous, in the service of good, for the protection of the innocent. But the other Odd wondered if the claim of righteous purpose, exerted so often in these past two years, was always true—or if it might be overused. There were nights when consideration of that issue would not allow sleep. In spite of all the doubt, my fury didn't abate.

On my knees behind the shrubbery, monitoring the driveway, I didn't like what I smelled. The offender wasn't the foliage with its tiny white flowers, which provided a green-leaf scent and a faint sweet fragrance similar to jasmine. The odor was mine, and it seemed to me that only part of it could be a consequence of all the sweating that I'd done and the chemicals in the gray snowflake ashes that had dissolved and stuck to my hair and jacket. Maybe part of it was the malodor of a deeper corruption.

If I progressed from being a righteous man to being a scourge, my destiny might not match Gypsy Mummy's prediction. Scourges assumed authority they had not been granted. They made a carefully reasoned decision to kill in greater numbers than were absolutely necessary to save themselves and the innocents who needed their protection. Scourges transgressed against social and sacred order. In *Hamlet,* the prince lacked the clarity of heart and the courage to be a minister of Truth, as he should have been, but he sure was a bang-up scourge, inflicting upon his kingdom more killing than necessary. Scourges themselves are always scourged. The prince did not survive the play. Moses scourged three thousand people—and did not live to see the promised land.

Crickets and toads had been singing in the nearby meadow that began where the mown lawn ended. They stopped abruptly, as if they had all forgotten their songs.

Forty-two

Since kneeling behind the shrubbery, I had avoided looking to the left, toward the Ainsworth house, or to the right, where flames from the gasoline fire unfurled like the flags of Hell. My eyes were somewhat dark-adapted once more.

Out there in the night, where the driveway turned from east to south and proceeded toward the residence, dark figures appeared. The brightly lighted residence no doubt compelled them to remove their night-vision goggles.

They were clustered together. Difficult to count. Closely grouped, they made one target. Tempting. But even if they remained in tight formation until they reached the front porch, I couldn't be sure of dropping them all. My weapon might not be set on burst-fire. I wouldn't know until I squeezed the trigger. I was too far away to stand up and pick them off one by one. They would scatter, and I would have lost the advantage of surprise. Besides, I didn't have sniper skills. I was a close-up killer.

I held my position until I was able to count them. Four. They ordered themselves into pairs as they came toward the house, which suggested that my idea of how they would do the job must be on the money.

The line of shrubs, defining the end of the lawn, grew waist-high, with a two-foot gap between each bush. I rose into a crouch and hurried toward the back of the house, not fully concealed. My powder-blue sport coat was definitely not the new black. I was better dressed for a prom than for secret ops. I counted on darkness. And the likelihood that they would be focused on the house rather than on shrubbery sixty feet to the west of it. Anyway, in about three seconds, I had put the house between me and them.

Nobody shouted or shot at me.

The back of the residence was as I remembered it. The veranda didn't wrap to this fourth side of the structure. A large flagstone patio instead. A round table with a big adjustable umbrella and six chairs. Two lounges for sunning, a small table between them. At the end of the patio farthest from the house stood an outdoor culinary center: large built-in barbecue, four gas burners under a steel cover, double sink, under-the-counter refrigerator, storage space.

I sprinted behind that open-air kitchen and crouched there, the combat rifle in both hands and ready.

From what Carl had said to Emory back at the fence between the orchard and Blue Sky Ranch, the cult had secretly photographed Lauren and the twins, perhaps at a distance, with a telephoto lens.

You seen the pictures—them two girls, their mother.

When they reconnoitered the area, considering possible targets for the C-4, they had found the Ainsworths, too, and had most likely decided at once to put Lauren and the girls on their itiner-

ary for a little sex, savagery, and satanic ceremony between demolition jobs. They would have scoped out the property; they would
know what to find on the back patio. They wouldn't have to
snoop around the outdoor kitchen in the dark, wondering what it
might be.

In spite of their soft-soled shoes, I heard them arrive. One of
them bumped against a piece of patio furniture, and the other
hissed his disapproval.

With caution, I eased up from a crouch, just until I could see
over the hood of the barbecue. The two cultists were facing away
from me, intent on the back door, silhouetted against the light
from the kitchen windows.

From the farther end of the house came a hard crash and the
sound of shattering glass as the other two creeps kicked open the
front door. No turning back now. Neither for them nor for me.

Forty-three

The doubt and the twinge of regret never came between the idea and the reality, when the decision to kill was reversible. At the moment between the motion and the act, I had the capacity only for fear and for a wild delight in my commitment to this hazardous deed. No, there was one thing more. I felt as well a terrible pride in my cunning, in my boldness.

From behind the patio culinary center, I rose to full height. The recoil proved to be not as bad as I expected. The weapon was set on burst-fire, after all, but the burst seemed to be three shots per trigger pull, which didn't produce quite the vicious spray of bullets that I envisioned. Nevertheless, the man on the left went down at once, and I targeted the second cultist.

His reactions were fine-tuned. He squeezed off two bursts as he swung toward me, though he had no chance of scoring a hit in the turn. He hoped to make me duck and thereby gain for himself a fateful second. I didn't duck, but returned two bursts for two, nailing his left side. He lost strength in his arms, so that his third and final volley went low, shattering through the ceramic-tile front of the outdoor kitchen, through the plywood or pressboard underneath, its energy spent in the guts of the under-the-counter refrigerator. I let off a last burst, and he was finished with his adventure at Blue Sky Ranch.

The racket had been louder than gunfire alone. If I was right about each pull of the trigger releasing three quick rounds, I had expended twelve. Perhaps fewer than half of those had been stopped by the two cultists. Others had split the wood siding on the back of the house and shattered windows and damaged the well-lighted kitchen that I could see through the missing panes of glass.

All of this had happened the instant after the two cultists at the front of the house had kicked open the door, alerting them that something had gone terribly wrong with their plan. They would either bail out or they would stay the course; and if the latter, they could no longer be taken by surprise, as the first two had been.

Unless I moved fast.

And had a little luck.

These people weren't Navy SEALs or Army Rangers, weren't trained by the best professional warriors in the world, weren't seasoned by a real war in which they had encountered an enemy who fought back. They lacked the honor of SEALs and Rangers, lacked ideals that stiffened the spine in times of peril. They were fanatics, driven by emotion rather than reason. Their commitment was to destruction instead of to the preservation of what was good, and this commitment made them feel dangerous, therefore powerful and superior. Being dangerous, however, wasn't the same as being powerful and certainly didn't support a claim to superiority. Like all barbarians, they were vulnerable to panic and confusion when the destruction they wished to wreak was visited instead upon them.

Even a fry cook in a powder-blue sport coat, who was unable to figure out the true and hidden nature of the world in spite of having been given plenty of hints, even *I* might triumph over them.

As the second cultist fell, he slammed his head against the edge of a patio table, incurring a superfluous final wound. By the time he kissed the flagstones, I was already running back the way I had come. This time I didn't rely on the cover of shrubbery, but stayed close to the house.

Most if not all of the downstairs lights were on, and as I passed each window, I scanned the room beyond. At the last one, I found what I wanted. The door-busting pair had moved out of the foyer but had gotten no farther than the living room, where the gunfire at the back of the house had surprised them and brought them to a brief halt. One of them started moving toward the archway that led to the hall.

I spent the eighteen rounds remaining in the magazine, and then dodged to the left of the window, standing with my back pressed to the house. I fumbled a spare magazine out of a sport-coat pocket, slapped it into the rifle.

As I looked up from that task, I saw headlights on the driveway, between the flanking oaks. But the cult's vehicle wasn't approaching. Backup wasn't on the way. The driver reversed as fast as he dared toward the county road. All the gunfire must have made him reconsider what duty required of him.

When I leaned to the shattered window and eased my head past the jamb, I saw a dead man lying in the living room. He must have removed his ski mask and goggles before entering the house. Shaved head. Face turned toward me. Mouth open. Eyes open. His expression wasn't one of pain or fear. He appeared to be puzzled.

There was no sign of the fourth cult member.

I didn't want to enter the house. I had nowhere else to go.

Forty-four

Proceeding with caution and proceeding slowly are sometimes two different things. In certain circumstances, momentum could be more important than caution, though it was never wise to dispense with wariness. I went up the steps and crossed the porch fast, cleared the open door in the usual fashion, and entered the foyer.

Directly ahead, the ground-floor hallway led to the kitchen at the back of the house. Living-room archway to the right. Past the archway, stairs also on the right. One flight visible, and the landing between floors. Two more doors on the right. Four doors on the left. Kitchen door closed at the farther end of the hall.

Silence. No blood on the floor. The fourth cultist had escaped the living room without being wounded.

I did not want to enter rooms to clear them and risk being cleared myself by a barrage fired through a window, felled by my own trick. The fourth cultist might be anywhere in the house . . . or he might be stalking me instead from outside.

By pushing a door open wide, I could scan most of a room and be reasonably content that no one lurked there. But the moment in the doorway, scanning, was an instant on the brink of death.

Yeats, the poet, wrote, *Many times man lives and dies / Between his two eternities.* The eternity before birth and the eternity after. Only in life do we die many times, from the mortal pain of loss and from all the griefs and fears with which this world can assail us. I wouldn't die in every doorway, perhaps only in one. I would, however, *expect* to die in each, and the expectation of death could, much like psychic magnetism, draw it to me.

Since I had returned to Pico Mundo, my usually keen intuition had been sharper and more reliable than ever. If I could not trust it without reservation on this night of nights, then when?

I passed doors without determining what lay behind them, passed rooms and perhaps a closet, and most likely a half-bath. At the third room on the left, I stopped. The door was neither closed nor open wide, but ajar. I stood by the jamb on the left and thrust the door open. When I heard something other than gunfire, I leaned forward and risked my face.

A study. Shelves of books. Sofa. Armchair and footstool. A handsome mahogany desk.

The fourth cultist stood behind the desk, at the farther end of the room. A woman. Dressed all in black like the others. She had put aside the hot ski mask, as well as the goggles that were of no use here. She stood with the stock of the rifle firmly in the crook of her right shoulder, aiming at the doorway. Perhaps what I had heard was her thin mewl of frustration, which issued from her again, as she worked the two-stage trigger without success. She pushed down repeatedly on the dual-paddle bolt catch, but either it failed to send the locked bolt forward or the bolt wasn't locked in the first place. Maybe she was out of ammunition. Whatever the case, she let loose a cry of vexation and threw the weapon at me, and it clattered to the floor short of the doorway.

I crossed the threshold, kicked the useless gun aside, and let her gaze into the muzzle of my combat rifle.

She preferred to stare at me, and with such hatred and anger that I could not doubt she wished me dead and by some method that would be intensely painful.

Returning her stare, I thought that my expression must have been a strange combination of dread and curiosity.

There might have been at least a bit of fear in her, too, because her contorted face reminded me of the faces of the drowned people in the submerged Pico Mundo of my dream.

But then it seemed that resignation took the place of rage. Her features relaxed. She shook her head. Wiped her face with one hand. Chewed her bottom lip for a moment. She let out a long sigh.

Regarding me now with weary indifference, she said, "Just do it already. Don't toy with me."

Although it is a cliché, appearances can be deceiving. Hers was so deceptive as to be fraud of the highest order. She was pretty, but her beauty alone was not the primary aspect of the deception. Skin so flawless that she wore no makeup, wide-set pellucid blue eyes that seemed incapable of guile, golden hair that an artist might bestow on paintings of angels, a brow so smooth it seemed never to have been furrowed by a negative emotion: She stood before me with an aura of childlike innocence that was belied only by the combat rifle with which she had tried to shoot me.

"Do it," she repeated.

I said, "What's your name?"

"Why do you care?"

"How old are you?"

She said nothing.

"You don't belong in this," I said.

"It's the only place I've ever belonged."

"With these maniacs?"

"They aren't maniacs."

"What are they, then?"

"Free," she said.

"Free? Free from what?"

"From everything."

"Freedom from everything is slavery."

"Oh? What am I enslaved to?"

"The void."

Her look of indifference was matched now by an insensibility in her voice that didn't fit well with the words she chose. "Just kill me, asshole."

I didn't pull the trigger. "All this tonight . . . what's it about?"

"Why do you care?"

"That's what I do. It's all I know. What's the point of being here if we don't care what happens?"

"The point is, there is no point." Whether her apathy was real or feigned, I could not tell. "To be and then not be." We stared at each other, as though the English we spoke was, in this instance, two different languages. Then she said, "Who *are* you?"

"Me? I'm nobody."

"You're somebody."

"Just a guy."

Her eyes widened slightly. "You're him."

"Nobody special."

Another silence. If she really didn't care how this ended, then it could end only in a way that would haunt me.

She said, "You can't kill a girl, can you?"

"I've killed a few."

"I don't believe you."

"It's true. I wish it weren't."

"But not an unarmed girl."

I didn't confirm her suspicion.

She smiled. "See how it is?"

"How is it?"

"I know what free is," she said. "You're not free. If you were free, I'd be dead now."

I understood her logic. It was the logic of the asylum.

"So I can just walk out of here," she said.

"No. I can't allow that."

"Why not? You have to have a good reason. Your way of thinking requires good reasons."

"You're a murderer."

"So are you," she said.

"No. I kill. You murder."

"What's the difference?"

"I kill murderers."

"Is this a riddle or something?"

"It's just the truth."

"I don't get it," she said.

With sorrow, I said, "No."

After a silence, she said, "Now what?"

I indicated a door framed by bookshelves. "Maybe that's a closet. Open it and show me."

She did as I asked, and it was a walk-in closet.

"You'll step in there," I told her. "I'll tip a chair under the knob to brace it, so you can't get out. Then I'll call the police."

"What if I won't?"

I thrust the rifle toward her. "Then I'll have to hurt you."

"Been established, hasn't it? You won't kill an unarmed girl."

"No. But I'll shoot to wound."

She studied me, trying to calculate a way out.

"Get in the closet."

She didn't move.

"Get in the closet."

When still she didn't move, I squeezed off a three-shot burst past her left hip, into the shelves of books.

"Four inches," I said. "That was the only difference between you walking normally or being crippled for the rest of your life."

Again her words were too edgy for her apathetic tone. "How many girls have you murdered, choirboy?"

"Killed," I corrected.

"How many? Are you ashamed to say how many?"

"Three."

"All justified, huh?"

"All in self-defense."

"That makes you feel righteous."

"No."

"Sleep like a baby, do you?"

"Not in a long time."

"You're him, all right."

"Like you, I'm nobody," I said. "We're two nobodies. But we're different."

"You're gonna find out we're somebodies," she said. "Some of us are geniuses."

"Geniuses create. They don't blow things up."

"Create, huh? Wait'll you see what some of us created."

"So tell me."

She hesitated, and I thought she almost began to share some secret that thrilled her. But then she held her tongue and stepped backward into the closet.

I crossed the room and started to close the door on her, and she blocked it with one foot. "Please don't. I'm claustrophobic, and I'm afraid of the dark."

"You *are* the dark," I said.

My mistake was getting too close to her. She was as lithe as an eel, as fast as a striking snake. She came in under the gun, and I've no idea from where she drew the knife.

She wanted to gut me, and I grabbed for her wrist, and although the blade didn't slice open my stomach, the point of it pierced my left palm. Before my eyes, the point exited the back of my hand—an inch or more of it gleaming and slick with blood. Before she could twist the knife and disable me with pain, I reared back to get the gun on her again and poked her with the muzzle and squeezed off a three-shot burst and at once another.

She fell back into the closet, landed on her rump, and knocked the back of her head against a shelf. She looked down at her torn stomach, tried to raise a hand to the wounds, but found perhaps that she was paralyzed below the neck.

She raised her head and met my eyes. The hatred and anger with which she'd first regarded me now returned and revealed the ugly face behind the mask of beauty. "Murderer."

I did not dispute the charge.

"See you in Hell, murderer."

"Maybe. But you're deceivers. All of you, deceivers. You've been deceiving me all night. One distraction after another. Sowing doubt. Hoping to sow despair. No more. I'm not listening anymore."

Her eyelids fluttered, almost closed, then opened wide. "Hey, dog. That's you. Just a dog. Know what?"

"What?"

Her voice grew thicker. "You a dog."

She was on her way out.

"You a dog?" she asked.

I didn't answer.

She found the strength to put a sneer in her voice. "Oh, yeah, you a dog."

"I didn't want this," I told her.

"Hey, dog, you got papers?"

A glaze dulled her eyes. She was only half here.

"You got papers?" she asked again. "You . . . just a dog."

And she was gone.

I put the rifle on the desk. The knife, a stiletto, hung from my left hand, stuck there. Not horrible pain. But bad enough. I gripped the yellow handle and with some care extracted the blade. On the way out, it felt as though it scraped a bone, and it must have touched a nerve, because I shivered head to foot and broke out in a sweat as cold as ice water.

Forty-five

After waking from the dream of the amaranth. The afternoon of the day that I would leave for Pico Mundo. The seaside cottage. Young Tim seeking seashells and playing in the surf. Annamaria and I on the sand side of the picket fence between yard and beach.

Then, as always, regardless of the place, the weather, she wore white athletic shoes, khaki pants, and a baggy sweater that could not conceal her pregnancy. Sometimes the sweater was pink, at other times yellow or blue or pale green, but it was always the same style. I had the strangest notion that Annamaria could have walked through a dusty marketplace crowded with women a thousand years before our time, two thousand, and have appeared to belong there, in spite of the shoes with rubber soles in an era before rubber, in spite of being clothed in fabrics unproducible then, in spite of the garments being in hues and having a consistency of color that no dye maker of that time could have achieved.

Watching Tim searching the shore for shells, she said, "Blossom Rosedale sold her house and wrapped up her affairs in Magic Beach. She'll be joining us here tonight for dinner."

"I wonder now," I said, "if she should have done that."

"She wants to be part of something that matters, odd one. And she believes that what you have been doing matters very much."

"But she was a part of Magic Beach. An important part. Everyone knew her, knew the art she created, and the quilts that won national awards."

"Being known by everyone is not the same as being loved."

"But she was loved. She had so many friends in Magic Beach."

Annamaria put a hand on my shoulder. She was petite, and her hands were delicate. Therefore, on those rare occasions when she placed a hand on my shoulder or took one of my hands in hers to impress upon me the importance of what she had to say, I was always surprised by the weight of her touch, by the strength of her grip.

"Young man, you have made many friends in your short life, and you are fortunate that a number of them love you, truly love you. But it's a rare person who can without reservation love someone with a face like the face that Blossom was left with after the fire."

"But in its own way, it's a beautiful face."

"Some people," she continued, "will be drawn to her because being her friend supports the image of themselves that they want others to have of them, makes them feel they're compassionate and tolerant and admirable. Such people may be her friends in a casual sense, they may even to some degree care about her. But when their true focus is always and all but entirely on themselves, they can't love her."

"Not all her friends can be like that," I said.

"Others will befriend her out of pity, but pity very often—not *always—comes with an unspoken and sometimes unrecognized element of contempt."*

I didn't even try to argue that point.

"Others," Annamaria said, "will befriend her out of sympathy, because they have suffered, too, though not as she has suffered. Sympathy is a nobler feeling than pity. But if sympathy is the principal reason that one person is drawn to another, there will always be an unbridgeable chasm between friendship and genuine love."

I was distressed to think that many of Blossom Rosedale's friends in Magic Beach might have been, for one reason or another, drawn to her because of her suffering, not mainly because of her clear quick mind and her great good heart. I refused to believe that there weren't many who truly loved her as she deserved to be loved.

When I expressed my distress to Annamaria, she patted my shoulder and then slipped her hands into the pockets of her roomy khaki pants. "Her mother died when she was four. Forty-five years have passed since her father set her on fire, when she was six. At fifty-one, why would she choose to dispose of her house, uproot herself, and come here to be part of your work if she didn't feel that, for the first time in her life, she was profoundly known for who she is, that she was at last cherished for who she truly is?"

And so we had come to one of those rare moments when I was speechless.

On the wet, compacted sand where the last of the purling surf reached before each rhythmic retreat, a sandpiper found something tasty and pecked the beach with a lack of skittishness that was unusual for its kind. The bird circled Tim, only a few feet

*from him, drawing closer each time it went around him, and the
boy stood watching it, amused and enchanted.*

"But I only knew Blossom for a few weeks," I said at last.

Annamaria smiled. "Isn't that remarkable?"

"If she wants to be part of . . . whatever it is I'm doing, what if
something happens? What if I'm not . . . doing it anymore?"

"You're too young to retire, odd one."

"You know what I mean, ma'am."

She watched the boy and the sandpiper, and I thought she
must be considering whether to be less mysterious than usual.
Finally she said, "If you're not doing what you do anymore, Blossom will find with Edie Fischer what she has found with you and
me."

"But Mrs. Fischer is eighty-six."

"She won't be retiring anytime soon, young man. Whatever
may happen in Pico Mundo, Edie Fischer will have work to do
for a long time. She will need a chauffeur, considering that you
proved not to be well suited for that job. She said you dawdled."

Tim stooped without frightening off the sandpiper. The bird
met his gaze. They stared at each other. Tim held out one hand,
palm up, and the bird regarded the hand for a moment before
continuing to peck the sand, now inches from the boy's right foot.

"The dream I had last night," I said, "ended with the amaranth."

"The flower that never dies."

"It died in my dream."

"Because that was just a dream. Things in dreams don't always mean what they seem to mean."

"It's from Greek mythology. The amaranth, I mean. There's no
such flower."

"The ancient Greeks were wise. They got many things right."

I said, "The big white flowers you always have floating in bowls. Like the one on the dinette table now. And the one in the living room. What are they?"

She appeared to be amused and yet dead serious when she said, "Amaranths."

"Where did you get them?"

"As I've said before, Oddie, I picked them from a tree in the neighborhood."

"Ma'am, I've walked the neighborhood a hundred times in the past couple of months, and I've never seen such flowers on a tree."

"Well, dear heart, you have to know where to look, and you have to be able to find a part of the neighborhood that not many people see."

As the sandpiper pecked tiny bits of whatever lunch from the beach, Tim had continued to hold out his hand. Now the bird regarded the offered palm once more, turned its head this way and that, and accepted the perch. Tim looked at us, astonished, as if to say, Do you see this?

"Remarkable," I said.

"As is everything around us, if we look."

The sandpiper flew from the hand, and Tim leaped to his feet to watch the bird soar skyward.

I said, "At dinner tonight with Blossom . . ."

"Yes?"

"Will you show me the trick with the amaranth? You've promised to show me, ma'am, but you never do."

"It is not a trick, odd one. It's better than that."

"So will you show me?"

"Not tonight. But soon."

Winging away, repeating its flight call—pjeev, pjeev, pjeev—*the sandpiper diminished to a dot, then vanished, but of course at the same moment it suddenly came into view of those who were farther north along the shore.*

"Ma'am?"

"Yes, Oddie?"

"Do you know the true and hidden nature of the world?"

"What do you think?"

"I think you do. I'll probably never understand it. Aside from English, I never was much good in school."

Forty-six

The puncture in my palm was more than an inch wide, but on the back of my hand, where the point of the blade had torn through, it was somewhat narrower. I bled freely, but not as voluminously as I would have bled if the nameless girl had severed an artery or vein when she attacked me. That was a bit of luck, because I had no time to go to a hospital emergency room.

In a washbasin drawer in the ground-floor half-bath at the Ainsworth house, I found first-aid supplies. Band-Aids, gauze pads, adhesive tape, rubbing alcohol, iodine . . .

A decorative container of liquid soap stood on the counter beside the sink. I turned the spigots, adjusted the water temperature so that it was warm but perhaps not so hot as to exacerbate the pain of the wound. The soap smelled of oranges. Lathering up proved to be about as much fun as sticking my hand in a wasps' nest.

After I rinsed off the soap, I kept my hands under the spout, though I could have stood there all night rinsing away the oozing blood. Maybe I was in shock, but I seemed to zone out as I watched the water foaming in the sink, the bubbles tinted pink and sparkling. I had set the temperature too hot, and the longer I kept my hand in gushing water, the more sharply the wound stung. Nevertheless, I stood there, watching the fast-flowing stream, grimacing at the torture but enduring it, because I was overcome by a sense that some revelation was impending, a revelation related to the water, the blood, the pain. There was something important that I knew—but didn't know I knew. Water, blood, pain . . .

The feeling passed, though not the pain. I was not a guy to whom revelations came easily.

Letting the water run in the sink, I poured rubbing alcohol and then iodine into both the entrance and exit wounds, all the while making shrill sounds of less than manly distress through my clenched teeth.

I used a small towel to wrap my left hand, to avoid dripping blood all over the marble countertop and the floor. With my right hand only, I prepared gauze pads. I found a bottle of thick and odorous fluid stoppered with a brush; it was used to paint shut small weeping wounds, creating a flexible sort of artificial skin, never meant for serious cuts into which bacteria might have been carried by a blade. My tetanus vaccination was current. Even if I might be trapping germs in the wound, I wasn't going to die of an infection. It took time for an infection to develop, and I doubted that I had enough hours left to accommodate one. The sealant dried swiftly, and I painted layer over layer. For the moment, anyway, the bleeding stopped. I applied the gauze pads and then wound adhesive tape around and around my hand.

Through all of that, I left the water running, listening to it rush into the sink and gurgle down the drain. In those sounds, there seemed to be words, a quick and liquid voice. I felt that everything depended on my understanding what was being said.

I wondered if being stabbed and having to kill the girl had left me in a state of shock that muddied my thinking. My skin was cold and clammy. A slight dizziness came and went and came again. Both were symptoms of a drop in blood pressure, which was one of the causes of physiological shock.

Bandaged, I watched the water for another half minute but then cranked it off when enlightenment did not come.

I was still cold and clammy, but the lightheadedness seemed to have passed.

I dropped the lid of the toilet. Sat. Fumbled my phone from a pocket. Held it in my injured hand. My good hand was shaking so that I had to concentrate to press the correct digits. Chief Porter had two cell phones. I figured he was fielding a lot of calls on the first one. I dialed the number that only Mrs. Porter and I knew. He answered, asked me to hold, and finished a call on the other phone.

When he came back to me, he sounded harried, which I'd never known him to be before. He knew about the explosions, of course, not just those that I had heard and seen, but another one at a warehouse at the opposite end of town from the Blue Sky Ranch.

"All hell's breaking loose tonight." He was furious. "These madmen, these goddamn *losers*."

"Sir, nothing that's happened so far is the main event. These are all distractions, to get your men spread thin."

"Distractions from the dam?"

"I don't think it's going to be the dam."

"I've got four men at Malo Suerte ever since I talked to you. If it's not the dam, I need them elsewhere."

I hesitated. "I don't know if it's the dam or not. I just don't know. Sir, there are three dead men and one dead woman here at Lauren Ainsworth's place."

"Not Lauren."

"No, sir. She and the girls are safe."

"Thank God."

"These are cultists. Two more are dead just inside the orchard fence that runs beside the Ainsworth driveway."

"Six altogether?"

"Six."

"Did you . . ."

"Yes, sir. I did. I did them all. They've forced me to be a killing machine, and I can't . . . I can't take much more of it." My voice broke, and for a moment, I couldn't piece it together again.

"Son, are you all right?"

My voice returned, but to my ear it didn't sound much like me. "She stabbed me in the hand, but that's okay. I can take more of that, but I can't take more killing."

"I'll be there right away, Oddie."

"No. No, sir. No. I'm leaving here as soon as I hang up. Did the CSI team finish in that motor home?"

"Yes. The coroner removed the bodies."

"You search the place, find anything?"

"Concealed gun closet. Weapons, ammo. Hundred thousand in cash. Passports and driver's licenses, their pictures but different names."

"Wolfgang, Jonathan, and Selene."

"Actually Woodrow, Jeremy, and Sibyl."

"What do you know about them?"

"We're working it. One or all three look to've been junkies. Forty hypodermic needles in the fridge, lots of ampules of drugs."

"What drug?"

"The lab is analyzing."

"You at the fairground?"

"Just left there to—"

"Go back. I'll meet you there. Maybe it's the dam, maybe something else. But the operation's being run from the carnival."

"Nothing can happen there that would put the town underwater."

"Remember, sometimes my dreams are symbolic, not literal."

Even in his silence, I could hear his alarm. Then he said, "There's ten, twelve thousand people in the fairgrounds tonight."

I looked at my watch. Ten minutes past ten o'clock.

"If anything's going to happen there," I said, "it might not be until the crowd is at its peak for the big drawing. Eleven forty-five might be the target time."

"*Might* doesn't cut it, Oddie. If they've moved that C-4 in here, I've got to evacuate this place *now*."

My hand throbbed like an abscessed tooth. "The cult will have people on the midway, Chief. The moment they see an evacuation starting, they'll move up the strike time."

"Maybe the timer's already set, and they can't change it."

"Or maybe they're using a cell phone as a detonator, all they have to do is make a call to it."

"Sonofabitch."

I stood up from the toilet, though it was an appropriate seat, considering that the cult seemed on the verge of flushing away

Pico Mundo. And more than this one town. Maybe much more. "I'm walking right along the edge of it, Chief."

"The edge of what?"

"The truth. Understanding. I can almost see it. I'll be there in twenty minutes."

"Not from where you are."

"Quarter to eleven at the latest."

"Leaves us just an hour."

"Meet me at a concession on the southwest side of the midway. Place called Face It."

"Wait a second. When you were on the midway earlier, did you see any bodachs?"

"No, sir."

"Not even one? Then nothing's going to happen at the carnival. If it was going to be blown sky-high, the place would be crawling with those bodachs of yours."

"I don't know, sir. I don't know anymore. Maybe they've learned that I can see them. Maybe they're manipulating me by staying out of sight. See you soon."

I terminated the call, stepped out of the half-bath into the ground-floor hallway, and discovered the gut-shot dead woman waiting for me.

Forty-seven

The spirits of really bad people seldom lingered this side of the Other Side. When their bodies died, most of them seemed to leave this world as if sucked out of it by the largest vacuum cleaner in the universe. The spirits that lingered were those of people who were basically good, regardless of what faults they might have had in life. On the day of the shootings at the Green Moon Mall, not long before Stormy's death, I had been confronted by the festering spirit of a man who'd been dead for a day and who felt that he had a score to settle with me. I had not since found myself the target of an assault by a ghost. Then the nameless girl in black, who had put a stiletto through my hand, suddenly appeared in the hallway and, no more subtle in death than in life, conveyed her anger by thrusting two fingers at me, the middle one on each hand.

The dead don't talk, but they have ways of getting their point across. In addition to rude gestures and more benign pantomime, they can go poltergeist, especially the bad ones. I had lost a perfectly good stereo system to a poltergeist when I was seventeen.

I had learned not to show fear in these cases. My fear empowers them. She glared at me, but I stared calmly back at her and said, "Go away. Aren't you eager to see what reward you'll get when you cross over?"

Earlier, in the study, after she had thrown her malfunctioning combat rifle at me, her face had been twisted by hatred and anger. Because she had reminded me of the faces of the drowned people in my dream, I had thought I also read fear in her features.

At the moment, there was no fear in her, only hatred and anger so griddle-hot that it might have fried an egg. Yet still I thought of the floating dead in that submerged Pico Mundo.

She put two fingers to my lips, apparently to indicate that she would tolerate no further talk from me. The fingers felt real to me, as did the touch of any spirit.

Cat-quick, she clawed at my right eye, as if to tear it from its socket. But no spirit could harm a living person by touch, not even those that were more radically evil than this one. This world belonged to the living, not to the dead. Their clawing fingers and their fists passed through us. Their bites could not draw blood.

When she realized that she couldn't blind or bleed me, her anger grew hotter, boiled into rage. Her beauty distorted like a reflection in a fun-house mirror. The deceptive look of childlike innocence that she had possessed earlier gave way to the truth of her: malice of an especially sinister and bitter degree, a venomous detestation of anyone who did not share her enthusiasm for cruelty, for murder, and who did not worship raw power as she did.

One option existed for some spirits to harm the living. If the malevolence in them was ripe enough, if they loathed every virtue and celebrated every abomination, they were sometimes able to convert their demonic rage into a fearsome energy that they could channel into anything made by the hand of man. We called them poltergeists.

The woman thrust her arms full length, hands palm-out, as if she were some enraptured faith healer proclaiming her power to a tent full of the desperate and gullible, but she didn't have healing in mind. Pulses of energy issued from her hands, visible but without effect on me, concentric rings of power that caused doors along the hallway to slam shut and crash open.

One of the two carpet runners peeled off the floor, undulated in the air, like some giant parasitic flatworm. It lashed the walls, knocked paintings off their hangers. When it flew at me, I ducked and felt it slap against my back as it ceased to be airborne and tumbled toward the kitchen.

The spirit herself exploded into frenzied motion, careening along the hallway, ricocheting from wall to wall, causing the lights to flicker and a groaning to arise within the walls, as if the wood studs were torquing behind the sheetrock. A table in the foyer rattled along the hardwood floor in a stiff-legged dance, and flung itself through the archway into the living room.

Poltergeists could express power but couldn't control it. They were blind fury, thrashing torment. They could harm a living person only by chance.

Nevertheless, I could still be knocked unconscious by a flying chair or struck dead by a bronze statue that had become a missile. To die triumphant, after defeating the cultists, would be all right, even perhaps desirable. But after I had come this far at such cost, to be decapitated by a round glass tabletop, flung like a discus, would be so infuriating that in death I might linger long enough to work off my anger with a little poltergeisting of my own, though I had nothing against the Ainsworths or their furniture.

The spirit did her whirling-dervish act, out of the hallway, into the living room. I heard bric-a-brac and light furniture and lamps being gathered up as if by a tornado, and I ran for the front door. A coffee-table book, a thick volume, flew past me, its glossy pages flapping like wings. Something cracked against the side of my head—a candy dish, which fell to the floor and shattered. I didn't see stars, like characters did in those old Chuck Jones cartoons, but I did see scores of little dark spots swarming in my vision, trying to coalesce and drop me blind to the floor. I kept going, however, and my vision cleared by the time I went through the front door, crossed the porch, and stumbled down the steps.

I didn't expect the spirit to follow me. Poltergeists usually thrash around like drunken politicians on a junket to some education conference at an offshore resort that is actually an anything-goes whorehouse. They exhaust themselves and wander off, having forgotten what they were doing or why they were there.

As I hurried to the stables that lay to the east, I thought the tumult in the residence was already subsiding. I shouted for Lauren, and after a minute she appeared in the darkness, wary and at first reluctant to switch on the flashlight.

"Where are the girls?" I asked.

The whites of Lauren's eyes appeared radiant in the night, owlish, and her voice trembled as she said, "All the shooting."

"It's finished."

Fortunately, either the spirit in the house had already worn itself out or its power had been spent to the extent that nothing more than pillows and afghans were being thrown around, the rage having faded to a hissy fit.

"What's happening," Lauren asked, "what the hell was that all about, the explosions, my God, the gunshots, *like machine guns*?"

"Where are the girls?" I asked again.

"I told them to wait, wait and be ready to run, till I was sure it was safe."

"You can't go back into the house. There are dead people in the house."

"What dead people?"

"Very bad dead people. Four of them. Two on the patio. You don't want the kids to see them. *You* don't want to see them. Is there a friend, family, you can stay with?"

She looked bewildered but nonetheless poised, and I could see from where the girls got their equanimity. "My sister, Arlene. She lives over in the heights. But what's this all about?"

"No time for that. Where in the house do you keep your car keys? I'll go in and get them for you."

"We keep them in the cars. There's no crime around here to worry about." She realized what she'd said, looked toward the house, then toward the huge gasoline fire in the distance. "Is it over, whatever it is?"

"No. We need to get out of here. You'll have to drive."

"All right."

"You'll have to drive *fast*."

I was holding up my left hand, and she saw the bandage. "What happened to you?"

"Stabbed. Maybe I could drive your second car if I had plenty of time. But driving the way I need to, I'd pull open the wound before I made it to the county road. Get the girls, come on, let's blow this place before something else happens."

When Lauren called them, Veronica and Victoria appeared with Muggs, the Labrador retriever.

In memory I heard the dying woman in the closet. *You a dog. Oh, yeah, you a dog.*

The girls didn't appear to be crying. Scared but stalwart. The dog wagged his tail.

The garage was a freestanding structure, separate from the house. We entered through the man-size door between two roll-ups. There were four vehicles. A Ford pickup with an extended bed. A Ford Expedition. A BMW. A 1947 Ford Sportsman Woody that Dave, her late husband, had fully restored and customized.

I thought Lauren would choose the BMW, for its power, but she wanted the Expedition. She told the girls to get in the back-seat, buckle up, and keep the dog lying on the seat between them, so that he wouldn't get hurt.

"When I say *fast*," I told her, "I mean to hell with speed limits. You've got to drop me off at the fairground before you take the girls to your sister's, and I need to be there already. Chief Wyatt Porter is waiting for me."

The resort to name-dropping was a little mortifying. But nearly everyone in Pico Mundo respected and admired the chief. Some people incorrectly thought of me as a hero, but my supposed heroics were old news. I figured that Lauren was more likely to go to extremes to help Chief Porter than she was to help a fry cook who was, let's face it, eccentric to the point of geekiness.

"Fast means *fast*. Yeah, I hear you," she said, as she went around to the driver's door. "I use the Expedition a lot more than any of the others. I can make it smoke."

I got into the passenger seat and closed the door. I drew the Glock from the shoulder rig under my sport coat and put it in my lap before engaging the safety harness. Then I picked it up, held it.

As she raised the big garage door with a remote, Lauren looked at the pistol, looked at me. "What's going to happen?"

"I don't know."

In the backseat, the twins were saying, "Good boy, good puppy, brave puppy."

Lauren started the engine. Popped the handbrake. Reversed out into the night. She turned the wheel hard, brought the Expedition around, shifted into drive, and powered away from the garage without taking the time to put down the door.

Forty-eight

Lauren Ainsworth might have made a pretty darn good NASCAR racer. Considering the extent to which she combined speed with caution, maybe it would be better to compare her to an ambulance driver. I knew the Expedition would have plenty of power, but I worried about its higher center of gravity, which could be a problem with any SUV. If she cornered too fast on a road not banked quite like it ought to be, we had a higher chance of rolling than we would have had with the BMW. We hadn't gone a mile before I stopped fretting about that, because she was in complete control, the Expedition a glove and she the hand within it.

Never taking her eyes off the highway, she said, "Who's blowing things up, what's happening at the fairground that you have to be there yesterday?"

"I need to think, Lauren. Sorry, but I need to think. I've got this brain-buster thing to figure out."

"You figure," she said. "Don't pay any mind to me."

The first thing I thought about was the woman cultist, how she had looked in the study, after she'd thrown aside the useless rifle.

Her face had been wrenched with anger and hatred. And yet she had reminded me of the drifting corpses in the dream, whose faces had been contorted in expressions of terror. Later, when she manifested in the hallway and went poltergeist, her hatred and rage had been still worse, demonic—and yet again I had thought of the drowners in the dream.

I remembered the last scene of that watery nightmare. The corpse of a little girl, maybe seven years old. Blond hair billowing around her head as the currents brought her alongside me. Her protruding, bloodshot eyes had rolled and focused on me. A froth of gas bubbles burst from her open mouth. And with them came a word: *Contumax.*

With that, I had exploded out of the dream, sitting straight up in bed, flailing at the sheets, heart racing. I had been terrified not merely by the vision of a drowned Pico Mundo, but also—and perhaps primarily—by that blond child who'd spoken the first word of the cult's two-word greeting. *Contumax. Potestas.* Her expression hadn't been one of extreme fright, had it? No. On reconsideration, her eyes had bulged and rolled like those of a maddened beast, and her expression had been one of white-hot rage, beyond rage, fury. But a child that young wouldn't be a member of the cult. She had frightened me awake, but she hadn't been what she appeared to be, hadn't been a threat, had been instead a victim.

I thought of Connie, sister to Ethan, the young woman who had painted me as a harlequin at Face It. Raven hair and celadon eyes. She had been in the dream, too, a drowned corpse drifting in the eerie light of the submerged town. I went to the cauldron of memory and tried to conjure that part of the dream in my mind's eye. The scene emerged: Connie's face but not as she was in life,

as she had been in the dream of death. Either I had misremem-
bered her expression when I woke from the nightmare, or I was
misremembering it now, for this time I saw not choking terror in
her face but extreme rage. And more than rage. Savage intent.
Hatred. Agony, too. And anguish. And fear, yes, but the fear
wasn't dominant, as I'd previously recalled; it was only one element in an extraordinary mien of twisted and tortured emotions.

We had reached a more populated portion of Pico Mundo, and
when Lauren turned a corner, traffic clogged the way ahead. At
once she hung a U-turn, arcing back into the intersection from
which we had just come, eliciting a Gershwin symphony of shrill
horn blasts as indignant drivers gave her the what-for. She swung
into a street that led in a direction we didn't want to go, turned
right into an alleyway that paralleled the jammed street and *did*
go the direction we wanted.

She said, "How crazy do I have to be? What's at stake, Oddie?
Tell me what's at stake."

"Everything," I said, somewhat surprised to hear such certainty in my voice. "Everything's at stake. Thousands of lives, the
whole town, maybe more than that, maybe much more."

She glanced at me, shocked. "Thousands?"

"Tens of thousands," I said, speaking intuitively now, better
understanding the dream.

She said, "Worse than the mall . . . back then."

"Much worse. Immeasurably worse."

The alley was narrow. Businesses backed up to it, some of
them restaurants that were still open and busy at that hour. If an
unwary kitchen staffer threw open a door and took a few quick
steps into the alleyway, we might not be able to stop in time if we
were going too fast.

She pressed down on the accelerator and at the same time began to pound the horn incessantly, warning off anyone who might be about to step in our way. The tires stuttered over cobblestones as old as any pavement in Pico Mundo, and we flashed past hulking Dumpsters with little room for error.

Trying to tune out the blaring horn, the racing engine, the periodic shriek of brakes, I returned to the brain-buster mystery that I needed to solve. If the faces of all the drowned people in the dream had not been fixed in expressions of terror . . . If fear and agony and anguish, although present, were lesser elements, and if their faces were frozen instead in screams of rage, contorted by hatred, were they the victims of violence or the perpetrators of it? Or could they somehow be both the victims and perpetrators?

As I'd told Chief Porter, certain of my prophetic dreams could be taken literally, but others were figurative. The meaning of them needed to be deciphered from symbolic imagery. And though I could make delicious fluffy pancakes every time I mixed the batter, I was not as reliably able to interpret my dreams.

Sometimes I wondered if I had everything backward, my life and purpose and meaning all backward. Maybe the best thing I had to offer was fry cookery of a high order, and maybe my paranormal abilities were nothing more than the equivalent of a talent for farting on command, better repressed than indulged. I, no less than anyone, was capable of self-delusion, of pride that led me to embrace a grander image of myself than was the truth.

If the people of Pico Mundo were destined to become both victims and perpetrators of violence, if I'd mistaken their expressions of rage-hatred-agony-anguish for terror, then perhaps I was wrong to think that the image of a flood should be taken literally, no matter how real it had seemed. Maybe the dam wouldn't be blown. Maybe there would be no tsunami from any source. *But then what did the water mean?*

"We're here," Lauren Ainsworth declared, pulling to a stop on the shoulder of the highway, across from the main entrance to the Maravilla County Fairgrounds.

My watch read 10:39, and I said, "You made incredible time, ma'am. I owe you one."

I holstered the Glock.

When I looked up, I saw that Lauren, who had been a rock until now, had stopped repressing her emotions. Tears streamed down her face. She leaned over the console, put an arm around my shoulders, and pulled me toward her until her forehead and mine met. "You don't owe me one, Oddie. I owe you everything. You saved our lives."

Because I still didn't know what horror was coming, she and the girls might yet be dead before the night was done. "Get the girls to your sister's house in the heights, ma'am. Maybe it'll be safer in the heights."

She kissed my cheek and let me go, but then the twins wanted to kiss me on the cheek, too. Also in tears, Veronica leaned forward from the back and then Victoria, weeping as well, but that wasn't the end of the good-byes.

Muggs scrambled off the backseat. Standing with his hind feet on the floor, he pawed forward between the front seats and came face-to-face with me. I would have been fine with a dog kiss, as long as it was on the cheek; but Muggs had something else in mind. His eyes met mine, and he grew very still, his gaze penetrating, his demeanor solemn. As when I had met Lou Donatella, the dwarf in a bear suit, I thought, *This is A Moment, stay with it.* Also as when I'd met that little person, I had no idea what I meant by *A Moment.*

Muggs and I remained eye-to-eye just long enough for the girls and their mother to recognize the strangeness of this final good-bye, if that's what it was. Then the dog shook his head, flapping his floppy ears, and terminated our moment with a sneeze.

"Got to go," I said, and threw open the passenger door.

Forty-nine

At this late hour, three of the ticket booths at the fairground were closed, leaving only the fourth and fifth. As previously, I went to ticket booth number four. The plump woman with long ringlets of auburn hair remained on duty. She was reading a paperback book, and when she put it aside to take my money, I saw that it was *The Last Good Bite* by P. Oswald Boone, my friend and mentor, which wasn't surprising, considering that he had sold more than a hundred million copies of his mysteries and that his fans were legion. Handing me an admission ticket, the cashier said, "Smart of you to come back. You should never have left before the big drawing. Got to be here to win. You're the one tonight, honey. You're the one tonight."

The midway was more crowded than I had ever seen it, the recent explosions having been too distant for the sound to penetrate the ceaseless whiz-bang and ballyhoo of the carnival. People waited in line at every ride, stood two-deep at the game booths, swarmed the concourse. I dodged and juked and slipped through the throng, using so many excuse-mes that I was glad they didn't cost anything.

The first people I saw when I arrived at the Face It tent were three lovely black girls in their late teens and early twenties, so similar that they must be sisters, two of them standing, one of them in the chair where Connie's mother worked on her face with a brush and sponge. The seated girl was being painted to match her sisters, and they were the bird women from my dream of the amaranth. In the dream, I had been lying on my back, clutching an urn full of ashes, and these three pretty girls with white-and-gold feathered faces had been standing close, looking down at me, as had been Blossom Rosedale and Terri Stambaugh, who was an Elvis fan of the first rank as well as my friend and boss from the Pico Mundo Grille.

Chief Porter stood on the farther side of the tent, talking to Connie. The artist saw me first and said, "You washed off your face."

"Yes, ma'am. I liked it so much I would have worn it for days, except when I left the fairground for a while, it kind of freaked out people."

"Want me to paint you again?"

"Thank you, no. I need to talk to the chief here."

She looked at my left hand. "Are you all right?"

I realized the wound had opened. Blood slowly soaked through the thickness of gauze I had taped over it.

"Nothing serious," I assured her. "Just an accident with a stapler."

"I wish my brother was here," Connie said. "You need an Ethan on your side."

Evidently, she didn't buy the stapler story. To give the chief and me privacy, she went to her mother's station to watch as the third bird woman's face was completed to perfection.

I expect that Wyatt Porter could maintain his cool through a volcanic eruption, although on this occasion he appeared undeniably harried. With his bloodhound jowls and his bagged, heavy-lidded eyes, he made people think of their favorite uncle. If you were perceptive, however, you saw a little bit of a Robert Mitchum look to him, and you knew that the avuncular face disguised a whip-smart no-nonsense hard-assed officer of the law. Now he had more of a Mitchum look than ever, as if anyone gave him the slightest reason to bust their chops, he would keep on punching even after he'd broken all his knuckles.

He said, "I told you ten or twelve thousand on the fairground, but now we have the gate count, and it's over fifteen thousand. Six of my guys plus nine state police are walking the midway, looking for something suspicious, all in plainclothes so they won't spook these crazy bastards into pushing the button early. Fifteen guys in a crowd of fifteen thousand, with no idea what 'suspicious' looks like in this case."

"Earlier, on the phone, sir, you said Wolfgang bought a couple of concessions. Maybe that's where it'll all go down."

Chief Porter shook his head. "That would be too easy. According to Lionel Sombra, Wolfgang—his real name was Woodrow Creel—hired longtime carnies to work his places, people that have been with Sombra Brothers in one role or another for fifteen, twenty years and more. Anyway, using the murder investigation as an excuse, about two hours ago, we closed both concessions for the night, sent the workers away. Left my guys, Taylor Pipes and Nick Korker, guarding both locations. It didn't seem to alarm these cultists, didn't cause them to pull the trigger." He indicated my bandaged hand, which I held down at my side, letting it drip. "That doesn't look good, son."

"Looks bad, but it doesn't hurt," I lied.

As Chief Porter watched fairgoers streaming past the open front of the Face It tent, a sea of humanity in its infinite variety, he said, "Doesn't seem right that these lunatics should look like anyone else. Can't you do your magnetism thing and draw a couple of them to you?"

"Don't have a name. Don't have a face. Don't have anything to focus on, sir. What about the other two who were executed in that motor home, Jonathan and Selene? Do you know anything about them?"

"Real names were Jeremy and Sibyl von Witzleben. Husband and wife. Both of them doctors of some kind."

The hundred different tunes issuing from attractions up and down the long midway had usually before seemed more festive than not, even if the many braided melodies were to the ear what a line of prose would be to the eye of a dyslexic reader. But now the music began to slide slowly into a sour disharmony.

"Those two," the chief continued, "had more stamps in their passports than a coyote has fleas. Spent most of last year down in Venezuela, which is a sewer these days. Food shortages, toilet-paper rationing, runaway inflation, death squads. Who in his right mind would want to spend a year there?"

"Doctors of what?"

"We're researching that. I'm waiting for a call."

We were standing near the front of the tent, and as we looked out at the midway, the razzle-dazzle of carnival lights seemed to be brighter and more frantic than before. The blinkers blinked faster. The pulsers pulsed faster. Waves of color chased one another faster, faster through the various fiber-optic designs.

Indicating the people on the concourse, the chief sounded as if frustration was about to make him scream. "Point me to one of these hateful bastards, Oddie. You see things I can't. You always have. See something for me. I really need you to see something for me, son."

My mind was still awash with the flood dream that evidently wasn't about a flood, the coyotes that had been something more than coyotes, the sandpiper that had flown from Tim's hand and vanished from our perspective only to come into view to people farther up the beach, the safe house that had appeared to be so Victorian but had been woven through with hidden high-tech defenses, the angelic face of the cult girl in Lauren's house and the vicious face of the same girl gone poltergeist. . . .

As the chief's cell phone rang and he answered it, I tried to sweep clean the junk shop that was my mind, and began to study the people on the concourse, mere feet away. He was right. I had always seen things he couldn't, things that no one else could see. Why not here, why not now, when it mattered so very much and so urgently?

He had several short questions for his caller and was terminating the call just as I saw two men ambling by as if they had never known a care in their entire lives, eating ice-cream bars dipped in chocolate and served on sticks, chatting and laughing and enjoying the flash and bustle of the carnival. They were in their twenties. Looked like surfer dudes from out of town. Blond and tanned and fit. Dressed in jeans and T-shirts. One of them had a red-and-black tattoo that began at his wrist and wound up his right arm, where it disappeared under the sleeve of his T-shirt. It was not an ordinary tattoo of a dragon or a snake or a mermaid, but a series of hieroglyphics, a statement of some kind, maybe a scrap of satanic prayer or a defiant pledge spelled in the singular symbols of the same pictographic language that I had seen on the coven's estate in Nevada, that had been painted on the tailgate of the Cadillac Escalade that tried to run me down during my motorcycle trip to Pico Mundo.

"Sir," I said, and by my tone alerted him. "See the surfer guys eating ice cream? The one with the tattoo, he's one of them. Which means the guy with him must be one of them, too."

"You're sure?"

"Yes."

Looking away from the cultists lest they notice his interest and take flight, Chief Porter unclipped a walkie-talkie from his belt. It was the size of a cell phone. He pressed SEND and held it down while he talked. To the fifteen plainclothes officers walking the midway, he said, "Contact. Outside the Face It tent." He described the two men. "Converge if you're nearby."

One designated respondent said, "Ten-four," to confirm that the message had been received.

"If they go in an attraction, off the concourse, maybe we can take them quietly. Squeeze them hard for information."

"Ten-four."

"That phone call," the chief said to me, "was a prelim report on Jeremy and Sibyl von Witzleben."

The ice-cream eaters had stopped to watch people playing a dart game involving a spinning wheel, an array of balloons, and a barker who distracted the players with amusing patter.

"The von Witzlebens were both microbiologists. She was also an epidemiologist, a specialist in epidemic diseases. He had an advanced degree in virology."

"What were they up to in Venezuela?" I wondered.

Having lost interest in the dart game, the ice-cream eaters meandered east along the concourse.

The chief said, "They were doing something that could be done only where the government, courts, and cops are all hugely corrupt."

The ice-cream eaters began to melt into the crowd.

"Damn, where are my guys? Gotta keep those two in sight till I can turn them over to plainclothes."

"I'll do it, sir."

"You don't have one of these," he said, indicating the walkie-talkie, "and you can't have mine."

As he hurried from the tent to trail the ice-cream eaters at a distance, all the thoughts and memories ricocheting through my head at last coalesced:

Standing at the sink in the half-bathroom at Lauren Ainsworth's house, watching the rushing water pour over the wound in my hand, the water too hot, exacerbating the pain, but I don't cool it down, because I'm gripped by a sense of a pending revelation related to the water and the blood and the pain, aware that there is something I know but do not know I know, something about blood and terrible pain and water. The plump cashier with the auburn hair saying, "You're the one tonight, honey, you're the one tonight." Gypsy Mummy and the four blank cards, four blank cards suggesting no future, no future at all, four when one would have conveyed the message. Perhaps the one thing I knew about the true and hidden nature of the world was that there were no coincidences. The Cadillac Escalade burning at the bottom of the desert arroyo. On the phone with Chief Porter, while he's telling me about Wolfgang and Jonathan and Selene, now known to be

Woodrow and Jeremy and Sibyl, and he says, "One or all three look to've been junkies ... hypodermic needles ... ampules of drugs." Being chased through the pitch-black department store, relying on my special guide dog, my psychic magnetism. Eye-to-eye with Muggs. Microbiologists, epidemiology, virology. Four blank cards, four predictions of death. The Four Horsemen of the Apocalypse: Pestilence, War, Famine, and Death. But no bo-dachs. Why no bodachs if mass murder is about to happen? The dying girl in the closet, saying, "You a dog. Oh, yeah, you a dog." Blood and terrible pain and water. Blind in the death-black de-partment store, led by my faithful guide dog, good old psychic magnetism, led to the man-made cave of suburban bats. A mini-mum of thirty percent of any colony of bats is infected with rabies. The auburn-haired woman in ticket booth number four, reading Ozzie Boone's The Last Good Bite, *a novel in which death by bats was the red herring. There are no coincidences. The dying girl saying, "Hey, dog, you got papers?"* Papers *meaning proof of vaccination. Hypodermic needles, ampules of some drug. No, ampules of a vaccine. Blood and terrible pain and water. Hydrophobia. Another name for rabies.* Hydrophobia. *More facts courtesy of Ozzie Boone: The victim of rabies suffers intense thirst, but any attempt to drink induces violent, agonizing spasms of the throat, hence the word* hydrophobia, *fear of water. Eye and facial muscles become paralyzed. Infected dogs foam at the mouth, are wild with rage and quick to bite. Venezuela, a dicta-torship, virtually a terrorist state. The first two of the Four Horse-men, Pestilence and War. Pestilence as a weapon in the silent war that is part of the true and hidden nature of the world. Wea-ponized rabies. The cultists vaccinated, the rest of us not. No bodachs because tonight involves only a quiet infection of thou-*

sands, no one aware, and the dying doesn't start for days, the dying and the violence, people raging like rabid dogs, which is when the bodachs would show up in legions. The sandpiper winging through the air, vanishing to one observer but visible to others. To infect the thousands on the midway, the weaponized rabies would have to be airborne, invisible to those who breathed it in, its presence known only to the vaccinated cultists.

The C-4 was a distraction.

The dam had never been a target.

Nothing had been what it appeared to be. Or, rather, everything had been more than it appeared to be.

Fifteen thousand infected. And then how many would *they* infect before their symptoms became apparent?

This wasn't only about Pico Mundo. The secret war fought all around us by armies little noticed was about to escalate.

"Norman, are you all right?"

I turned to Connie, who had put a hand on my shoulder. My horror must have been evident, because she flinched as if something about my face, my eyes, frightened her.

"No, you're not all right—are you?"

"The man Wolfgang Schmidt," I said. "Did you know him?"

"*Did* I know him? Has something happened to him?"

News of the three brutal murders in the carnie park had not spread to every corner of the midway in the three hours since they occurred, probably because Wyatt Porter had done his best to keep a lid on it.

"Do you know him?" I asked.

"I know who he is. But I don't know him."

"He bought two concessions."

"Some say he never was from a carnie family. Norman, your hand needs medical attention."

"What concessions did he buy?"

"They belonged to Solly Nickles. Solly got lung cancer and it went fast with him. His kids didn't want a carnival life, so he took the best offer. Schmidt overpaid."

"*Which* concessions, Connie?"

"The duck shoot and the fun house."

In my mind's eye, I saw the facade of the fun house: the giant dimensional sculpture of an ogre's face, twenty feet from chin to crown, almost as wide, detailed and scary but hokey at the same time, its crazed eyes rolling in its sockets. Periodically a growl issued from its open mouth, a growl and a strong blast of compressed air that traveled twenty feet into the promenade, mussing patrons' hair and startling them.

I stepped out of the tent, not quite into the throng, scanning the crowd for Chief Porter. The pumping calliope, the hundred other musics, the laughter and screams of the marks on the thrill rides, the smells and dazzling lights made me a little dizzy. I could not see the chief. He had followed the ice-cream eaters out of sight.

Behind me, Connie said, "Norman, what's wrong?"

The fun house was east along this leg of the concourse.

I glanced at my wristwatch. Eleven o'clock.

"Norman, your hand."

Forty-five minutes. Unless someone got nervous for whatever reason and pulled the trigger sooner.

I pressed forward through the resisting crowd, east toward the fun house.

Fifty

The midway crowd was bigger than a crowd, a throng, bigger than a throng, a multitude, the ceaseless press and crush of human flesh. People of all kinds and ages. Senior citizens with canes and hearing aids and bifocals. Teenagers in groups, dressed and accessorized in rebellion and yet dressed alike, some intent on texting or playing games on their phones even with the riotous carnival clamoring for their attention and their dollars all around them. Children eating cotton candy and ice cream and popcorn, children who should have been home in bed but were here with their parents, children with painted faces, none of them painted like Death, yet each of them a dead child walking if the cult succeeded. Short men with tall women. Fat women with skinny men. The gay, the straight, and the confused. Democrats and Republicans and those who, if asked, would shout *Neither!* The rich and the poor. All races, all creeds, all targets for those who did not believe that life was precious.

By the time I reached the fun house, I still had not seen Chief Porter or the two men he was tailing. In the giant face of the ogre, the eyes were not rolling as before, but were fixed straight ahead. The sculpted beast no longer issued threatening roars accompanied by great blasts of breath. The eerie music had been silenced. The lights that previously pulsed and flashed were dark now. A sign, hanging from a cord strung between two stanchions on the entrance ramp simply declared CLOSED.

I didn't think it wise to enter the attraction by way of the ramp, in plain view of everyone on the concourse. Some people might recognize me, and a few of them might be cult members.

In truth, I assumed that it wouldn't be wise to enter the fun house by any means whatsoever. But I was exhausted and bleeding and terrified. It wasn't possible for me to buy an ice cream and go to the carousel instead and ride around on one of the swan benches provided among the horses for those who were in no condition to climb into a saddle and hold on to a brass pole.

Acting as if I was a person of authority in the Sombra Brothers operation, with my bleeding left hand thrust under my sport coat as if soothing an acidic stomach or doing a Napoleon imitation, I left the concourse. I walked between the fun house and the Wall of Death, which featured performances by a motorcycle daredevil riding at high speed, parallel to the ground, around the wall of a circular arena about fifteen feet deep, doing tricks, while the patrons on tiered bleachers looked down at him, waiting for something to go wrong that would turn him into Jell-O in a costume. They were between shows, but gasoline fumes lingered from the previous one.

Most of the carnival's attractions were in tents, but the fun house had board walls with a canvas roof. They had probably put it up and torn it down a thousand times without incident, but I doubted that there was a structural engineer in the world who, upon a close inspection of the place, wouldn't have the vapors. Images of ghosts, vampires, and werewolves covered the side wall, but they were no more scary than Mickey Mouse.

At the back of the structure, a loosely fitted wooden door was labeled KEEP OUT / EMPLOYEES ONLY. Although few marks ever ventured behind the attractions, the former owner, Solly Nickles, evidently believed in consistency of presentation; the words on the door looked as if they had been written by the finger of a skeleton using blood for paint.

I thought the door would be locked but it wasn't. I couldn't decide if that was a good or bad thing.

When I stepped inside, I found myself in a small vestibule with a ten-foot ladder nailed to the wall in front of me. Four steps to my left. Four to my right. Each set of steps led to a door.

I tried the door on the left. It opened awkwardly outward, because above it on the inner side hung a lighted EMERGENCY EXIT sign. Beyond lay a narrow corridor in which the walls, floor, and ceiling were painted flat black. This fun house was a walk-through rather than a ride-through palace of thrills and chills, a black maze in which monsters popped from walls or dropped from ceilings, triggered by motion detectors. Ordinarily, the maze would be all but pitch-black, but at the moment a string of work lights revealed the way. Hanging overhead were rubber spiders the size of poodles, vaguely luminescent.

I could hear the noises of the carnival and the boisterous crowd, but no sound that seemed to come from within the fun house.

I tried the door on the right and found the same situation, although instead of spiders, there were shrunken heads.

Chief Porter had said that he'd assigned Taylor Pipes and Nick Korker to keep watch at the two attractions. I knew them both. Nice guys.

I almost called out, but then decided to keep silent.

In my mind's eye, I summoned Taylor's and Nick's faces. I concentrated on their names, and psychic magnetism drew me to the ladder. I needed both hands, and the pain in my left made an ordeal of ascension. I left a slick of blood on the rungs, which worried me, not because I might be losing a critical amount of it, which I wasn't, but because I was trying to be quiet and was pretty much succeeding—though the blood left a trail that could be noticed and followed.

Ten feet above the floor of the vestibule, the ladder brought me to an opening about four feet wide and a little over six high. Rungs in the walls provided grips to swing safely off the ladder and onto my feet. The walls were painted light gray there, and a string of small work lights ran end to end. No rubber spiders or shrunken heads or other claptrap cluttered the space. I assumed that the maze lay under me and that this passageway allowed an employee to travel from one end of the fun house to the other without encountering customers.

I stood listening but, as far as I could tell, still heard no sound that originated within those walls. All the noise filtering in from the carnival, however, would surely mask the scrapes and clicks and creaks of anyone who might be moving as cautiously through the structure as I was.

The gray corridor ended in another ladder that led down a four-foot-square shaft. Although my left hand wasn't growing numb and the pain remained as bad as ever, it became stiffer by the minute and less useful to me. As much as possible, I tried to grip with just my fingers, rather than wrap the skewered palm around the rungs, but the descent became a sweat-inducing heart-knocking gruesome little journey.

At the bottom waited another door. When I opened it, I found Taylor Pipes's body.

Fifty-one

He had been shot once in the back. There wasn't much blood because the round had gone through his heart, stopping it in an instant. He hadn't drawn his weapon. Taylor Pipes had been smart and quick, not a guy who allowed himself to be shot from behind.

The room in which he'd met his end measured perhaps ten feet from the door by which I'd entered to the front wall of the fun house, maybe twenty-five feet from side to side. I was behind the head of the ogre, looking at a reverse mold of the beastly face. From the midway, you couldn't discern that it had been cast in two pieces, but from this perspective, the joining bolts and the center seam were evident. The backs of the eyeballs, which rolled ominously when the face came to life, were maybe six feet above me, and the mouth just above floor level.

In addition to the door beyond which lay the ladder to the high gray corridor, four other doors offered choices, a pair that flanked the first, and one at each end of the space. Between the doors were trick mirrors. In this one, I swelled fat. In the next, I shrank thin as a pencil. Here, I stood with a huge head and diminutive body.

There, I had an immense body and a head no bigger than a base-ball. In another, my body and head were sinuous, twisting, as if I were a vaporous genie writhing out of a well-rubbed lamp. In every mirror, I bled from my left hand, and in every mirror, I held the Glock in my right.

I assumed the four doors through which I had not entered all led to different sections of the maze and that patrons returned more than once to this space behind the ogre's head as they tried to find their way out. The cultist who had taken Taylor by sur-prise might have left the fun house for some reason or he might still be lurking elsewhere within it. In either case, there were five doors by which he could return at any moment.

Turning from the last mirror, I saw what had been so import-ant to me in the dream of the amaranth: what I had thought of as the urn, a stainless-steel cylinder about half again as tall and half again as wide as a carton of milk.

The object stood beside a heavy-duty electric air compressor and associated equipment that, even to a mechanical ignoramus like me, couldn't be mistaken for anything other than the source of the ogre's blasts of breath that accompanied his roars of rage. A four-inch-diameter tube led from the compressor to the monster's mouth.

The urn could be nothing else than a container of the weapon-ized rabies virus suspended in some medium that would effi-ciently convey it into the ogre's exhalations, whereupon it would be spewed with force across the crowded concourse, through the happy bustling crowd, toward the many rides and the other attractions in the center of the midway. The medium would be odorless and tasteless but might appear as a faint mist.

Because Ozzie Boone had written a novel about a killer virus and because he was incapable of withholding from his friends the numerous fascinating details of the research he did for a novel, I knew a few things about viruses, just as I knew more than I ever wanted to know about bats, liver flukes, the incidence of psychopathic tendencies in clowns, and the capacity of hogs to be trained to kill.

Bacteria were exceedingly small creatures, but viruses were smaller still. Big viruses were one-fifth the size of the average bacterium, but the vast majority of them were orders of magnitude smaller. The flu virus measured eighty thousandths of a millionth of a meter in diameter. Viruses were so tiny, they couldn't be seen with ordinary microscopes. Their structure wasn't known until the invention of the electron microscope in 1933. Billions of viruses could fit into one drop of water.

Viruses have none of our five senses. But they have one sense, the only one they need: an unexplained ability to detect the chemical composition of the cell surface of whichever species make the best hosts for them. Detecting it, they are drawn to it. You might say that viruses have one sense, and that it is pretty much the same one that I call psychic magnetism.

For those who don't believe the world is a mysterious and deeply layered place, brood on *that* awhile.

The urn could hold megatrillions of the weaponized rabies virus, enough perhaps to infect the entire population of the planet. Pico Mundo might be the locus from which a plague spread across several counties in California and Nevada before being contained, or across the nation, or across the world.

From the top of that shiny cylinder of death sprouted a nozzle encircled by what appeared to be a rotating petcock currently in the closed position. A rubber tube connected the nozzle to a hole that had been drilled in the four-inch-diameter out-feed pipe through which the compressor released jets of the ogre's breath into the world beyond.

I knelt beside the cylinder and was about to pluck that tube from the nozzle when the door at the west end of the room flew open and a little man appeared there. Lou Donatella wasn't dressed as a bear cub this time, but pretty much like me, except that he had the good taste not to wear a powder-blue sport coat. Holding the pistol in a two-hand grip, he squeezed off three shots, killing the man behind me, who I had not heard come out of one of the other doors.

More often than I could count in my eventful life, I had been taken by surprise, but never more so than by Lou's in-the-nick-of-time arrival. After our brief encounter in the carnie camp-ground, he had decided to ally himself with me.

Our eyes met in shared amazement and astonishment, which were not the same thing, which I knew to be true because Ozzie Boone had explained the difference to me.

When he spoke, Lou revealed that he possessed psychic abilities, as I had thought that he might: "I foresaw this much, but not what comes next."

I tore the rubber tube from the urn just as one of the mirrors, which proved to be a hidden door, flew open like the lid of a jack-in-the-box, and a cultist shot me. Lou shot the cultist, and in turn the cultist shot Lou dead. Although I'd taken a bullet in the right side of my chest and could not get my breath, I had the strength and balance to shoot the cultist, finishing the job that my short comrade had started.

Aside from dying, there was nothing left for me to do but take the stainless-steel cylinder, the urn in the amaranth dream, where

the cultists couldn't get their murderous hands on it, to Chief
Wyatt Porter, who would know what to do, who always knew
what to do, who was one of the two surrogate fathers who had
always been there for me when my real father could not be both-
ered.

Fifty-two

Leaving the fun house by the door through which Lou Donatella had entered to save me, I turned right because to turn left would be to go into the maze. A short passageway brought me to the ramp that served as the public entrance. Having dropped my pistol to be able to hold the cylinder of weaponized rabies with both arms, I staggered down the ramp, sidled past the stanchions that supported the CLOSED sign, and turned left into surging multitudes.

I shouted at people to get out of my way, declared that I was wounded and dying, and they took me seriously when they noticed all the blood. They took me even more seriously when I shouted that I was *diseased* and dying, which was a bald-faced lie, but in crisis you say what you have to say and worry later about whether you screwed up or not. The people who were attracted by the novelty of seeing a man die from a gunshot were repelled by the prospect of contracting the disease with which I might be infected.

At that moment, I saw something that I first thought must be a hallucination, a consequence of blood loss and shock. Among the people in the crowd, there were some into whom I could look, as if I had X-ray vision, though it was only their hearts that were visible to me. Hearts not red, but black. Hearts not of muscle, but of metal, cardiac machines ticking and thumping and glistening with oil. I am sure that, if autopsied, their hearts would have looked unremarkable. What I saw was the hidden truth of them. From each of those dark and seemingly robotic hearts, a black filament, an umbilical invisible to ordinary eyes, snaked away into the carnival. Snaked away through the whirling amusements and the blinking lights, as if to some puppeteer in concealment. Somehow I knew that not all of them were cultists, that many of them did evil to their fellow men without the need of an organization to support them. When I looked up into their faces, I saw in every case what they did not see in their mirrors: eyes that were like pools of oil, without color. And if they didn't know me for who and what I was, an entity of terrible power looked through their eyes from its remote lair and knew me, and caused them, one after another, to smile in pleasure at the sight of my suffering. I turned my eyes from them and did not look again.

In this world, Evil works through countless surrogates. Its name is Legion. But Good works through surrogates, as well, and they are legion, too.

The rest of my time on the midway ticked away pretty much as in the dream of the amaranth that I have already recounted. Somehow I found the strength to lumber forward while the carnival around me blurred and became a place without detail, where those luminous smears of red and blue and gold and white and green whirled and pulsed, swooped toward me and soared as if they were shapeless birds of light. Screams and panicked shouting. Tortured and shrill music. I see no need to describe the pandemonium again.

Pain? Oh, yes. Devastating pain. Like nothing I had ever known before. And a frightening sense of walking a high wire, of falling for a moment, but then finding myself on the wire again, falling into a black void but then rebounding from it once more.

Blossom Rosedale appeared, as she had in the dream, and helped me to stay on my feet. I had never seen the Happy Monster cry before, and I told her not to weep now, told her that I knew to what I was coming, that I had been coming to it for almost two years, and that whatever the place might prove to be, I was not afraid. If I didn't say all that, I thought I did, but she continued to cry as she helped me along.

I didn't see the cultist behind us, the last assassin, who would have shot me and no doubt Blossom, too. Chief Wyatt Porter, who had always been there when I needed him, was there again. He loomed as in the dream, the muzzle of his service pistol swelling until it looked like the mouth of a cannon. He shot the lunatic before the lunatic could shoot us.

Just like the transition in the dream, I found myself lying on a hard surface, but unlike in the dream, I knew that I rested on the table where Connie, sister to Ethan, kept her array of paints and brushes and sponges, in the Face It tent. She had swept all of her things to the floor with one arm, and they had placed me upon the table to await the paramedics who were already racing to the scene.

All the noise of the carnival had faded, and there were only soft voices, murmuring and weeping when no weeping was necessary. The three lovely black girls stood by me, looking down with solemn brown eyes, their faces painted with white-and-gold feathers, their hands upon my arms, my brow, as if to hold me to the world of the living. Terri Stambaugh was there, too, for she had been at the carnival that night. Terri and Blossom Rosedale, as in the dream.

Someone said that everyone should stay back, so as not to stress me, but I said no. I said I wanted to see them all, to see people. I wanted to see not just the people I loved and the people I knew, but also the people I didn't know. I wanted to see people, because people had been my life, the good and bad, but always so many more good people than bad. They had been my life, and I did not want to die without the faces of people as the last thing I saw of that beautiful and mysterious world.

In the dream, Wyatt Porter had not been by the table on which I was lying, but he appeared there in the fulfillment of the dream, as did Edie Fischer and Connie and Connie's mother. And I loved them all, those I knew and those I didn't.

I think the last thing I said was, "Where is Annamaria?"

As in the dream, I closed my eyes and opened them and found myself alone. I seemed to be paralyzed. Couldn't move a finger. Panic took me for a moment. But then Annamaria spoke, and her voice at once calmed me, though I couldn't see her.

"Well, young man, you have had quite a day."

With dreamlike fluidity, I somehow transitioned to a chair in the Face It tent, alone with Annamaria, the table between us.

I was no longer in pain.

On the table stood a wide shallow bowl containing an inch of water, and in the water floated a beautiful white flower bigger than a cantaloupe, its petals radiant and as thick as wax.

"The flower," said Annamaria, "is the amaranth."

She proceeded one by one to pluck the petals from the bloom, until she had completely deconstructed it. A couple of hundred pieces of the amaranth lay scattered on the table around the bowl.

"You always said that you wanted to see the flower trick," she reminded me. "But it is not a trick. I have no trick to show you. This is only what is."

" 'This is only what is,' " I said. "Still enigmatic."

She smiled and shook her head. "No more enigma."

The debris of petals on the table stirred, although no hand touched them. Before my eyes, the bloom reassembled and became again the exquisite flower that she had taken apart.

As the last petal reattached itself, the tiny bell around my neck began tinkling sweetly, the silver clapper beating against the silver strike and silver lip.

"Who are you?" I asked.

"You know what an avatar is, young man."

"Yes, I know. It's the form in which a deity visits Earth."

"I am no deity. I am no avatar in that sense, but I have been for you—and others before you—something like an avatar. I am only human. Once long ago, I gave birth to a daughter, and later she gave birth to a little boy, and I am now for eternity a universal mother, a mother to love those who, like you, were unloved by their mothers on Earth. You are, young man, as fine a son as any mother could wish to have, and you need not be afraid of what will happen now."

The silver bell rang one more time, and suddenly I felt as if I were the flower, being dismantled as it had been, pieces of myself falling away, showering away into a terrible darkness, until nothing remained of me. Nothing remained, and yet I was aware in the utterly lightless void.

Before me appeared a form in the void, and it was, of all things, a golden question mark. It might have been an inch high or a thousand miles from dot to upper curve. Because I had no body, I had no sense of perspective.

The question mark remained before me—or above me, or below me—long enough that I began to wonder if I was supposed to respond to it somehow. As I considered what to say, the question mark morphed into a golden exclamation point, like the one on the cell phone that I'd been given by Edie Fischer.

After a moment, the exclamation point exploded soundlessly into a rushing abundance of light. The black void vanished around me, and I found myself flying through a smooth blue realm of radiance with no detectable source, gliding as if on wings, though still I had no body. The blue gave way to the crystalline light of the Mojave, and suddenly I was standing in downtown Pico Mundo on a sun-drenched day. The jacaranda trees were in bloom, and birds were singing, and the air smelled clean and sweet.

I was dressed now in my customary attire: sneakers, blue jeans, and a white T-shirt. No bandage wrapped my left hand, and I bore no wounds.

The town lay in an unnatural quiet, the silence of cemeteries. No vehicles plied the streets. No pedestrians. No sign of a living soul. I felt that I must be alone, having returned to my hometown after all of humanity had been killed off, and a deep uneasiness overcame me.

I started walking, not certain where I should go. Within half a block, I heard hurried footsteps, heels clicking against a sidewalk in the preternatural silence. I couldn't quite discern from which direction they approached.

Uncertain who or what might be rushing toward me, I halted.

A moment later, Lou Donatella turned the corner; he waved at me. He wasn't dressed either as a bear cub or as he had been dressed when he burst into the fun house to save me. Like me, Lou wore sneakers, blue jeans, and a white T-shirt, though on his shirt were the words LITTLE IS BIG.

Still disoriented, I thought that I had returned to my role as a counselor for the lingering spirits who would not move on to the Other Side.

Then Lou said, "Hey, dude!"

If I could *hear* the dead, not just see them, I had to be dead, as well. But like the amaranth . . . dead and not dead.

Lou grabbed my hand and pumped it with both of his and said, "Big orientation meeting at the movie theater on the square this evening. Can't wait for it. See you there, pal." He hurried past me, engaged in some task I could not imagine. As I looked after him, he turned once and shook two fists in the air, and laughed, and said, "Isn't this great?" before he continued on his way.

I watched him until he turned another corner, and gradually an understanding came to me. Or I wanted to believe that it was an understanding, a perception of truth, and not just a wild hope.

At a run, fast as I could go, I headed toward the house in which Stormy had rented an apartment. In *this* Pico Mundo, I could run much faster than in the old, and without tiring.

When eventually I turned a corner into the street where she had lived, I found the sidewalk opposite her apartment house lined with people whom I'd known. All of them were people who had died and lingered, who had finally crossed over with my help. An old school teacher of mine. A high-school friend who had died young. A young prostitute who had been shot to death at a place once called the Church of the Whispering Comet Topless Bar, Adult Bookstore, and Burger Heaven. There were dozens of them, scores, including Mr. Elvis Presley and Mr. Frank Sinatra. They were all dressed in sneakers and blue jeans and white T-shirts, both the men and women, but each of their outfits had a detail or two different from the others. This one wore his cuffs rolled. That one wore his sleeves rolled. This one sported an em-broidered flower on her shirt.

They started waving when they saw me, and I was so excited to see them that I almost dashed across the street to shake their hands and hug them. But of all the people I have loved, there was one for whom my love had been most pure, and I could not stop until I knew for sure that Gypsy Mummy's promise had been kept.

I raced up the steps to the front door of the house, the one that featured a large oval of leaded glass here as it did in the other Pico Mundo. She didn't wait for me to go inside and knock at her apartment, but flung open the door and came into my arms on the stoop. I lifted her off her feet and turned in a circle with her, as-tonished, amazed, in a state of bliss that I thought I would never know again.

Stormy Llewellyn in sneakers and blue jeans and a white T-shirt, with pink military-style epaulets sewn on the shoulders. Beautiful Stormy whole and radiant and laughing down at me as I looked up into her face.

She said, "What took you so long, griddle boy?"

Before I could answer, she said, "Put me down, put me down, come on, I have to show you."

When I put her down, she took me by the hand and led me

through the front door, into the house, along the hallway, through the door to her apartment. The place was as it had been in the other Pico Mundo: the old floor lamps with silk shades and beaded fringes, the Stickley-style chairs with the contrasting Victorian footstools, the Maxfield Parrish prints and the carnival-glass vases.

She talked excitedly all the way along the hall and into the apartment: "What did I tell you, odd one? Boot camp! And what did I say followed boot camp? A life in service! And what did I say that life of service would be?"

"You said it would be a great adventure, greater than all the adventure-story writers in the history of the world could imagine. You said it would out-Tolkien Tolkien, and that after it comes the third and eternal life."

"You did listen, after all," she said. "Sometimes I wondered, griddle boy."

She tore open a coat-closet door and took from it something like a crossbow, though it was a work of art, apparently made of silver and elegantly engraved from the stock to the stirrup.

She said excitedly, "No guns here, Oddie. No guns. I know you'll like no guns. They wouldn't be useful, anyway."

She handed me as well a quiver of short arrows that were tipped in silver.

"No one here kills other people. That's all over and done with, all those terrible things. No more of that. No one eats the animals, and the animals don't eat us. Wait'll you talk to one. To an animal, I mean. It's the freakiest thing, but good freaky."

From the closet she took a second quiver of short arrows, these tipped in gold, and handed it to me.

Bewildered, I said, "What is all this for?"

"It's sort of like Purgatory here, but not stuffy and sorrowful, the way we always thought it would be. Atonement, oh, yeah, we've got atonement to do, buddy, you better believe it, but the way we do it is nothing like you'd expect. The true and hidden nature of the world is as true here as it was back where we came from, but here it's not *hidden*."

I put the crossbow on a nearby armchair, the quivers with it, and said, "But what are we at war with?"

"Oh, my adorable fry cook, wait till you see them. They're the most hideous terrifying creatures, and wickedly cunning, and there's ever so much that can go wrong. But what you always know now, what we all know here, is exactly what we're fighting *for* and how right it is to fight for it. Now kiss me."

I did.

That is as much as I can say to those who are not yet here, but I suspect that my friend and mentor and surrogate father, Mr. Ozzie Boone, who loved me as if I were his own son, will in his inimitable way add a chapter fifty-three.

Fifty-three

Earlier in the night, the sky had pulsed with distant heat lightning along the southern horizon. We had no expectation of rain, however, and the weather report had said that the storm would never cross the county line.

In the last hour of the day, I was ensconced in my custom-built armchair, which had been constructed to serve me without any fear whatsoever of collapse until I attained the magnificent weight of five hundred pounds, if I ever did.

My cat, Terrible Chester, curled on the sofa, alternately snoozing and glaring at me with what might have been mistaken for contempt, though I knew it to be a kind of amused and gentle scorn.

Oblivious of the cult's heinous bombings in distant parts of Pico Mundo, I sipped Caymus Cabernet Sauvignon, nibbled champagne cheese, and for the third time read *Bleak House,* which I found to be anything but bleak. I was on page 102 when, precisely at 11:19, the meteorologists were proved wrong. Such a flash of lightning scorched the night and flared so brightly at every window that, had gravity not been a special challenge to me, I would have shot to my feet in alarm. Even as an immediate and equally bright second flash followed the first, an unprecedented crash of thunder shook the house from chimney top to foundation, vibrating in the windowpanes. The second peal outdid the first, and on the top of the side table next to my chair, my wineglass wobbled and almost tipped over.

As a novelist but also as a man who has never tried to extinguish the child in himself, I love spectacle. Abandoning wine and cheese and Mr. Dickens, I managed to ascend from the armchair with my usual strained dignity and made my way to the front door and then onto the porch.

Never in my considerable experience had a sky been so crazed with storm light, great bolts beyond counting, crackling across the heavens in curious patterns, one bolt arcing to the next, revealing the clouds in such a way as to make it appear that they were in fact the crumbled and tumbling remains of some great and ancient stone city sliding down a mountainside to bury Pico Mundo in ruins. When the rain came a moment later, it fell in torrents that the word *cloudburst* cannot begin to describe. Throughout the rainfall, the lightning did not cease, nor the thunder—until the entire spectacle ended in an instant. Stunned, I looked at my watch and saw that it was 11:22 to the second. The entire storm lasted precisely three minutes. An hour later, when I returned to the porch, the sky had entirely cleared, and an infinity of stars shone brightly. I found that abbreviated tempest remarkable.

I do not often sleep well. Sleep seems to me to be a preview of death, and I do not like to be reminded of that coming attraction.

At one o'clock in the morning, in the darkness of that dismal May, as I sat reading *Bleak House,* Wyatt and Karla Porter rang the doorbell and brought me news of the dear boy's death. I almost died myself to hear of it. I wanted to die, and for once not by eating myself into the grave. We held one another in silence for a moment; I am large enough to be hugged by two at once. When I could speak, I asked when Oddie had passed, but then I answered the question before they had a chance to respond—"It was at eleven-nineteen"—and they confirmed my intuition.

We sat around the kitchen table for a while, with coffee and memories, as we would do often in the days that followed. More than once, I put the lie to my image as a hard-boiled writer of tough-guy mysteries when I succumbed to choking grief.

After Wyatt and Karla left, with night yet remaining and with the dawn unwelcome, I could not read Dickens or taste the wine or want the cheese. I went into my office, intending to unlock the metal cabinet in which I kept the seven manuscripts that Oddie had written, the accounts of his adventures, memoirs beginning with the story of the shootings at the Green Moon Mall and the death of Stormy.

He had written much in a little time, for he was as gifted with language and story as with his sixth sense, though because of his singular humility, he would never have taken such praise seriously. For obvious reasons, the seven books were not to be published until his death.

I didn't unlock the cabinet that night, for when I entered my office, I found my computer humming, though I had switched it off hours before. The printer pumped out pages, of what I could not imagine.

Mystified, I took the stack already in the tray and found that in my hands I held his eighth and final manuscript. I am certain you can imagine that my reaction included amazement and astonishment, but exceeded them. Amazement and astonishment express the momentary overwhelming of the mind by something beyond expectation. Amazement is an emotional response, astonishment an intellectual one. Wonder, yes, in wonder I waited for the manuscript to finish printing, and in wonder I carried it to the kitchen, where I brewed another pot of coffee and sat to read in another fortified chair.

There was no title page, because he had never titled his books. He left that to me. Instead, the top sheet had this simple message: *Sir, here is the last of it, a pile of strange pages. You will think they can't have been written in the few hours since my death, but I do not live in time anymore. I can accomplish a lifetime of work in what would seem, from your side of the veil, to be mere minutes. I know that you will take my passing hard, because you are a kind man with a tender heart. But don't mourn for me. As you will learn from this story, all is well. The promise that mattered has been kept, and I have found work that, believe it or not, I enjoy even a great deal more than being a fry cook at the Pico Mundo Grille. I will miss you terribly until I see you.*

—*Odd Thomas.*

Amazement, astonishment, wonder, and now awe. In awe, one's mind yields to something grand in character, formidable in power. I yielded without reservation.

Terrible Chester was not a cat who found it necessary or even just pleasant to console or be consoled. But as I sat at the kitchen table, reading my beloved friend's manuscript, Chester sprang into my generous lap and curled there and slept until I turned the final page.

As with the other seven memoirs, I have now changed a few of the names. For instance, those enemies of Edie Fischer who do

not already know her real name should not be told it, and I con-
cocted this nom de guerre to conceal her true identity in both this
volume and in the one that came before it, *Deeply Odd*. I made no
other alterations.

For this final book, I never considered any title but *Saint Odd*.
Oh, how he would dislike the saint part! He would want me to
call it *The Fry Cook Meets His End* or *Odd as Ever,* or perhaps
Fumbling My Way to Eternity. But what other word so well fits
a young man who would give his life to save a friend or even an
innocent stranger, and who, in giving it, would think he had not
done enough?

I have his ashes in a mortuary urn. I keep them on the mantel
above the living-room fireplace, where Stormy's ashes are in an
urn beside his. I look up at them from time to time when I am
reading, and I smile to think that he would make jokes about the
hard-boiled mystery writer being a sentimental basket case. I
carry in my wallet the fortune-teller's card that he carried in his—
YOU ARE DESTINED TO BE TOGETHER FOREVER—and I dare to
believe that it means not just Odd and Stormy, but all of us.

About the Author

DEAN KOONTZ, the author of many #1 *New York Times* bestsellers, lives in Southern California with his wife, Gerda, their golden retriever, Anna, and the enduring spirit of their golden, Trixie.

www.deankoontz.com

Facebook.com/Dean Koontz Official

@deankoontz

Correspondence for the author should be addressed to:

Dean Koontz

P.O. Box 9529

Newport Beach, California 92658